Praise for COLD WIND

"[With] rich character development and an inside look at an untamed environment where community determines survival. Fans of the first book will do well to follow up with this one." —*Booklist*

"Appealing . . . Fans of light regional mysteries will be satisfied." —*Publishers Weekly*

"Suspense-filled [and] uniquely thrilling." —*BookPage*

Praise for THIN ICE

"[A] riveting story with an unusual setting and cast of characters." —*Library Journal* (starred review / Pick of the Month)

"[With] murder, mayhem and heroics . . . [and] an intriguing cast of characters." —*Anchorage Daily News* on *Thin Ice*

"A page-turner with an unusual location and a coda that provides more questions than answers." —*Kirkus Reviews*

"Readers are left wondering up to the last exciting page what the answers are, and will eagerly await the second in this new Alaska mysteries series from the author of the Scottish Bookshop mysteries." —*Booklist*

"Riveting. Suspenseful and intriguing . . . Shelton's fans are sure to enjoy this compelling departure from her typical writing style." —Shelf Awareness

"*Thin Ice* proves to be a riveting start to an unstoppable series. Fans of Louise Penny's Three Pines will love Shelton's new Alaska Wild series." —Susan Furlong, bestselling author of the Bone Gap Travellers novels

"A stunning new series that folds a compelling mystery inside a heart-stopping thriller and features a heroine vivid and tough enough to carry both." —Wendall Thomas, Macavity and Lefty Award–nominated author of the Cyd Redondo Mysteries

"Creepily atmospheric with plenty of bone-chilling twists . . . With touches of Stephen King's *Misery* amongst the vast expanse of wilderness. *Thin Ice* is sure to keep you turning the page and just may keep you up all night."
—Ellie Alexander, author of the Bakeshop Mysteries

Praise for Paige Shelton's Scottish Bookshop Mysteries

"Captivating . . . Ghostly pubs and blustery winter scenes help create a suitably sinister atmosphere, while distinctive characters and judicious use of Scottish dialect add to the story's appeal." —*Publishers Weekly* on *Deadly Editions*

"Filled with literary references that will tickle bibliophiles."
—*Kirkus Reviews* on *Deadly Editions*

"Vivid descriptions of Edinburgh enhance the well-crafted plot. Cozy fans will look forward to the further adventures of smart and intuitive Delaney."
—*Publishers Weekly* on *The Stolen Letter*

ALSO BY PAIGE SHELTON

DARK
NIGHT

A MYSTERY

PAIGE SHELTON

St. Martin's Paperbacks

Published in the United States by St. Martin's Paperbacks, an imprint of St. Martin's Publishing Group

DARK NIGHT

For information, address St. Martin's Publishing Group, 120 Broadway, New York, NY 10271.

www.stmartins.com

Library of Congress Catalog Card Number: 2021042840

ISBN: 978-1-250-85011-9

Our books may be purchased in bulk for promotional, educational, or business use. Please contact your local bookseller or the Macmillan Corporate and Premium Sales Department at 1-800-221-7945, ext. 5442, or by email at MacmillanSpecialMarkets@macmillan.com.

Printed in the United States of America

Minotaur hardcover edition published 2021
St. Martin's Paperbacks edition / November 2022

10 9 8 7 6 5 4 3 2 1

For Barbara,
and all the Iditarod calendars she sent us over the years

One

None of you Rivers people ever listen.
  I put my fingers to my temples and squeezed my eyes shut.

As the Benedict, Alaska, days had become shorter and the nights longer and darker, the words had been with me. They'd haunted me, awakened me from deep dream-filled sleeps. I'd felt the distraction of them as I worked, gritted my teeth, trying to push them away.

Their continual play through my mind was doing me no good. They weren't soothing words. They were the stuff of bad times, memories that had taken on a life of their own now and were bubbling up more and more all the time.

Those words weren't the worst part.

Seven months ago, a man named Travis Walker kidnapped me, took me from my home in St. Louis, and kept me in his van for three days, during which he hurt and tortured me. For a long time, I'd forgotten most of what happened during those seemingly endless days. It was only a few months ago, about the time the police learned his real name, that I started to remember more, including his saying those words. Lots more started to resurface after that. Moments in the van, smells, noises, his voice. Even more of the sickening fear. The countryside passing by as he drove, the road signs—we'd gone all through Missouri.

I thought he'd taken me because of my career as a thriller writer. That he was an unhinged fan of my dark and disturbing books, written under my pseudonym, Elizabeth Fairchild. But those words meant that not only had he known my real name—the name I was now using to hide from him—but that maybe he'd known me for a long time, been aware of my entire family.

My father had disappeared when I was seven, and though my mother, Mill Rivers, had spent most of her life searching for Dad, she was now off the radar, too, after allegedly shooting Walker in the parking lot of a Piggly Wiggly.

I'd come to the conclusion that those seven words, along with a few other pieces of evidence, *might* also mean that Travis Walker had something to do with my father's disappearance.

They also might mean nothing at all, could have just been part of Walker's cruel manipulations.

There was even a possibility that the memory was a glitch. Though I was fairly certain my mind was putting things together correctly, there was no guarantee. I could be misremembering. I'd done it before. With my mom on the run and my kidnapper still on the loose, the idea that my mind was playing tricks on me didn't seem unwarranted.

I'd escaped the van, witnesses saying I flung myself out of it, though I still don't remember that part. Because of the impact, I'd needed brain surgery to clear a subdural hematoma, but there didn't appear to be any lingering brain damage. Since I'd also run from the hospital in St. Louis, Missouri, where I was being treated and observed, though, I couldn't know for sure.

Mostly I just wanted Travis's voice to leave my head, leave me alone.

Inside my room at the Benedict House, a halfway house for female felons, where I was also living, I stood from my desk chair. I'd been working on notes for my next book, or at least trying to. Most of the time I wrote my novels in a small hunting shed out in the woods that housed the community one-sheet newspaper, the *Petition,* that I also put together every week—it made a good cover for my real job, since there was only one local who knew who I was: the police chief, Gril Samuels. But inspiration had struck this evening.

Unfortunately, as it waned, Travis Walker's words had come back full force. Again.

I pulled back the curtain from the room's window. The view was of an open plot of land that led to the woods; to-night all I saw was darkness. If there was a moon, it was hidden behind thick clouds. Any artificial light from the small downtown businesses didn't eke its way back here, behind the buildings.

I closed the curtain. I was antsy, not able to think about reading something for pleasure. I'd loaded some old television sitcoms onto my laptop, but the idea of watching something funny made my skin crawl. I needed to *do* something. Exercise?

Though that would have helped, I decided to opt for some civilization instead. I pulled on a hat, grabbed my coat, and left the room, still double-checking the lock on the door, even after all these months. Actually, triple-checking.

The rest of the Benedict House was quiet. My landlord and the woman who ran it, Viola, was probably in her office or her room. It wasn't required that we check in with each other as we came and went, but I often let her know what my plans were.

Tonight I just wanted to go.

I slipped on my boots from a pile we left by the front door. These were my newest pair. I'd purchased them from the mercantile two weeks earlier, and I didn't think I'd worn anything else since.

I glanced down the hallway toward Viola's rooms, but didn't hear or see her, or smell anything coming from the kitchen.

We'd had a resident through Christmas, but Ellen had done so well that with a break in the weather, she was flown back to Juneau and then Anchorage to forge a new life. She'd come to the Benedict House a strung-out junkie but left a cleaned-up woman with a goal to succeed. She'd wished to stay longer because she'd ended up enjoying her time at the house, but she hadn't been allowed to make those sorts of decisions for herself. Viola had heard that she was still on track. We both hoped she'd be okay, and frankly, we missed her, not to mention her bread-baking skills.

I stepped out and into the cold. The ground was covered in snow, hiding the mud that had come earlier in the season. It was frozen solid now, and the crunchy snow wasn't easy to walk or drive through.

The small downtown was set up in an L-shape. I glanced over to the other leg, seeing that all the businesses had their lights on. CAFÉ, BAR, and MERCANTILE were open. I wasn't hungry (a rare occurrence since I'd moved to Alaska), but a drink sounded good.

As I hitched up my coat collar, though, I was stopped short by a double glimmer coming toward me from in front of the buildings.

I gasped lightly and zeroed in on the approaching threat.

The shine came from two eyes. I froze in place as my own eyes adjusted to the diluted darkness. There were no street-lights, but the business windows helped take away some of the gloom.

Was it a bear?

A second later, I realized it was too short. A wolf? No,

that wasn't it, either, and I didn't sense it was on the attack, at any rate.

With relief, I realized it was a dog, one I'd seen from a distance before. A husky, part of one of the local musher's teams. I hadn't met the man, who I'd heard was always training for the Iditarod, but I'd seen this particular dog—Gus, I thought his name was—a few times.

"Gus?" I said hesitantly.

He trotted directly to me, sat, and smiled upward.

"Hello," I said as I patted his head. I laughed. "Aren't you ferocious?"

Gus's tail wagged appreciatively.

"Gus?" a voice hailed from the other side of the buildings.

"He's here," I called back. "Over by Benedict House."

I heard the crunch of boots before a man emerged from the shadows. Maybe in his late sixties, he moved well but with a hitch to his quick step. "He's friendly."

"I know," I said as he stopped next to the dog.

"Gus, Gus, Gus." The man reached for the dog's collar and gently pulled the animal toward him. He looked up at me. "This is maybe the greatest dog I've ever known, but he's also the smartest and loves to find new ways to escape. I apologize if he bothered you."

"He didn't." I extended my hand. "I'm Beth Rivers."

With his free hand, we shook. "Elijah Wyatt. I'm not sure how we haven't met yet. You must not have needed a tow."

"You're pretty popular around here. I haven't needed a tow yet, but maybe someday."

"I've heard of your . . . your scar." He smiled sheepishly. "Wow, that was terribly inappropriate. I'm sorry."

"Don't worry about it. It's hard to miss."

My hair, now white from the trauma of being kidnapped, had grown out some from the hospital bathroom haircut I'd given myself, but the scar would probably always be obvious. I didn't care what I looked like as long as it wasn't brown-haired novelist Elizabeth Fairchild.

It was difficult to see Elijah clearly, and even though I had heard of him, I didn't think I'd noticed him out and about. I shopped at the mercantile and Tochco's, our local version of Costco, but if he'd been there at the same time I had, I didn't remember him.

In the shadows I saw gray hair tufting out under his cap. His wrinkled face was friendly in a Jimmy Stewart way and I immediately got good vibes from him. He seemed like a nice guy.

Of course, he took care of a bunch of sled dogs. How could anyone who cared for a team of dogs not be a good guy? I'd also heard about his operating our one local tow truck—outfitted with a front blade. He voluntarily plowed our two main streets.

"I'm headed over to the bar for a drink. Want to join me?" I said.

This was just the way things were done around Benedict. I wasn't being flirtatious or asking him on a date. You just formed friendships quickly here.

"Gosh, maybe I'll stop by later. I need to get Gus back and check on my other dogs, but I'd love to come by if it works out."

"Sounds good. I would love to meet your other dogs someday."

Gus laughed. "They're a ragtag group if ever there was one, but they're the best. Come over anytime. I'm back behind Tochco's. The Tochco folks let me use their landline."

"Thanks, I will." I'd heard that part, too—that if you needed a tow, you called Tochco's and somehow Elijah would get the message. Landlines were sparse in Benedict, but not as sparse as cell and internet signals.

As I watched him lead the dog away and out around the

buildings, I listened for the sound of a vehicle engine but didn't hear one. He must have set out on foot the couple of miles from Tochco's in search of the dog. Traveling such a way wasn't unheard of out here, but I wondered if I should have offered them a ride home.

I hurried to the path Elijah had taken but couldn't see him or the dog when I turned the corner. I debated running back to my truck and trying to catch up, but it wasn't currently snowing. They'd be okay, and Elijah was probably grateful to have a way for Gus to burn off some energy.

Meeting Gus and Elijah had made the haunting mantra disappear for a while—I knew this because it nudged its way back into my head just as I turned around again, heading toward the bar.

"Go away," I said quietly with gritted teeth as I opened the door.

Maybe something else would distract me.

Two

"No new parolees?" Benny, Viola's sister and the woman who ran the bar, said. She took her job seriously and not only could she make any drink in the book but was the best listener and secret keeper in town.

"Nope, but it's not because Viola is in trouble." I put the celery stalk back into my tall Bloody Mary. I sat up on the stool some so Benny could hear me better. It was noisy and crowded tonight. "They were supposed to send over two women, but they missed the last ferry a couple of weeks ago, so they made other arrangements. No one is mad at Viola anymore. We are one hundred percent sure."

Viola had gotten into some trouble a few months earlier because she missed some pertinent information about one of the parolees, more often referred to by her as "clients." Her position as the person who ran the Benedict House had been temporarily jeopardized, but all had been forgiven. Someone in a high position of power had realized that Viola did lots more good than bad. Besides, who else was going to be in charge of the halfway house out in the middle of Nowhere, Alaska?

Once winter set in, the ferry from Juneau was scheduled to run only once a week, if weather conditions permitted.

Though it wasn't currently snowing, I hadn't heard that trips had been resumed on any sort of regular schedule since the one two weeks earlier.

"Is Viola upset?" Benny frowned.

"She's not upset, but she's at a loss. There are plenty of projects she could work on. She keeps talking about winterizing the windows, but she likes to have a client or two. Now she has to redirect her energies."

Benny nodded. "My sister doesn't like to redirect, and I know she hates doing the windows."

I nodded.

The Benedict House was at one time a Russian church. Then it became an inn until it was deemed not quite up to earthquake safety standards to house paying guests. The authorities figured it would work just fine for female criminals, however. Viola somehow knew how to rule with a firm but kind hand. She had been in charge of many parolees over the years, though because of the mistakes she'd made, she had to prove herself once again with Ellen. She'd been told she was back in everybody's good graces, but you can't control the weather.

Viola and Benny had run away from a bad family situation in Juneau when they were kids, landing in Benedict. They'd both found their way in this small, primitive community, and they were loved and beloved, treated with quiet respect. I'd come to recognize that the dynamics of the community wouldn't be in sync if they weren't here. They made a good difference.

I noticed that Benny kept glancing down at the other end of the bar.

I leaned over and looked. A man sat there, someone I'd never seen before. Middle-aged, he was still wrapped in his winter gear, like I was. Those who'd lived in Benedict for a while might take off their coat when going inside, but those of us who were still getting our Alaska bearings kept wrapped up for a bit.

"Is he new?" I asked, wondering if he'd managed to catch the ferry that Viola's potential clients had missed.

"Sort of." She frowned. "He's the census guy, but he's been here a couple months."

"Really? We have a census guy in town? I missed this."

"We do. I guess our lack of internet access makes us a target for invasive bureaucracy."

I almost laughed, but I realized soon enough that she wasn't kidding. "It's not good he's here?" I said doubtfully.

The expression on Benny's face was distinctly distasteful. "We don't take kindly to such nosiness." Benny sniffed.

I cocked my head as I processed her words. She was right; this community didn't like any nosiness, which was one of the reasons I loved it so much.

I understood the importance of the census and the census takers. I knew how community decisions were made because of the survey's results, how historical records could be useful. But I also knew that the residents of Benedict, Alaska, my new home, didn't like to be asked many questions, particularly personal ones that might include things like how many people lived in a residence, what their real names and actual ages were, and what folks did for a living. In fact, I was living my own lie, and now, knowing what I knew, I would run the other way if I saw that man coming toward me. With a ping of insight, I realized that I'd lived my lie for so long now that it didn't really feel like much of a lie until I gave it some thought.

We were *all* a secretive bunch. It wasn't just me.

"Sure," I said a long moment later, my mind now wandering to something I'd found on my desk about four months ago. It had rattled me. Someone had left a note with Travis

Walker's name and an alleged address, supposedly in Milton, Missouri, my hometown. I'd taken the appropriate next step of searching for the address—and found nothing. Not even an abandoned lot, no thick Missouri woods. Nothing. The address simply didn't exist. I'd followed up by sending the contents of the note to the detective in St. Louis heading up the search to find my abductor, but Detective Majors hadn't come up with any answers either.

Who else other than Gril knew to leave that note on my desk, knew my tie to Travis Walker, an identity that had only recently surfaced at the time? That unanswered question had almost sent me on the run again, but Gril had convinced me to stay. He'd figure it out, he'd said. But he hadn't; no one had. My suspicion about . . . everyone . . . had waned over time, but every now and then, like right now, as we were discussing a man who made it his business to record addresses and other details, a new wave of disquiet zipped through me.

"You say he's been here a couple of months?" I asked.

"Give or take."

Benny picked up a glass and wiped it dry with a clean dishcloth. "He was in here last night. And he's here again. He's only drinking while he's here, not working, but if he starts asking folks things, I'll kick him out. He'll scare everyone away."

"Where's he staying?" I asked.

"With Gril."

"Really? The census man is staying with the police chief?"

Benny shrugged. "Had to stay somewhere."

"The census is a good thing, you know." I wasn't sure if I was trying to convince her or myself.

"We have about five hundred residents; that's all anyone needs to write down about us. We live here for a variety of reasons, but none of them are about wanting to share our personal stuff with anyone, particularly red-tape bureaucratic government people. Dodge him, Beth. Don't give him answers if you can avoid it."

I nodded and reached for the celery stalk again. "Sure thing." Didn't have to tell me twice.

I suddenly had the urge to hurry and finish my drink, get back to my room, and close the door. I'd sit there or lie there and just let the mantra torture me some. The two of us would make for an insomnia-filled night, but at least the curious census man wouldn't be there, too.

"Beth?" Benny said.

I jumped back to the moment. "Sorry, my mind wandered." I cleared my throat. "I met Elijah Wyatt and his dog Gus tonight."

Benny nodded knowingly. "Gus got out again?"

"Yes."

"He's the smartest dog." Benny squinted. "You haven't met Elijah before now?"

"No. I spend a lot of time working."

"You do. How's it going? Are you getting any business? How many offices have you organized lately?"

The main character in my first thriller novel organized offices for a living. The story took place over a twenty-four-hour period of terror, with her locked inside a high-rise with a psychopath. The book was still a big seller. I'd used her job as my cover for why I spent so much time at the *Petition* building. There I could access the library's internet and do my "organizing" job via my laptop. I doubted many people believed that I was actually doing what I said, but as it was Benedict, no one questioned me too much.

Ellen, the recently departed client, had figured out who I was almost immediately. She'd kept my secret as far as I knew, though, and I had talked to her about the note with the address. I believed her when she told me she hadn't had anything to do with it.

News outlets still interested in the story had shared his name, along with a picture of Travis and a warning for people to be on the lookout. A picture of me was included, too, the old me, stating that my representatives said I was still busy recovering and writing. This was mostly a true story.

"Sometimes a couple, sometimes none," I said in answer to Benny's question. "I don't need a lot of money to live on."

In fact, I had plenty of money, but I hadn't spent much since moving to Benedict. It was not a lavish lifestyle.

When I wasn't freaking out about someone else knowing who I was, though, I enjoyed the level of comfort I found living in Benedict—the ease, the sense of isolation. Even if we didn't all know one another well, I sort of knew who many people were, and I knew they *weren't* Travis Walker.

"That's good," Benny said. "I'm glad you're able to just do your thing."

Recently, I had educated myself about the different types of stalkers. Travis had wanted to own me. I was his to do with whatever he pleased, and his failed attempt at rape had only made him angrier. Travis Walker had been evil, arrogant, and psychopathic. But I still didn't know his true motives for wanting me. Until he was captured and successfully questioned, no one would.

For all I could tell, the detective still working the case in St. Louis didn't have much more than she'd had earlier. Walker was in the wind. He'd escaped the law so far, even after being shot by my mother. I was losing faith that the police would ever succeed, but at least I knew Walker wasn't here in Benedict. He wasn't currently in this bar. Having his picture had helped, too. Since escaping that van, I appreciated my moments of safety and security; I was grateful for all of them, even if I was always on the lookout for the person who could take them away again. I was always grateful *not* to see him in the room.

I jumped a little as the door to the bar suddenly burst open. It wasn't an uncommon occurrence because of the wind, but this time it was accompanied by noises that garnered everyone's attention.

"Help!" a woman said.

"Claudia!" voices answered.

It seemed the crowd became one as we all moved toward the woman who'd come through the door. When I saw her, my initial reaction was that there was something wrong with her face. It took another half a step toward her to realize that one eye and her forehead were bloody and swollen.

I elbowed my way closer. Again, I didn't know her, but had seen her around.

"Claudia, what happened?" Benny said as she took Claudia's arm and led her to a chair. Before Claudia could answer, Benny aimed her voice to the rest of us. "Someone grab some ice from behind the bar." She took the dishcloth she'd been using and held it to the blood on Claudia's forehead.

I was too focused on the blood seeping into the fabric to go back for the ice. I knelt in front of her.

"Beth, get some ice," Benny said. I didn't move. "Jesus, someone get some ice, and step back, give us some room. You've all seen blood before. Give us some air!"

I still didn't move.

"Beth!" Benny said.

I took off the knit cap I'd been wearing. Released from the cap, my hair was wild, completely out of control, but it was how I communicated to Benny what even I didn't quite understand. I was compelled to look at Claudia to see if she could use more than a dishcloth and ice. I needed—*needed*—to see if she required something more, like brain surgery; not that I could determine such a thing anyway.

Nevertheless, I couldn't stop myself from attempting to understand.

Benny's eyebrows came together over her critical gaze at me. "What?"

"Lift up the dishcloth. I need to see the injury," I said.

"Are you a doctor?"

"No." I pointed at my scar.

And for some reason, Benny understood. She stopped scowling and nodded, then lifted the dishcloth.

Yes, it was a long gash, but I could tell immediately that it wasn't deep. There were other injuries, though—a black eye that seemed to be swelling even as I studied it. The corner of Claudia's mouth was also cut and bloody, but not gushing.

My nonmedical diagnosis was that she didn't need brain surgery, but my diagnosis didn't mean much of anything.

"You want me to get ahold of Dr. Powder?" I asked Benny.

Our one local medical professional, Dr. Powder, a fit man in his sixties, was gifted with compassion and patience, as well as a keen eye. I'd seen him inspecting my scar, but he'd never pushed me to explain it beyond the lie I'd told most everyone, that I'd fallen off a horse in Colorado.

Benny nodded as she put the dishcloth back over the gash. As I stood, she said, "Hang on, Beth, just help me get her to the back room. She could use some privacy."

With us on either side of her, Benny and I guided Claudia to Benny's back room, the place where Benny sometimes slept and, conveniently, the room where Dr. Powder saw patients when they couldn't make it out to his house on the west side of town. Benny's landline phone was in the room, too.

Gingerly we set Claudia on the bed. She leaned back against the wall but remained sitting up. Benny grabbed the phone, an old-fashioned rotary model, and dialed some numbers. A few moments later Dr. Powder was on the way.

One of the regulars opened the office door and handed in

some ice wrapped in another dishcloth, as well as a bottle of ibuprofen and an unopened bottle of vodka. I stayed next to Claudia, but Benny brought the items over to the bed.

"Who's tending the bar?" I asked Benny.

"Someone will take care of things," she said. She was correct; someone would. It's what we did in Benedict. "All right, Claudia, tell me what happened. Did that son of a bitch do this to you?"

Tears filled Claudia's eyes. "It wasn't like that, Benny. He thought . . . he thought he was in trouble. I didn't explain it all well enough. It wasn't his fault."

It was textbook victim denial, and I didn't even know the circumstances.

"Dammit, Claudia," Benny said gently, "it's never his fault, is it?"

Claudia's face scrunched up and tears flowed more freely down her cheeks. "I know. I know."

"What happened?" Benny asked.

"It's the winter, you know how it is." Claudia sniffed. "He's been holed up in our house for a month with nothing to do, and he sprained his ankle a while ago. You *know* how it is."

"Yeah, yeah, I know how it is," Benny said, gently again, but without conviction.

"It was that census man. He came by today," Claudia continued.

"Yeah?"

"Yes, he came in, and at first Ned was okay, happy to have someone else to talk to. Right?"

"Sure." Benny held the ice up to the swelling eye.

"Ned didn't quite understand what the census was, you know. But then the man started asking all those questions, Ned got uncomfortable, and then he asked how many people live in our house. Ned got upset, wondering what he was getting at."

Benny sent me a quick glance before she looked back at Claudia. "Y'all have someone staying with you?"

She didn't want to answer, but she did a moment later. "Sometimes."

"Who?"

Claudia shook her head.

"Claudia, what's going on? Who is it, and why would Ned want to keep them a secret?"

"I can't tell you, Benny, I just can't."

It was difficult for me to understand how old Claudia was, but I guessed early to mid-twenties. When I'd seen her around it had been with a man. He'd seemed young, too, smallish—not someone I would have ever guessed brutalized his wife, but of course that's rarely obvious.

"Claudia, just tell me who. Come on," Benny urged.

I realized that this was why Claudia was at the bar. I didn't know where she lived, but she'd come here specifically because she knew Benny would help her, maybe intervene with Gril regarding what might need to be done with Ned. It was probably an established pattern. I suddenly understood that Benny and Claudia had been through something like this before.

Claudia lowered her voice and her eyes. "It's Ned's sister, Lucy."

"Lucy . . . last name Withers?" Benny asked.

"That's her. Do you know her?"

"I do not. Who is she and why is she a secret?"

Claudia sighed. "She snuck over from Juneau. She's . . . wanted by the police. She took some things and was arrested, but got away and came over on the ferry a couple weeks ago. We've been letting her stay with us."

I suspected that if her husband hadn't beaten her, Claudia wouldn't have told on her sister-in-law, but she was just angry enough to spill the beans, even if the three of us in the room knew she might regret it, try to somehow recant it.

"Okay, we have to get that part figured out. You know that, don't you? I have to make some other calls. You understand?" Benny said.

"I get it."

Benny nodded and grabbed the phone again. She dialed the police station, but no one was there this late. She left a message that either Gril or Donner, the park ranger who was also part of our local law enforcement team, would get tomorrow morning. She tried Dr. Powder again, managing to catch him before he'd left, and asked him to pick up Gril on his way in. He told her he was already planning on it.

"Stay here tonight. You'll be safe," Benny said to Claudia after she hung up the phone.

"Thanks, Benny." Claudia was visibly relieved.

I'd watched them with a strange sense that this was all probably none of my business, but it somehow needed to be.

I'd heard the stories about what the winters here could do to people. When cold and darkness set in, people are forced to stay inside, stay in their homes. It could be too much for some people.

I was lucky because I lived in a room close to the bar and café, as well as the mercantile. Even in the worst weather, I could find a different place to go, someone else to talk to. So many Benedict residents lived away from the tiny downtown, the hub of our small civilization. It was just the day before that my friend Orin had told me about a walk that took place with spring thaw—the *Death Walk,* he called it. There was no other way to see if everyone was okay, had survived the winter, than to check on everyone personally, one by one.

Those who were alive all met downtown in search of

those who didn't show up for the search. Most of the time, everyone was found—some a little worse for the wear, some not too bad off. As spring came on, most everyone returned to normal, felt better, as darkness, literally and figuratively, lifted.

Even those who'd lived in Benedict the longest could be in danger of mental health issues. Just because they hadn't had any before didn't mean they wouldn't at some point.

The reason Orin had told me about the march was because he wanted me to post the date of the spring gathering in the *Petition*. Sure, it wasn't scheduled for four months, but the sooner everyone knew about it, could mark it on their calendars, the better. Orin mentioned that for some folks, just knowing the date helped, gave them something to look forward to.

Thoughts of being stuck in my home caused goose bumps to rise under all my winter gear. I didn't know what exactly was getting to me—the present conditions or the idea that I didn't ever want to be stuck, trapped, ever again. My reaction was too personal.

"Beth?" Benny said. "You okay?"

"Yes," I answered.

"Head on home if you want. I got this."

I looked at Claudia. We'd never even met before now, but I didn't think I could leave.

"I'm good," I said with a nod.

I wasn't, not all the way at least, but they didn't need to know that. And they didn't need to know that leaving right now might be even worse for me than staying and understanding, or maybe just lending a hand.

Three

Benny managed to convince the customers that the bar needed to close early—which wasn't an easy task, for a couple of reasons. Folks liked the socializing, and it had started snowing in a big, gusty way. This storm "had teeth," I heard a few people say. Going outside in the weather sounded much less appealing than riding it out inside for a while.

The last one out the door was the census man, whose name I learned was Doug Vitner, with most people just calling him Vitner. When he heard Gril was on his way with the doctor, he thought maybe he'd leave the vehicle he'd borrowed from the airport's small fleet of vans and catch a ride back to his room with his host, who surely knew how to drive through a storm better than he did.

But Benny told Vitner to leave anyway, that the police had business there that evening. He could figure out how to get back to Gril's just fine. I thought she was being a little harsh, but I kept that opinion to myself. To be fair, Gril's cabin wasn't too far away, just off the main road. I knew that the road had been cleared earlier that day—probably by Elijah. Thinking about him and Gus, I calculated that they had surely made it home before the storm.

Vitner was none too pleased, and he muttered some curse words in Benny's direction as he pulled a scarf tighter around his neck.

"Excuse me?" Benny had said.

"You heard me," Vitner said before he glared in my direction a beat too long. Finally, he pushed the door open and disappeared into the storm.

Neither Benny nor I commented about him further after he left.

I was surprised that she didn't ask me to leave, too. I didn't offer to go. I wondered if the shiver that had run through me earlier had given her the impression that I wasn't well and needed a watchful eye or two on me. When she asked Viola to join us, Benny might have considered that no one else would be at the Benedict House to make sure I was okay.

Gril and Dr. Powder arrived half an hour or so later, both of them making their way to the back room to Claudia and kicking the rest of us out into the front part of the bar.

Gril joined Viola, Benny, and me at our table a short time later.

"Claudia's okay," he said. "But we all know what happens next with Ned. He'll still be dangerous for a while. His wintertime violence has only gotten worse over the few years they've been here."

"She can stay here," Benny offered. "I'll stay, too."

"She can stay with me . . ."—Viola nodded in my direction—"us."

"There's more." Gril looked at Viola. "It sounds like we have a felon in town, which isn't uncommon, I know, but we weren't aware of this one until tonight. Ned's sister, Lucy, snuck over on the ferry a couple weeks ago. She's bad news, theft—armed, probably, though from what I can glean so far, she hasn't shot at anyone. I'll check with Juneau police tonight or in the morning. Donner is on his way here, and he and I will head over to Ned and Claudia's to pick Lucy up. I doubt she's left the house in this storm and don't know where she would go anyway."

"That's only going to make Ned angrier," I added.

"We know, so . . . here's what I'd like to do. Well, what I'd really like to do is take both Lucy and Ned into custody and keep them at the police station, but the heater isn't working like it should over there. It would be dangerous and irresponsible to do such a thing. Besides, I don't have much of a way to secure a prisoner, and I'm thinking Lucy and Ned shouldn't stay together. We'll let Ned stay at his house for now; he's got a sprained ankle, so he won't run, I don't think. I want Claudia to stay here at the bar or go home with you, Benny—but Donner will stay here, too. Vi, I want you to lock Lucy in one of your rooms at the Benedict House for the night. I'll figure out how to get her back to Juneau tomorrow. There might be a ferry coming over, I heard. I want to send Ned back to Juneau, too. We can't keep doing this with Ned and Claudia. It's only getting worse."

I hadn't known about Ned and Claudia before now, but I saw how tonight's events had preyed on Gril, and he wasn't easily tired.

I heard the moan of the wind outside and couldn't imagine the weather would clear enough by tomorrow for a ferry run.

"You can just kick Ned out of town?" I asked.

"Yes. I'll have him taken in over there for assault. Hopefully I can get it all done, or at least get him out of here, before Claudia changes her story. I'm not sure what I'll be able to accomplish, but I'll try."

"Gril," Benny said, "I don't know if it will help, but Ned was in here yesterday afternoon. He couldn't walk well, because of that hurt ankle, so I made sure he had a seat. I served him only one drink, but he must have been drinking beforehand. He got out of control, obnoxious, quickly. I had to kick him out. He broke a chair. I don't know, maybe that will give you more."

"He was violent?" Gril asked.

"Well, toward the chair. I didn't give him much of a chance to be violent toward any of the customers."

"Good to know." Gril stood.

Benny bit her bottom lip, glanced at the door, and then back at Gril. "I'm pretty sure I closed up with plenty of time for everyone to get home before the storm."

Gril nodded.

"I met Elijah Wyatt tonight. I don't know the timing of everything exactly, but I think he and his dog, Gus, had ample time to make it home," I interjected.

"I'll check on them," Gril said. He looked at Viola. "You okay babysitting Lucy?"

"Of course." Viola nodded once.

Gril looked at me. "You might want to stay someplace else tonight. To repeat, I really don't think she's violent, but it might not be worth the risk. You could stay here or bunk up in the *Petition* shed—heater works great out there."

"Viola is armed," I said, without mentioning the shed's tin roof and how noisy it was during storms.

"But you're not," Gril said.

I nodded. "I'll be fine. Does Claudia have a concussion?"

The other three looked at me with questioning eyes.

"Um. Well, no. She's fine. Doesn't even need stitches," Gril said.

Not needing stitches in Benedict was different from not needing stitches in other parts of the world where medical care was easier and Alaskan snowstorms didn't keep travel to a minimum. Viola had cut her hand a week earlier during another storm. She'd had me superglue it together, but there was no question that stitches would have been in order. However, we were both pleased with my handiwork.

"Good. I'm happy to hear she's going to be okay," I said.

Gril shook his head. "If her husband doesn't kill her first. Again, I'd like to get him out of here or her out of here, but I doubt she'll want to leave. I can do more to force him."

It was difficult for the Juneau police to send resources in this direction. Juneau had its own problems, and though I'd met a medical examiner from there, I hadn't met any actual officers of the law. Travel was risky, and once here, as I was seeing now, getting back over in the winter wasn't easy or predictable.

The Harvington brothers operated the small airstrip on the edge of town, but I'd heard they hadn't had a plane up since they'd delivered Ellen back to Juneau. Isolation was what I'd wanted, and I'd found the perfect spot.

But Benedict folks would always have to take care of Benedict folks.

The door to the bar flew open again and Donner came through. He was covered in a patchwork of ice, his beard catching the light and sparkling.

"Damn, it's getting bad out there," Viola said.

"It is," Donner agreed.

Gril shook his head again as he stood. "Let's get this over with, Donner. Powder will stay as long as you want him to, Benny."

"I think he should head back home before the roads are completely impassable," Benny said.

"Your call," Gril said. "You're armed, too?"

"Yes, sir."

I didn't know that Benny also had a weapon, but her sister wore her gun proudly in a holster on her hip. Benny wasn't quite as obvious.

"All right. Let's go, Donner." Gril zipped his coat.

I watched as the two of them went back out into the snow. As the door closed and the residual chill filled the air inside,

I had a sense that there must be another way or other ways to take care of the situation. It all seemed so precarious.

But there were no other options right now, only making do with what we had. I trusted the people in charge, but when darkness and storms intervened, sometimes even the best choices couldn't help but seem like the wrong ones.

Four

The storm raged on as Viola and I sat in the Benedict House's dining room, drinking coffee and snacking on whatever we could find in the pantry. Viola didn't stock the cupboards when there weren't clients in house to do the cooking. We both ate most of our meals at the small restaurant downtown or threw together sandwiches and canned soup.

"How are you and your fella?" Viola asked as she topped off our coffees for the third, or maybe the fourth, time.

"My fella?" I asked before I realized that she was talking about the only man I'd dated since moving to Benedict. Tex Southern, a man with a life so different from mine that as much as we liked each other, we couldn't quite figure out how to work with the differences. "You mean Tex?"

"Of course I mean Tex. Who else has there been?"

"No one. I mean, Tex isn't really someone, either."

"Why? What's the problem? I heard you two seemed to get along."

I wondered who'd told her such a thing, but the possibilities were endless. Gossip was a way of life in Benedict.

"We live far away from each other. He has daughters; I don't even have a pet."

"I thought you liked his girls."

"I do! A lot, actually, but that doesn't change the fact that I've never spent much time around children." In fact, even when I was one myself, I didn't spend much time around children. I was always either with my mother, on the road in search of my father, or with my grandfather, a small-town Missouri police chief, but I couldn't tell Viola those details.

"Do you like him?" Viola asked.

"Vi, I haven't seen him in a month. He lives twenty miles away and the weather has made travel less than ideal."

"*Pfft*. Twenty miles is nothing. Do you like him?"

I looked at her. "Yes, I do like him, but I don't know if it's a love match, you know."

"What's missing?"

"Again, we haven't seen each other in a month. In fact, we only had a few dates." Five, to be exact, and they'd all been enjoyable, if more or less platonic.

"You can use the landline in my office, you know. He has one, right?"

"He does."

It had crossed my mind a time or two that I could call Tex, but that had seemed somehow strange, maybe not grown-up. I had my own phone, a burner, but I used it rarely because of the spotty cell phone coverage.

"Use my phone. Call him." She leaned forward and put her elbows on the table. "You're not one of those women who needs the man to make all the moves, are you?"

"No," I said. "Not even a little bit. It's just all so much more . . . work here."

Viola shrugged. "Your life, I suppose."

She didn't know the half of it. She had no idea what my life truly was. What I also couldn't tell her was that even though spending time with someone who didn't live right next door out here was work, it was the lie I'd continued to live that made it even more difficult. I hadn't told Tex the truth of who I was, either. That was the real reason I hadn't pursued a deeper relationship. I'd read the signals. I'd seen his interest, but a lie gets worse the longer it goes on. I liked him too much to continue to hide my real self around him.

The people in my new home of Benedict had been introduced to me as Beth Rivers from Colorado. The irony was that that was my real name, but certainly not who I was best known as, Elizabeth Fairchild from St. Louis, Missouri. I didn't look much like the author photo inside my books anymore, a woman with a happy, successful glint in her eyes. When I looked in the mirror these days, I could see a now-dull gaze in my reflection.

I'd never been to Colorado. My escape from the hospital in St. Louis where I'd been recovering from the brain surgery had been assisted by Detective Majors, the woman on the case in Missouri. I thought she was good at her job, but apparently she wasn't as good at being a detective as Travis Walker was at hiding from the police.

"Maybe I'll give him a call," I said.

"Good idea."

We heard the front door open and then voices approaching.

"'Bout time." Viola stood. "Want to just wait here while I get her settled?"

"No," I answered quickly. The deep curiosity about the state of Claudia's injuries was still with me. I wanted as many details as possible in regard to what was going on. Details were powerful things.

"All right, stay back some. Do as Gril and I say. If we tell you to vamoose, vamoose. Got it?"

"Yes."

Viola adjusted the holster on her hips and led the way out of the dining room and into the entryway, a comfortable space still furnished with a cherrywood key box from the days the building was an inn.

It was crowded tonight, and a spray of snow spread from the doorway all the way to the counter.

Gril and Donner stood on either side of a woman about my age, around thirty.

"Let go of my arm, assholes," she spat as she squirmed.

Neither Gril nor Donner let go.

"What is this hoity-toity—and I'm being sarcastic here, in case y'all are too thick to get it—place?" Lucy asked.

"You'll be staying here this evening, Ms. Withers," Gril informed her. He shook his head at Donner. "We'll all be staying here this evening."

"Well, aren't I the lucky one? Who the fuck are you two?" Lucy looked at Viola and me.

"I am your worst nightmare," Viola said.

I didn't offer up my name but suppressed a smile at Viola's Clint Eastwood–esque answer.

Lucy looked Viola up and down, took in this big woman with a gun. She tried to keep her jaw jutted forward, her eyes critical, but I saw the brief waver as she realized who was in charge.

"Come with me." Viola stepped forward and grabbed Lucy's arm. Viola looked at Gril. "I got her. You two go have some coffee."

Viola led Lucy down the hallway and into a room next to hers. Clients are usually taken up to the second floor, but it appeared Lucy was going to get some special attention.

Once they were shut inside the room, I looked at Gril. "Is this okay?"

Gril shrugged. "We don't have a lot of choices."

Donner stepped around Gril and me and made his way into the dining room. "Was the coffee a genuine offer?"

I nodded, and a short time later, after he brewed a fresh pot, we were pouring new cups.

"I could have just let her stay with Ned overnight.

She probably wouldn't have gone out in the weather, but I couldn't risk it," Gril said. "We need a better holding facility, but frankly, we've not had many issues. This is certainly a rare case."

"How was Ned?"

Gril and Donner shared a frown.

"Upset," Gril said. "I left him home if only to keep everyone away from everyone else."

"Will he search for Claudia tonight?" I asked.

"Doubt it." Gril shook his head. "It's brutal out there. Ned is a violent bully, but he's also a self-preservationist and he does have a hurt ankle."

"Will he cool down?" I lifted my mug, enjoying Donner's strong coffee.

"He always does, eventually. Then he always heats up again, too," Donner said.

"Other times, Claudia has begged me to let him be," Gril added. "Ultimately, she's afraid of trying to live on her own."

"It's a real concern for some people," I said.

"Right. But I think those sorts of fears compound in the winter." Gril looked at me. "Believe it or not, there are some folks who love this time of year, the isolation."

I nodded. "You are staying here overnight?"

"I am," he said. "Donner's heading over to the bar to stay with Benny and Claudia."

I sat back in my chair and regarded the two weary men. "You know, not many people would get the care you're giving Claudia. You're going above and beyond."

Donner smiled under his thick beard. I'd come to recognize the expression via the turning up of the corners of his eyes; it was next to impossible to see his mouth. "Best police chief in Alaska."

Gril huffed. "Brownnoser."

Donner stood. "I'll head over to Benny's. Hopefully, the ferry will be running tomorrow."

"Cross your fingers," Gril said. "Thanks for all your help tonight."

"Yes, sir. Thanks for the coffee, Beth. Call the landline at the bar if anyone here needs anything."

"What do you suppose Viola is doing in there with Lucy?" I asked Gril after Donner left.

"Laying down the law."

"Is any of this legal?"

"Not technically, but it'll all be fine. We have to keep as many people safe as we can. Because of our circumstances, we can't always follow exact procedure, but we do our best."

I nodded. Whatever secrets they wanted me to keep regarding their methods, I was on board.

Gril sat forward on his chair and glanced quickly toward the hallway before he spoke quietly. "I have something I need to talk to you about."

"Oh?" I looked toward the hallway, too; there was no one approaching. We'd heard Donner leave and would hear the front door open again if he came back. We would know when Viola came out of Lucy's room.

"I heard from the detective on your case today."

"Today?" I hadn't received a phone call or an email from Detective Majors, but I'd only checked first thing in the morning. It was after midnight now, so technically that was yesterday morning.

Gril nodded. "Your mother. Have you heard from her?"

"Not for months."

Gril squinted.

"I'm not lying, Gril. Not for months." I looked toward the hallway again. "Not since she shot—allegedly shot—Walker in the grocery store parking lot."

"Right."

She'd gotten away, too, gone underground. She'd done this sort of thing before—gone into hiding after doing something she shouldn't have been doing, though this was her first time shooting someone, as far as I knew. Her disappearing act wasn't unusual to me, which was probably the strangest thing of all. I truly hadn't heard from Mill Rivers in months.

Gril rubbed his short gray scraggly beard as he inspected me.

"I really haven't heard from her, Gril. Why do you ask?"

"Detective Majors thinks she's tracked Mill to Juneau."

I choked on air. "What?"

"The police got a tip. A woman visiting Juneau made a fuss outside a gift shop. The woman was asked to show her ID. The ID she showed the officer wasn't in your mother's name, but the cop was sharp. He watched the woman as she sorted through some cards, caught the name on another ID. He saw it gave Millicent as a first name, and Missouri as the residence state. Majors has asked to be notified by police from other states when there are any potential sightings. The Juneau officer made a call."

"So either the woman was Mill or she has Mill's identification? Any description?"

"Tall, skinny, about sixty probably, with curly dark hair."

"That could be Mill."

Gril frowned. "Majors wanted to give me a heads-up and asked me to talk to you. I didn't sense any urgency this morning, but now that a ferry might be coming over tomorrow and with everything else that will keep me distracted, I thought I should let you know."

The wind howled, rattling every part of the building.

"There's no way the ferry will be over tomorrow," I said.

Gril shrugged. "All indications are that the weather will clear in a couple of hours and it will be safe for travel shortly after that."

I *had* witnessed some surprisingly quick weather changes. "Is it possible she tracked me down?"

"Don't know. She's been searching for your father for years, still hasn't found him."

"But she might have found me?" Gril knew what I was really saying—if Mill could find me, anyone could.

And of course there was a specific someone I didn't want doing any such thing.

Gril put his hand on my arm. "I'm still seeing the manifests, Beth. Not only that, I've given the ferry folks a picture of Walker, asked them to be on the lookout. The Harvingtons won't bring over anyone who looks like him. They'll let me know if any other planes bring someone like him here. In fact, they called me when that census man, Vitner, stopped by the airport right after he disembarked the ferry. They were suspicious. It's why Vitner's staying with me. I wanted to make sure."

I thought about the man I'd seen tonight for the first time and gave a nervous laugh. "I hadn't even known he was here until tonight. I don't see much resemblance to Walker, aside from maybe age."

"I'm just trying to tell you that I'm watching everything. Closely."

The picture I'd received of my stalker was from an earlier arrest, for things other than stalking. I couldn't remember not knowing what he looked like now. The image of his face was burned into my mind.

In fact, there *was* a slight resemblance between Walker and Vitner—not only age, but their short brown hair, average weight. But I'd seen Vitner's eyes, and though they weren't friendly when he'd been talking to Benny, they weren't evil like Walker's. No, it wasn't the same person, no matter what my imagination might try to make of it.

"I appreciate it, Gril."

"I'll be at the ferry tomorrow—if it comes in, that is. Do you want me to give them an additional heads-up, a description of your mother? Do you want her to stay away if she is in fact trying to get here? Shoot, Beth, I think there's a chance that she might even be on it tomorrow, if that was her they talked to."

I couldn't accept that idea, but I knew I needed to remember that with Mill, anything at all was possible. I pondered a moment. Was she really trying to get to me? Sure, I wouldn't mind seeing her, but she and I weren't made to be around each other for an extended time period. I was curious, though. What had she done, what else had she been up to? How had she managed . . . everything?

"No, it's okay. She would never hurt me or anyone in Benedict. I still can't believe she might be that close by. This must be just a strange set of circumstances that won't turn out to be what they appear. Right?"

"I don't know."

I looked at Gril. We sat together for a long few minutes, both of us deep in our thoughts. A big wave of exhaustion came over me and I realized that whether or not I processed or accepted what he was saying, whatever was going to happen was going to happen.

"I'd better get some rest. I'll go with you to the ferry—if it comes in, of course. If Mill Rivers is on her way to town, she'd love a real welcome," I finally said, the seeds of possibility taking deeper root.

She wouldn't come here, though, would she? She'd want to remain under the radar. Gril heard my sarcasm but shrugged and nodded before he poured himself another cup of coffee and I went to bed.

Five

I woke up facedown on the floor. It was still dark and cold, but I couldn't get an immediate grasp on the time. At least I wasn't confused as to where I was. I was in my room in the Benedict House, but waking up on the floor wasn't normal at all.

I sat up and leaned against the side of the mattress. I'd fallen out of bed? I didn't remember any other time in my life that I'd done such a thing, and I didn't remember this fall. I'd awakened because of the cold, not because of the impact of hitting the floor or any resulting pain.

My head cleared some more, and I lifted myself up and back onto the bed. I grabbed the clock I'd put on the nightstand—burner phones didn't work as well as smartphones when it came to clocks and alarms. It was close to four A.M., that almost-end-of-the-night point when it's hard to get back to sleep because you were going to get up in a couple of hours anyway.

I pushed away the confusion. I needed to take stock.

I realized my bare feet were colder than the rest of me. I should wear socks to bed. I tucked myself back under the thick bedcovers and pulled them up around my chin. The sheets were cold, too, as if I hadn't been in them for at least a good few minutes. Everything would warm up quickly.

How long had I been on the floor? The Benedict House's furnace did a good job, but the inside winter air was cool, with drafts blowing here and there. My feet were still downright icy.

A noise, a thud, sounded from somewhere, but I couldn't immediately determine if it came from inside or out. A duplicate noise pulled me back out of the bed, and I went to the window, peeling back the curtain.

The storm had let up, but the darkness was still thick. I couldn't make out any distinct shapes.

Like the downtown area, the Benedict House was an L-shaped structure, though made up of two stories. Outside my window, I could see the other part of the el, where Viola's room was located. Through the gloom, I noticed that Viola's light was on, as well as the light for the room where Lucy was being kept.

I heard the noise again, but now I was sure it came from inside the building. Doors were probably opening and closing. I'd heard that plenty of times, but there was something different about these thuds that made me wonder what else was going on.

I switched on the lamp on my nightstand and squinted as my eyes adjusted again. I pulled thick socks over my feet and slipped into some tennis shoes. I threw more sweats over the sweats I was already wearing and a cap onto my head before I went to my door.

When I went to unlock the thumb latch, I stopped in my tracks. It was not turned appropriately. I slowed down, wondering if I'd left it unlocked. This could happen—but it hadn't happened to me since I'd been in Alaska. In fact, I'd been obsessive about making sure all the locks in my life were secured tightly, to the point of checking and rechecking them. I couldn't remember if I'd followed my normal rituals once I'd made it to my room sometime after midnight. I'd been so tired.

I turned the knob and the door opened. Maybe I'd just moved too quickly in my distracted state and earlier exhaustion. Maybe it had been unlocked during the night. I looked at the spot on the floor where I'd awakened, but there were no answers there. What had happened to result in my being there—and had it included leaving my room?

This would not matter to most people, wouldn't have mattered to me before Travis Walker. Most people would either not notice or chalk it up to temporary carelessness, not obsess over it.

But I'd lived through something that most people hadn't. Instead of a second or two of rolling my eyes at myself, I felt a deep well of shame dig its way through my gut. This was not what someone who cared about her well-being did.

Shit.

With my hand still on the doorknob, I closed my eyes and breathed in and out, telling myself this wasn't the big deal I was making it.

I'd come far enough in whatever recovery I was making to know my reaction wasn't appropriate, that there was nothing to be ashamed of—I would do better next time, and all's well that ends well, right?

It wasn't that easy to get from A to B, but I would. Eventually. And from now on, I would damn well go back to making sure my door was locked.

I touched the key in my pocket before I stepped into the hallway and pulled the door shut. I locked the door and checked it twice.

Viola kept the lights in the hallways on all the time but dimmed them at night. I could see up toward the front door, but not down into the other part, where Viola's room and office, as well as the dining room and kitchen, were. I didn't know if Viola had provided Gril with a room or if he was still in the dining room.

As I came around to the small lobby, I looked at the mat by the front door where we kept the shoes and boots—heavy on boots this time of year. My eyes landed on mine, the ones I'd recently purchased that had become my favorites. I'd worn them earlier, but had taken them off when Viola and I had first come home.

They were shinier than I'd expect after sitting there for so many hours. I crouched and grabbed them, realizing that they were indeed wet and cold. I looked at the pair Viola had had on earlier—damp but not soaked, and not nearly as cold as mine.

"What in the world?" I muttered. Had someone worn my boots outside after I had tonight? Or was this normal residual moisture? I'd never checked my boots at four in the morning before.

I put them back and shook off a new sense of discombobulation. "You're just out of sorts," I muttered again to myself.

The front door opened wide. The cold wind brought in some icy air as well as Gril. The weather had calmed, but not died down completely.

"Beth, what are you doing?" Gril asked.

"I heard something."

"What?" Gril's hand fell to the gun at his side.

"Just thuds, maybe doors closing."

"Did someone leave?"

"Um, I don't know what's going on. Where were you?"

"I heard something, too, a while ago, though."

"Doors?"

"No, not doors." Gril moved past me and walked quickly down the hallway toward Viola's room.

He knocked once. "I'm coming in, Viola." He pushed the

door open just as I caught up to him and looked over his shoulder.

No one was in the room.

"Vi?" Gril went through and to the bathroom.

I was close behind. The bathroom door was open, but she wasn't in there, either.

Gril turned and pushed past me, making his way next door to Lucy's room. He pulled a key out of his pocket and used it to open Lucy's door. I recognized it as a master key for all the rooms, and my strange mind wondered if maybe Gril had unlocked my door earlier. I pushed away the idea.

"Coming in, Lucy," Gril announced as he pushed through again.

Lucy sat up in the bed, her eyes blinking in confusion. "The fuck?" She pulled the quilt up around her neck.

"Have you been in here the whole time?" Gril asked.

"What do you mean, the whole time? Like, since that crazy bitch threw me in here and threatened to shoot me if I even thought about leaving? Yeah, I've been in here *that* whole time. I'm not as stupid as the rest of you look. Also, I was locked in. How about that? Seems like some civil rights might have been violated here."

Boy, wasn't she likable.

I glanced around the room as Gril checked the bathroom. Not only had Viola left Lucy a glass of water, but a mostly clean plate, with some bread crusts, sat on the nightstand. A hairbrush and some scrunchies were there, too; Lucy's hair was pulled up with a bright pink one.

There was no sign of torture or obvious injury. She seemed fine, well taken care of.

Viola wasn't in there.

"Where's Viola?" Gril asked.

"How would I know?" Lucy said as she sniffed.

Gril looked at her a long moment. "Go back to sleep." He

then directed me out of the room and pulled the door behind him.

"Light?" Lucy asked before it closed.

He didn't reopen it to flip the switch for her, but he did double-check that it locked again.

We heard noises coming from the stairs and turned to see Viola come from the stairway. She was dressed in sweats, too, but she had a scarf around her neck. Her nose was bright red.

"What's going on?" Gril asked.

"A couple windows sprung open up there. I had to get them closed and locked. Wasn't easy. What's going on down here? Lucy okay?"

"She's fine," Gril said.

Viola looked at him as if his questions, his reactions, weren't quite what she expected, but maybe she didn't know he'd left the building and that made her think differently. I wasn't going to bring that part up yet.

"You okay?" Viola asked Gril.

"Just couldn't find you."

"I didn't think to let you know I was going up there. Next time I will."

Again, Gril didn't tell her he'd been out of the building. Again, I wasn't going to, either, even if I didn't quite understand why.

"What are you doing out of bed?" Viola asked me.

"I heard noises—probably you upstairs with the windows."

Viola squinted. "Probably."

We stood there a long moment, each of us most likely waiting for whatever the others felt they needed to say.

"Get some rest," Gril finally said. "Ferry will be here at noon if it comes in." He turned and walked back into the dining room.

Viola eyed him and then sent me a questioning glance. "Go to bed, Beth," she said before she went back into her own room.

I stood in the hallway by myself for a long moment. What in the world had just happened? Where had Gril been?

Why were my boots so wet?

Had I truly not locked my door?

And I'd fallen out of bed? What in the world?

I shook my head at myself and finally went back to my room. Things were always weirder at night. Despite all the activity and the strange hour, I *was* able to get back to sleep, after checking the lock on my door a few times and then finally placing a chair under the knob—something I hadn't done for months. It was the best choice, at least for a little while.

Six

Next time I woke up, it was already nine-thirty. Even though that was much later than normal for me, I lay in bed a moment as my mind replayed the strange events from the long night before. It had all seemed so bizarre, ramped-up spookiness with the wind blowing outside.

Had I truly fallen out of bed?

I thought about the moments when Gril came back inside, the frostiness of my wet boots, and Viola's appearance from the stairway and subsequent claim to be closing windows upstairs. If I examined the events one by one, nothing was suspicious, but there had been such a layer of mystery to everything that I couldn't shake the notion that something else had been going on, though I couldn't guess what.

The wind wasn't blowing hard enough to shake the rafters anymore, and light framed the thick curtains over the window. That helped push away most of my leftover apprehension, but not all of it.

I got out of bed and made my way to the window. The sun rose at about nine and then set again at around three-thirty this time of year. And, boy, was it there this morning. I squinted as I took in the bright blue sky. I wondered at the current temperature; the high today would probably be about freezing.

I hurried to get ready, still somewhat off from the night's activities, but I couldn't deny that I felt a thread of excitement because of the possibility that the ferry was coming over, though not just because there was a remote chance that my mother would be on it. I relished the idea that the maritime highway might see some traffic again, even if temporarily. Just seeing the ferry gave me a connection to the rest of the world that I didn't even know I craved until I'd watched it dock two weeks earlier. I had no desire to leave Benedict yet, but the ferry's back-and-forth journey instilled me with the confidence that I could.

And yes, the other part of my excitement was because of Mill. If she truly had been in Juneau because she'd figured out where I was, she'd been looking for a chance to get here. She'd know that today might be her day. A part of me dreaded her coming to Benedict, but another part of me would be happy to see her. That anticipation and my lifelong curiosity regarding how she still hadn't been caught in any of her exploits gave me real hope that I'd see her soon. However, her days of freedom might be over, too, though Gril didn't behave as if he wanted to arrest her. I wished for a way to contact her, maybe warn her, at least find out if she really was in Juneau.

I moved the chair away from the door, pleased to see the bolt was still locked, and went back out into the now brightly lit hallway.

Breakfast smells came from the kitchen, and a sense of the newness of another day propelled me forward. Pep found its way into my step.

"Gril?" I said when I entered the kitchen.

"Morning. Want something to eat?"

"You're cooking?" I didn't ask where he got the groceries, but he'd probably ventured to the café for things.

"I am. Why not?"

"You're the police chief."

"And my prisoner, if we can go so far as to call her that, is four doors away. I was awake. Everyone needs to eat. Go grab Viola and ask her to bring Lucy."

I nodded and made my way to Viola's room, surprised that she wasn't up yet. Even with a late night, she was usually out of her room by six.

She opened the door as I arrived. "You cooking?"

"Nope. Gril."

"Ah." She adjusted the holster. "I'll grab Lucy. The sooner we get her out of here, the better."

"Was she trouble?" I asked.

"She's made of trouble," Viola said. "But no, she wasn't extra trouble."

I followed her to Lucy's door, noting to myself that I wouldn't be surprised if the room was empty.

But it wasn't empty. Lucy was there, her hair still up in the scrunchie as she sat on the edge of the bed. "Jesus. About time. I thought you all were going to just let me smell the food. I'm starving."

"I'm just here to make sure you're okay. I didn't offer you food," Viola said.

I started at her words. She was tough, but never mean.

"You can kiss my ass, then."

Viola put her hands on her hips and shook her head. "The chief told me to let you eat. If it had been up to me, I just don't know."

"Whatever," Lucy said. She looked at me. "Who are you? You're like a sad puppy or a shadow or something. Do you have a name?"

I lifted an eyebrow but didn't say anything. Maybe Viola's meanness was justified.

"Let's go." Viola led us the short distance to the dining room.

Viola instructed Lucy to sit down as I grabbed the silverware. I was used to helping the clients with cooking and setting the table, so it was a familiar routine, even though Gril had never joined us before.

"A policeman who can cook. How . . . weird," Lucy said.

"Actually, I'm the chief. How was your night, Lucy?"

"Cold, windy, noisy, and full of interruptions. Why do you ask?"

"Just being polite."

Lucy snorted. "I don't believe that at all."

We sat together around a table and didn't waste a moment digging into the delicious food. We were all hungry. My familiar sense of bottomless hunger was back, and for a few bites I couldn't have cared less who I was eating with and what they might have done the night before.

"Care to share more of the details of what got you in trouble in Juneau?" Gril asked a moment later.

"Here?" Lucy said. "In front of everyone? Why?"

"Again, just being polite."

"No you're not. But it doesn't matter. I'm not going to tell anyone much of anything until I get an attorney."

"Did you witness your brother beating up his wife?" Viola asked.

We all looked at Lucy. Gril didn't seem to be bothered by Viola's jumping in.

"My brother didn't touch her."

"How'd she get the black eye then, the cuts?" Viola asked.

Lucy shrugged. "Ran into a door or something."

"Eat your breakfast," Gril said.

A few more silent bites later, the front door opened and we heard Donner. "Gril?"

The tone of that one word grabbed our attention—something was wrong.

"Back here." Gril scooted the chair back and stood, wiping a napkin over his mouth.

Donner was there a moment later. "We have a problem."

"What's up?" Gril moved around the table.

Donner surveyed the dining room, his eyes landing first on me, then Viola, and finally Lucy. "Shit."

"Donner, what's going on?" Gril asked.

Donner took a deep breath, but it didn't appear to calm him any, if that had been his goal. "You gotta come with me, Chief. Everyone else stay here. Right here. Do not leave the Benedict House until we come back."

"Let's go."

The men were out of the building only a few seconds later.

"Finish up," Viola said to Lucy. "You're going back to your room."

"What?" Lucy said, her mouth still full of food.

"You have approximately one minute to eat whatever you can." Viola looked at her watch. "Go."

"You are violating one constitutional right of mine after another." Her mouth was still full.

"You don't even know what the Constitution is," Viola said. "Forty-five seconds."

Lucy shoved more food in her mouth, and true to her word, Viola had her relocked in her room before the minute was up.

"What about the window in her room?" I asked after she confirmed the door was locked. The idea that she'd try to escape seemed more real in the daytime.

Viola went around me and into her own room. She gathered her winter gear, wrapping her face in the same scarf I'd seen her in the night before. "She might try to run, but she won't get far. It's cold, and anyone who talks tough like she does is truly a wimp. I'm not too worried. She'd probably go right back to Ned's anyway. Ned's a shit, and he'd give her up if the choice was between him and her. Go to your room and make sure the door's locked or head on off to the *Petition,* if you need to get out of here. Sorry to disrupt your breakfast, but I want you to be away from Lucy for now."

"Why?"

"Don't know her, don't like her, and don't trust her."

"Where are you going?"

"To see what's going on."

"Donner said to stay here."

"Don't care."

"I'm coming with you."

"Gril has asked me specifically to make sure you mind your own business."

"I don't care, either," I said as I took off in a jog to my room to grab my gear. "Just give me fifteen seconds."

Viola stopped by the front door and looked at her watch. "Go."

I donned sunglasses as Viola put on her Indiana Jones fedora. The biting cold air tingled my face, and the brightness caused my eyes to water even behind the dark lenses. I wished I'd grabbed a scarf, too. But I forgot about it when we spotted the small crowd a couple of seconds later.

"Stay behind me," Viola said as we took off, our boots crunching in the icy snow.

I stuck close to her as we made our way toward the sculpture of Ben, the bear, which announced our small downtown.

"Back!" Gril demanded as we approached. "I mean it, stay back!"

The sculpture resided at the front of the small downtown.

It was of an adult-sized black bear. It was cute, which of course some bears were, particularly from a safe distance. But this one was cuter than any of the black or grizzly bears I'd seen around Benedict, and I'd seen quite a few by now. The sculpture's mouth was turned up at the corners, welcoming anyone who came to visit. At the moment it was the only creature in the area with a smile. Something was clearly wrong.

Gril, Donner, Benny, and Claudia were gathered together a yard or so away from the back end of Ben, their attention either on something in front of the sculpture or, in Claudia's case, at the ground around her feet. Her hand was over her mouth. Even from a distance, I could see her wide-eyed look of fear or perhaps shock, but I couldn't see what was causing the reaction. Benny held on to Claudia's arm.

"What's going on, Gril?" Viola asked.

If it had been anyone else who asked, he probably wouldn't have answered. He looked back at us, at Viola specifically, his mouth in a straight serious line. He paused a moment longer, but then said, "We've got a body, Vi."

Viola mumbled some curse words before she spoke aloud again. "Who is it?"

"It's Ned!" Claudia shrieked. "It's my Ned!"

"Shit," Viola said quietly.

"This is a crime scene," Donner said as he looked at us. Even though he wore sunglasses, too, I could see his strained expression. "We've already contaminated it. Stay back so you don't add to the problem."

"What happened?" The words jumped out of my mouth. I took a step closer to the scene, but Viola put her hand out to stop me. I couldn't see anything—no body, not even a spatter of blood.

For a long moment, no one said anything as Claudia wailed.

"He was murdered," Benny finally said. "Stabbed, we think."

"Murdered?" Viola said. "Are you sure? The weather last night. The elements . . ."

Donner shook his head slowly. "No, not the elements. It was murder."

Claudia cried out again.

I craned my neck again, but still couldn't see anything. I glanced all around. I didn't see anyone else outside. Was Ned's body noticed by someone driving by along one of the main roads that intersected only about twenty feet from Ben? But we were the only ones out there. Maybe no one had driven by yet. There had been a storm the night before. Maybe everyone was still inside their homes.

"Who found him?" I asked.

Donner and Gril looked at each other, but neither of them answered.

"Gril?" I urged.

No one answered.

Viola looked at me, her hand on her gun. "You stay right there. We're going to get Claudia inside. Don't move until I tell you to." She walked toward her sister. "Let's get them out of here, Benny. Gril and Donner have work to do."

Benny and Viola guided Claudia toward the bar. Viola nodded that I should go with them as they came back by. I hurried to open the door to the bar, sending another fleeting glance out toward the sculpture, but I still couldn't see anything unusual. I wished I could.

I looked around yet again and knew there was something I should be noticing. I told myself to look, *really* look.

I finally saw it. The two main roads had been plowed. Elijah might have seen Ned's body. Is that how he was found? Had Elijah called the police? If so, why wasn't he here still? When had he plowed?

It was just one of the questions crashing around in my mind. I had about a million others, but I was afraid to focus on them. They all had something to do with the strange things that had happened overnight. What had really occurred during that storm, and had something I heard or seen been tied to a murder?

One more time I looked out toward Ben.

I wished I could be as bold as I'd been the night before with Benny as she attended to Claudia. But I couldn't. My curiosity was still there, but this time there was raw fear, too.

I took a deep breath and then followed the other women inside.

Seven

Claudia was inconsolable. Viola made another call to Dr. Powder, who returned to the bar to examine Claudia again and administer a sedative. He also confirmed that Ned Withers was in fact dead, though I didn't think there'd been any doubt. After he finished up, Viola, Benny, and I sat in the front of the bar—leaving the door to the back room open in case Claudia awakened again.

Benny kept the CLOSED sign lit, but since the whole downtown square was cordoned off as a crime scene, no one could make it even as far as the door anyway.

"How long do you think it will take them?" Benny asked Viola. "I'm sorry about Ned, but I'm sure people will start to get antsy in an hour or so; some folks will need to get their stuff done before the sun sets."

"I'm not sure. I know Gril has been on the phone with Juneau authorities. He had too much to handle as of last night, but now, with a murder, he's trying to get some help. If Juneau wants to send people over, it could be a while."

It was just before noon. We still had a few hours of light.

"The ferry?" I asked.

"It should be here in about an hour. It did leave Juneau,

but a little late, and Ned wasn't found until after it disembarked. Any investigators will need to fly over if they're coming," Viola said. "The ferry will turn right around and head back, so folks will have to be ready to go, including any crime scene folks, if they don't want to fly back—and that's more unpredictable. Planes get grounded all the time, at Mother Nature's whim. It all makes for some precarious planning."

"Who found Ned?" I asked.

"Donner, I think." Viola looked at Benny, who was nodding.

"How did someone not see him sooner?"

"Oh, he . . . it . . ."—Benny cringed—"you couldn't see him from any spot except if you were looking right by Ben. He bled a lot, but everything was contained. The way the snow's been plowed, the amount on the ground. He was just well hidden, kind of in a hole, but not something that was dug, just a well of sorts."

I nodded. "What about whoever plowed this morning? Elijah?"

"If the roads were done this morning, they would have been done by Elijah," Viola added. "But he would have done them in the dark. I didn't even look out that way. Had they been plowed?"

"I think so," I said.

"Let's remember to tell Gril, just in case," Viola said. "Maybe Elijah saw something."

"Elijah wouldn't have seen him. No one would unless they were right there," Benny said again.

"Why was Donner right there?" I asked.

Benny shrugged. "Don't know."

Viola squinted at me. "What's on your mind, Beth?"

"I'm just trying to understand."

I was, but there was more. I'd heard sounds last night. Gril said he had, too. Had the noises I'd heard really been Viola closing windows? Had Gril ever figured out what he might have heard? Or did he just tell me he thought he'd heard something? Why would he do that?

When Donner and Gril and I sat around a dining table in the Benedict House the night before, they'd talked about Ned and how it was time to put an end to his behavior. They went out in the storm to talk to him, while at the same time mentioning they didn't think he would go anywhere. What really happened last night, and was I willing to mention my thoughts to anyone? I didn't know yet, but I sure didn't like feeling suspicious about any of these people. They were my friends—my family, almost.

"What happened, Benz?" Viola asked her sister. "Can you give us any more details?"

Benny took a deep breath. "Donner went outside, said he was going to go do a quick look around, see if anything got damaged in last night's wind. Then he was going to get Gril, check on Lucy. Claudia and I were just sitting here, up front, having pretzels for breakfast, when Donner made a noise— like a yell or something. Claudia and I ran outside. He was up by Ben, so we hurried to get to him. I tried to pull Claudia back once we saw Ned's body, but she fought me. Donner went to fetch Gril."

"What . . . what did the body look like?" I interjected.

"What do you mean?" Viola asked.

"I guess I'd like to know what happened to him."

Benny nodded as if she understood. Maybe she did. She seemed to understand me when I needed to see Claudia's injuries. "Lots of blood came from his chest. Someone stabbed him right in the heart. I could . . . I could see the wound."

"Anything else? What was he wearing?" I asked.

"He was dressed for the storm," Benny continued. "My

guess is that someone got him when he was on his way to find Claudia. He would have thought she was with me, and the bar would be a good place to start his search."

"So no one really knows what time it happened?" I asked.

"I don't think so."

"Did he have a weapon with him that you could see?"

"Didn't see one. In fact, when I looked at the wound, I wondered about the size of the knife. It had to be huge."

I nodded. There were some large knives in the Benedict House's kitchen. Viola kept them locked up when she had clients in residence, but with just us two there, she'd left the knife drawer unlocked. I had a sudden urge to go check the drawer, but I'd do it later.

"Did anything happen here last night after we all left?" Viola asked.

Benny bit her bottom lip and looked toward the bar's front door.

"What?" Viola urged.

Benny turned back to her sister and nodded. "Yes, but it didn't seem overly strange, certainly not the precursor or aftermath of murder."

"What happened?" Viola asked again.

"I was sleeping on the floor in the back room with Claudia. I woke up and she wasn't in the bed. I came out here, but neither she nor Donner were anywhere to be seen. I stepped outside, out front, and found Donner walking back from the direction of the Benedict House. I asked where Claudia was, but he said he didn't know, seemed surprised I didn't know. We found her around the other end of the buildings, having a smoke."

"What time was this?" Viola asked.

"Between four and five sometime."

"I don't think he came inside the Benedict House. It was

windy out there," Viola said. "I was closing some windows up on the second floor a little earlier than that. She was smoking outside? You'd've probably let her smoke inside."

Benny nodded. "I think she just didn't want me to know she smokes, and it had stopped snowing."

"Did you see Gril anywhere?" I asked.

"No. Why?" Benny said.

I steeled myself. This was going to be difficult, but it needed to be done. "I heard Viola last night. I went to explore what was going on. Gril was coming into the Benedict House shortly after I left my room."

"So he'd left the building?" Viola said.

"I guess, but I don't know when or why."

It was Viola's turn to bite her bottom lip. "I didn't hear any of that. Maybe Donner did come inside, and I missed that, too. I thought I saw something out there, but that was earlier, about three. I had to turn on the lights in a room where I was shutting the window, so I couldn't see outside very well, but I wondered if I saw a flashlight moving around out toward Ben last night. I shrugged it off when it seemed to disappear."

"You were up there a long time," I said.

Viola nodded distractedly and then asked Benny a question. "Was there a flashlight by Ned?"

"Not that I saw."

"What about footprints?" Viola asked. "There was plenty of new snow."

"And we all walked through it," Benny said. "But, sure, I noticed some prints on the other side of Ned's body—thought they might belong to him."

Viola nodded.

I thought about sharing other details of my own night, but they didn't need to know I'd fallen out of bed. My paranoia over my potentially unlocked door was embarrassing. The mention of footprints brought a mental image of my wet boots to mind. I looked down at them on my feet now, but there was no sign of anything suspicious on them, no blood spots that I could see. I knew I hadn't killed Ned. I did, however, have the sudden urge to check the boots more closely, but I didn't.

"I'm just going to take a peek out there at what they're doing. I'll stay back. I just want to see." I stood.

No one stopped me.

I opened the door, and the light, now muted by cloud cover, still almost blinded me because of how dark it was inside the bar. I remained in the doorway as I watched.

Gril and Donner were there, joined by a man named Ruke, whom I'd purchased my truck from—though actually it had been his sister's. Ruke, a local Tlingit, wasn't technically a medicine man, but nonetheless worked with alternative and herbal remedies. Early on, he had warned me that his intuition told him I should stay out of Glacier Bay, the location that was the main reason this small town saw so many tourists during the summertime. I'd listened and had barely even put a toe in the water. I'd been in Alaska and near Glacier Bay for this whole time and hadn't seen one glacier. It wasn't long ago that Viola told me I'd better hurry up and go look at them before they all melted.

Ruke grabbed some folded plastic from the back of his truck, a much newer and nicer version of the one he'd sold me. As he unfolded it, I realized it was a body bag.

Because the sculpture was in the way, I couldn't see everything as the men bent, crouched, and lifted.

"Gril?" I called from the doorway.

He stood up and looked at me.

"Want me to look?" I asked.

"No. It's all obvious. We just need the weapon, which is nowhere in sight."

No one thought our conversation was strange. By now most everyone knew I'd worked with my grandfather and had ultimately helped him to solve crimes. Everyone but Gril thought that had all happened somewhere in Colorado, not Missouri, but no one questioned my assistance anymore. It was the Benedict way to use all available resources anyway.

"Okay," I said as Gril got back to work.

I was disappointed, though as much out of a compulsive curiosity as a desire to be helpful. It was the same urge I'd felt to examine Claudia's wounds. I wished I'd been asked to look. I wanted to see the gore.

I swallowed hard. At least I was aware that this level of interest wasn't necessarily normal.

The three men had Ned's body zipped inside the bag and loaded into the back of Ruke's truck quickly and efficiently. Ruke hopped in and started the engine.

"Where will Ruke take Ned's body?" I asked over my shoulder.

"To one of the freezers for now," Viola said. "Sounds like the Juneau folks won't be coming after all. I doubt they'd be moving Ned if someone was on their way."

I turned around. "Which freezer?"

"Don't know, but probably the airport. No one is using it for fish at the moment."

I shut the door and went back to join the women.

"Who would have killed Ned?" I asked as I sat down.

Benny and Viola looked at each other.

"Lots of folks, I suppose," Viola said quietly after she glanced at the back-room door.

"But mostly Claudia?" I said.

Viola and Benny shared another look before Viola shook her head.

"No, in fact, I don't think Claudia would have killed Ned,"

she said. "Ned was horrible to her, but in her mind, he was good to her, too—took care of her, made sure she had a roof over her head and food on the table. Sometimes ugly, complicated things get made uglier and more complicated by our remoteness, and I'm sure he'd convinced Claudia that she'd never be able to make it without him. As is typical for assholes of his flavor, he was also jealous and overly sensitive. Any man who might have let his eyes linger on Claudia a moment too long was someone Ned felt the need to challenge, puff up to. You know the type."

I nodded.

"Anyway, Claudia's a pretty young thing," Viola continued. "Even though I know that's not appropriate to say anymore. She is, and she's a pretty young thing in the wilds of Alaska where there aren't as many women as men. Men's eyes are gonna linger."

"Some women's, too," Benny said.

We turned to look at her, mostly out of curiosity.

"I mean, she's not my type, but you know what I'm saying."

"Yeah," Viola said.

Part of why I'd come to like Benedict so much was because it was a place where you truly got to be yourself and you were accepted for who you were, as long as you weren't, as Viola had just called Ned, an asshole. Most folks weren't.

Gril opened the door. "We're done out here. For now."

We stood and the three of us spoke at once.

Gril held up his hand. "We don't have any other information. No, no Juneau people are coming to help. They figure I can handle it, which is just their way of telling me they don't have the energy to get here and do the work. That's all right. We'll get this sorted out. There might be some boot prints, but it's hard to tell. Donner's going to take some impressions, so the area near Ben is still off-limits, but business as usual may resume." He looked toward the back room. "How's Claudia?"

"Sedated," Viola said.

"Probably for the best," Gril said.

"She can stay here," Benny added. "I'll keep an eye on her."

Gril nodded. "I need to get Lucy figured out and then we'll focus on what Claudia's going to do next. I don't think she killed Ned, but I need to question her officially and then find out about any other family she might have, if we can. See if there's anyone we can call for her."

"Oh no," I said. "Lucy has no idea her brother was killed, does she?"

"No, and that's . . . I will let her know." Gril looked at Viola. "I need to get down to the dock for the ferry first. I hate to keep the bad news from Lucy, but for now don't tell her. I'd like to gauge her reaction myself. Okay?"

"Sure," Viola said.

Gril looked at me. "I'm going now. You still want to come?"

Viola and Benny seemed confused.

"What's going on?" Viola asked.

"There's a chance Beth's mother is on the ferry," Gril said.

My heart sunk at his words. This was not how I wanted others to learn my secrets.

"Really? Why didn't you say something?" Viola said. "I'll get a room ready, just in case."

Viola stepped around Gril and headed back to the Benedict House. I realized that he hadn't in fact spilled my secrets, but gave me a chance to keep them, even if I needed to massage them a little. My mother could visit, and now I wouldn't have to keep her hidden. Meeting her at the ferry meant I could prep her with the right story. If she was truly on that boat, that is. Surely she wasn't.

I would have to take a closer look at my boots and check the knife drawer later. Gril was ready to go. As Benny went back toward the bar, I sent Gril a strained smile with a nod.

"Let's go," he said, with no smiles to give back.

Eight

I stayed on the dock, leaning against the corner of the railing, and observed the goings-on below. It was cold and windy, but the sky was still cloudless and the sun warmed my face just enough to keep me from shivering.

But when people began to disembark, my nerves zipped to alert and got the best of me. My mouth seemed dry, and I could feel my heartbeat speed up. Was it possible that my mother was on that boat?

Gril hurried down the gangplank to meet the captain, who handed over a clipboard. Gril scrutinized it closely, flipping a page up and over and checking once more, running his finger down the length of it. He did the same once again, then looked up at me and shook his head as he gave a thumbs-up.

She wasn't on board. Relief and disappointment swept through me at once. But just because her name wasn't listed on the passenger manifest didn't mean for sure she wasn't on the ferry. Apparently she had a few other IDs, so there was still a chance she would show. It was too soon to know for sure.

I tried to relax as I watched the passengers disembark, and Gril and the captain fell into conversation.

I recognized some folks as locals. Dressed in heavy winter gear, most of them walked with their heads down, seemingly weary and in a hurry to get home. I wondered what they'd done with themselves in Juneau for two weeks, but didn't know any of them well enough to ask.

No one looked like Travis Walker. Not even slightly. I did it automatically—put every man I saw through a Travis filter. He was so very ordinary that I sometimes did a double take, but today there were no Travis Walkers. More relief.

Gril shook hands with the captain and then made his way toward me.

"No one named Millicent Rivers, but we'll wait a second to see if she's aboard. The captain wasn't looking for anyone with her features, and there were plenty of passengers today."

"What do people do if they get stuck in Juneau?"

"Make do." He shrugged. "Our current problem is that the captain just got word that the ferry might not head back to Juneau today. They were going to turn around pretty quickly, but now they're going to wait it out a bit. Some bad weather has hit the city. That gives me a chance to talk to Lucy first, but if the weather doesn't calm down, I won't be able to get her out of here today."

"Could the Harvingtons help?"

"It's possible, but again, the weather will dictate. I guess we'll see."

"What will you do if you can't get Lucy back?"

"Don't know yet, working on another plan—"

"Hey!" a voice called from the ship's gangplank.

I knew it immediately. Though I truly did love my mother, and a moment earlier I'd felt some sadness that her name hadn't been on the passenger manifest, a sense of dread washed through me at hearing her call.

Gril and I turned toward the voice.

"Darlin'!" Mill smiled and waved in our direction, an

unlit cigarette hanging from the corner of her mouth. "You came to greet me! Hold on, I'm coming."

"Your mother, I presume," Gril said.

"Yes. That's her." I blinked back some unexpected tears and told myself to keep it together. What was with all the conflicting emotions? Maybe everyone felt this way about their mother, but I doubted it.

Millicent Rivers was here. She was on the run from the law, which was something I hadn't forgotten, and I was about to introduce her to the local lawman. Just another day in the Rivers family. *The family who never listens.* I buried that thought.

"Looks like you have two fugitives in town," I said to Gril.

"Looks that way." He rubbed his chin. "Okay, I'll give you two a minute. Meet me up by my truck."

I nodded as he turned away. I wondered what in the world he was going to do with her—what I was going to do with her. I watched my mother make her way to me. She moved as if she hadn't a care in the world. She smiled at me around the cigarette, her eyes bright with happiness and the only kind of love that she knew how to express. I couldn't define it really, but I knew it was more about her than anyone else, which honestly was fine.

She smelled like maple syrup and cigarette smoke as she pulled me into a hug. She'd probably had pancakes at McDonald's in Juneau. It was her favorite breakfast.

"You look so good!" she said when she pulled back. "You look healthy."

"Wait until I take my cap off." I blinked away the tears. "You look good, too, the same."

"Did you know I was coming because of the run-in I had with the cop in Juneau?"

"Kind of."

Mill smiled. "Good. My plan worked then."

"How did you find me?" I asked.

"I'll tell you later, but don't worry, no one else can do what I do. You know that."

She truly did look like the same woman who'd stayed by my bedside through my surgery and recovery. It hadn't been a year yet but felt like an eon had passed. In the hospital, I hadn't told her I was running away, and I was surprised she hadn't held it against me. If she had, she wouldn't have done all the things she'd done over the last few months. She wouldn't be here.

Well, she might be here. She was on the lam, and maybe she'd just run out of places to go.

"Gus!" A voice called from behind.

I know that voice, I thought as I turned to greet the dog running directly at me.

"Look out, baby girl," Mill said as she grabbed my arm, preparing to pull me out of harm's way.

I braced myself, but the dog did not knock me over. Instead, he came to a skidding halt and looked up at me with the smile I'd seen for the first time the night before. It was even bigger and brighter in the daylight.

"Hello." This time I didn't hesitate to scratch behind his ears.

I didn't know if he recognized me or if he was simply the friendliest dog I'd ever met, but he leaned into my hands.

"Oh my goodness, Gus!" Elijah was there a few seconds later, holding a leash. "I can't believe he got away. I must not have latched this thing." He realized who I was. "Oh, you again. That's why he took off. He took a quick liking to you. I'm so sorry."

"It's okay. He's a great dog."

"He is, but goodness, he's work." Elijah hooked the leash onto Gus's collar. Immediately, the dog sat right next to Elijah.

"Elijah Wyatt," he said as he extended his hand to Mill.

"Good to meet you. I'm this girl's mom. Just call me Mill, everybody does," she said as she pulled the still-unlit cigarette out of her mouth with one hand and shook Elijah's with the other.

"Good to meet you, Mill."

They held each other's gaze a moment as if sharing a mutual curiosity. I was briefly taken aback, befuddled at the idea that my mother might actually be curious about a man other than my father. I was well past the age such things should surprise me, but her search for my father as I'd grown up must have stunted or delayed that maturity.

Elijah looked at me. "Hey, again, I'm sorry about Gus."

"Don't be," I said. "I want to meet all your dogs."

Elijah looked almost the same in the daylight, though a little more wrinkled and weathered. In a good way, a way that made me return his easy smile. He and Mill *were* close to the same age.

"Come by anytime. Excuse me for now, though. Hopefully, there's a new sled with my name on it on that ferry," he said.

"Good luck!" I said as Elijah and Gus took off toward the passenger bridge and gangplank. Gus behaved, but as we observed, it was easy to see he was a powerful dog.

"That dog's a handful," Mill observed.

I smiled as I turned back to her. "Mill, the only person who knows who I am is the police chief, and he also knows you're on the run from the law."

Mill nodded agreeably. "That who you were talking to a minute ago?"

"Yes. He's waiting at his truck for us."

"Got it. I'll talk to him. He didn't arrest me right away, so there's hope there. You and he get along?"

"Very well. He's a good man."

She looked at me and frowned. "Not many of those around anymore, I suppose." Briefly, she turned her gaze toward the ship. I wondered who she was thinking about, or if she was just wistfully looking into her past. She glanced back at me before I could ask.

I didn't argue with her, but I could have. I'd met more good people—men and women—in this primitive world than I could ever have predicted I would know. If she was here for any length of time, she'd see that, too, but some part of me hoped she wouldn't stay too long.

She reached into her jacket pocket and pulled out a lighter. She reinserted the cigarette, lit it, and took a puff. "Think I'll be arrested?"

"Well, we haven't discussed it. Other emergencies have been his priority."

Mill smiled. "That's good news, girlie. I bet I can work with that. Come on, let's go get our charm on, you got me?"

I smiled. I didn't know who to feel sorrier for, me or Gril. Maybe Viola. The idea that Mill might finally meet her match with Viola also made me smile to myself.

"All right, everyone knows me as Beth Rivers," I said as we began walking.

"See, I was right all those years ago when I told you to use a pseudonym, though I never could have predicted this." She looked around.

The ocean was on one side, a road that led into the woods was on the other, and a giant sky was above.

"It's something here, isn't it?" I observed.

"It's a beautiful place, but I'll tell you more about that later." She winked and then took off toward the truck.

I caught up with her. "Again, remember, only Gril knows who I am or what happened."

"I hear you, but I'm surprised that no one has put it together. You do look different, but still, you're famous."

"A woman who was here temporarily did," I said, thinking about Ellen. "And there's a guy who runs the library, Orin, who did some special ops work in a previous life. I suspect he knows, but I'm not sure."

"Oooh, special ops. I'd like to meet him."

Maybe I needed to feel sorry for Orin, too. "Okay. How long are you staying?"

Mill laughed. "I suppose that depends on how my conversation with your police chief goes." She looked back toward the ferry. "And the availability of transportation."

"My landlord is getting a room ready."

"Sounds fancy."

She knew nothing about my existence here. It wasn't all that long ago that she'd found a phone number on Detective Majors's desk that had my initials, *B.R,* written next to it. It was Viola's office phone number. With the area code, she could then figure out that I was in Alaska, but there was no way to uncover anything more specific. Because the Benedict House was a halfway house for felons, the number was kept as hidden as any number could be these days. Mill had had to use some other skills to narrow down exactly where in this vast state I was staying.

No one other than Gril knew a thing about her, and he didn't know nearly the half of it. She could be a challenge for all of us.

Gril was in the driver's seat of his truck, the motor running. I opened the passenger door as Mill stood next to me.

"Gril, this is my mom, Mill. Mill, this is Gril." I cleared my throat at the rhyme that I hadn't picked up on until that moment.

"Pleasure." Mill had already toed out the cigarette next to the truck. She stepped forward and held out her hand.

They shook as I looked back at the cigarette on the ground and then hurried to grab it. I'd done that same sort of thing all through Missouri as I'd grown up with my mother, picked up her discarded cigarettes. Nothing changes sometimes, even after it seems everything has.

"Mill, nice to meet you," Gril said. He got right to business. "Here's the deal. You are wanted by police officials, and I am fully aware of that situation. Because Beth has been a wonderful addition to our community, I'm going to look the other way for a couple weeks, pretend I don't see you, unless you cause trouble. You need to head back in a couple weeks though, if the ferry is running—I'm sorry about that if you both planned on a longer visit, but I'm already going to be breaking some big rules. Keep a low profile, don't cause me any trouble, and everything will be fine. Okay?"

Mill nodded respectfully. "You're mighty kind to look the other way. I accept your terms. Thank you."

She hopped into the truck, taking up the middle of the bench seat. She looked at me and patted the passenger side. "Hop in, hun."

I processed how surprisingly easy those few moments had been, and how everything was probably about to get more complicated because my mother was here.

And then I hopped in.

Nine

There wasn't much small talk as Gril drove us the short distance back downtown. My mother was pretty good at reading a room, and though she didn't always conform, she knew that for now silence was far better than almost anything that might come out of her mouth.

Donner was still working next to Ben as we passed by on our way to the Benedict House's small parking lot. We all glanced over at him, but no one said anything. From that angle, I could see some red-stained snow, though not as much as I might have expected. I noticed the corners of Mill's mouth turn up a little when she saw the bear, down when she realized there was something that looked like blood at its feet. Her eyebrows came together as she looked at me, but I just gave her a tiny shake of my head. I knew Gril wouldn't want to share the events of the morning with her.

Unbothered, she turned her attention to the quaint downtown and smiled again.

We thanked Gril for the ride, but he exited the truck, too, and came inside with us. Viola was in the lobby when we walked in. She met us with a strained smile aimed at Gril as he took off toward Lucy's room.

"Howdy, you must be Beth's mom," Viola said as she extended a hand. "I'm Viola."

Mill looked at me with raised eyebrows, playing along with my earlier comments about keeping secrets.

"This is my mom, Mill," I said. It would be too difficult to try to use anything else.

"Pleasure to meet you. Beth has told me some great things about you." Mill's gaze skirted over the gun, but mostly she kept her own eyes on Viola's.

I'd never told my mother one thing about Viola.

"Same," Viola said, both of them being polite, both of them knowing it, too.

I held back my own strained smile. "Everything okay?" I asked Viola.

"Sure, sure." She looked back at Mill. "I put the room next to Beth's together. You're welcome to stay as long as you like. The kitchen isn't well stocked, but make yourself at home with whatever you can find."

"Thank you, Viola," Mill said.

I looked at my mother; her tone was more genuine than I thought I'd ever heard. Was she simply glad to be away from police nipping at her heels? It would be unlike her to be concerned about getting caught, but she *had* shot at someone this time.

Previously, she'd been so cavalier about her run-ins with the police that I hadn't considered how she might have changed. But I should have, because nothing had been the same—for me or her—since Travis.

"You're welcome. If you two will excuse me, I'm going to see if I can help Gril. Let me know if you need anything."

Viola set off toward Lucy's room, too.

"What's going on?" Mill asked me quietly.

I waited until we couldn't see Viola anymore and then

signaled her to follow me into the kitchen. She did without comment.

I hurried to the knife drawer and pulled on the handle. It was locked.

"Shoot," I said.

"What?" Mill asked. "I can get in there if you really want me to."

Though I didn't know exactly how she'd do it, for a moment I considered her offer, but then made the right decision and shook my head. "No. It's probably been locked for a while."

"What's in there?"

"Knives."

"Okay?"

After another moment I shook my head again. "Come on, let's get you settled, and I'll tell you what's going on."

There were only three rooms on the bottom floor of the short wing of the Benedict House where my room was located. I'd seen the inside of the one directly next to mine, but it had looked nothing like it did now. Before, it held the same furniture as mine, but there had been no bedding, nothing welcoming.

In the short time I'd been with Gril, Viola had transformed the space into an inviting winter oasis, with bedding similar to my own as well as fresh towels, some wrapped soap, and a couple of bottles of shampoo and conditioner. I appreciated the effort.

"You really did know I was coming?" Mill said as we looked around the space.

I closed the door to her room. "Only since recently." I sat down on the edge of the bed and took off my boots. "Help me look at these."

Mill stood in front of me with her fists on her hips. "Why? What am I looking for?"

"I don't know. Blood, maybe."

"Bethie?"

"Just look. I'll tell you everything, but please look first."

Mill grabbed the boot I wasn't inspecting and gave it a thorough once-over. "Clean as a whistle."

We traded, and a few minutes later, we agreed that there was nothing suspicious on either boot.

Mill sat on the edge of the bed next to me. "What's up?"

I nodded and took a deep breath. The adrenaline that I'd felt, the anxiety about my boots somehow being on the feet of whoever killed Ned, was fizzling out. There was no blood on either of them. The relief was real, but it was slow spreading.

"First, Mill, how did you find me?" I asked.

"Okay. That's fair. We'll start there. Once I figured out what state you were in, and after my run-in, I just caught the first flight out of the lower forty-eight and got up here. I spent some time in Anchorage and really enjoyed it. I used my time there to learn what I could about Alaska, and let me tell you, you certainly didn't pick the safest place to hide. It's dangerous out here."

"It's a little primitive."

"That's putting it mildly."

"So you've been in Alaska since you shot—"

"Yes, since I shot your abductor. If I'd done it right, I would have faced the music, Bethie, but he's still alive. I had to lay low until the heat cooled some. I have to go back and finish the job."

"Mill, you don't have to," I interrupted. "I'd rather you were okay, not in jail, not being chased."

"Too late, I'm afraid. Your police chief knows the trouble I'm in—the Juneau police might figure out more, too. My freedom is short-lived, but I'm willing to accept that if I do the job right." She put up her hand. "No, do not even argue with me about this. It's my life, I'll do what I want."

"I know, Mill, but I'm okay." I finally took off my hat. "I look funny, but I'm okay."

Mill's eyes grew big for an instant and then she smiled. I cocked my head as I inspected her face and she inspected mine.

In fact she also looked a little different, softer around the edges. Alaska had been good for her. Or something had.

Mill put her hand on my cheek. "You look great."

"So do you," I said, not hiding the surprise in my voice.

Mill laughed. "However, I'm going to cut your hair."

I laughed, too, and put the hat back on. "You've been in Anchorage this whole time?"

"No, when I realized you'd probably go someplace less populated but probably not as wintery as some of the northern towns, I took off to Homer. I really loved it, and I explored every corner of that place before I gave up on the idea that I might find you there. Anyway, it was by chance that I figured out you were here. I was at a bar up in Homer and I heard a couple of folks talking about a little publication called the *Petition*."

"What?" I said.

"Yes, they were from here, and they were looking at it, talking about some classes that were coming up and how they wanted to be back home in time. They left the paper on the table."

"Really?"

"I was just curious, so I picked it up, and a few sentences in, I knew you'd written it."

"You did?"

"Of course. I know your writing voice better than anyone. I can't say I was one hundred percent, but I was pretty sure. I figured out how to get here, but then the weather wasn't cooperating. So I spent some time in Juneau and enjoyed it there, too. That place is haunted, you know?"

"I don't know. You've seen lots more of Alaska than I have." I slipped on my boots.

"You need to get out some then, see the sights. It's quite the state."

I shook my head at my mother. "You are amazing, you know that, don't you?"

"Hell yes, I know that." She pulled out her cigarettes. "But I bet I can't smoke in here."

"I'm afraid not."

"Care to step outside with me for a minute, tell me what's going on with that bearded park ranger and why it looked like he was processing a bloody crime scene?"

I sighed. "Sure."

Viola had left Mill's key on a small table by the door. Mill grabbed it as we walked by. She made sure the door was locked after we exited the room.

"This has been my room since I got here," I said as I waved my hand that way. I lowered my voice and continued, "This is a halfway house. I didn't mean to get a room here, but I was in a hurry using a computer in Dr. Genero's office in the hospital. It just worked out."

"Nice job," Mill said, true admiration lining her voice.

Suddenly she stopped walking, her focus on my doorknob. She pointed. "What's that?"

I looked at the knob, noticing a reddish-brown stain about the size of a dime along its rounded edge. "I . . ." I stepped closer and leaned over to look at it. Adrenaline zipped through me again. "It looks like blood."

"Are you hurt?" Mill asked.

Later I would realize that the edge had come back to her voice with that one small question. It was the edge I was used to. It had been missing since she disembarked the ferry.

I stood straight and looked at my hands. "I don't think so."

Mill's eyebrows came together as she nodded toward

the Benedict House's front door. "What's going on out there?"

I looked at her as I worked to understand the moment—her tone as well as the stain on my doorknob. I opened my mouth to tell her about the murder, but the words wouldn't find their way out of my mouth.

Mill frowned and then put her finger up to her lips as if telling me to shush. A second later she licked a finger and ran it over the stain on the doorknob.

I held back a gasp as my hand went to my mouth. Had she just destroyed possible evidence? "What are you doing?" I whispered.

Mill sent me a steely gaze and then grabbed the tail of her shirt, wiping it over the knob, too. "All right, dollie, I could use a smoke. Let's head outside."

I worked to regain my composure before I followed my mother's saunter outside.

Ten

We were in such a hurry that I didn't notice the wails until we'd made it outside. They came from inside, in the direction of Lucy's room.

"Someone's upset." Mill lit a cigarette.

We walked to the end of the boardwalk in front of the Benedict House, toward the unpopulated parking lot. Mill didn't *like* to be polite about her smoking, but she was most of the time anyway.

"I think that's Lucy. She's in the other small wing." We weren't close to her room's window, but the wails still reached us nonetheless. I looked out toward Ben. Donner was gone now. "Something happened last night."

"I figured as much."

"There was a murder."

"Well, shit, Beth. Have anything to do with Walker, you think?"

"Oh, no. Not at all, though I understand your concern. There was an incident when I first moved here and I wondered, too . . . but no, this was a domestic problem, maybe made worse by yet another fugitive from the law."

"I'm not the only fugitive in town?"

"Probably not by a long shot, but I only know for sure of one other."

"Deets, darlin'?"

Mill smoked and listened intently as I told her about the events of the last twenty-four hours. Lucy's wail calmed, but we heard raised voices a time or two.

After I finished relaying the deets, Mill's first question caught me off guard. "You fell out of bed?"

"It appears that way."

"I've never known you once to do that. Do you hurt anywhere, like you have a bruise?"

"No." I shrugged.

Her other questions were about my wet boots and the potential blood on my doorknob, the stain that Mill had removed without any hesitation whatsoever.

Though there was no one around to hear us, I kept my voice low as I said, "What if that was Ned's blood?"

"My thoughts exactly," Mill said. "No matter whose blood it was, though, I wasn't about to let it stay on your doorknob to be found by someone. I mean, I'm sure Gril is a good guy, but I never trust the police, you know that."

I hesitated.

"Gril *is* a good guy, isn't he?"

"He's been wonderful, but I don't understand what was really going on last night when he came inside."

"He probably was just checking things out," she said, though not confidently.

"Maybe . . ."

"What are you thinking?"

"It was just something I saw between him and Donner, a shared look. And they were adamant that they were going to check on Ned last night, even though they thought he'd just stay home because of the storm."

Mill took a long drag and blew out smoke. "But Ned didn't. He went looking for his wife, right?"

"I think that's what they think now."

Mill nodded. "I hear you. But who knows what really happened, you know. If Gril or the park ranger killed Ned, maybe he deserved it."

"I don't disagree."

"But?"

"I guess I don't want to believe Gril would do such a thing."

"He's leaving me alone for a while. I suspect he's good at knowing the right thing to do."

I didn't argue or point out the flaws in her logic. "Yes, but what if the blood on my doorknob led to the actual killer? I didn't kill Ned."

"You fell out of bed, and your boots were wetter than you thought they should be. You had us inspect them. I'm no math genius, but I've known police officers to add stuff up wrong and I don't want any answers to lead to you. And if the lawmen had something to do with the murder, then they might be looking for any opportunity to shine a light of guilt on someone else."

I didn't want to think Gril was like that, but I couldn't deny that Mill had a good point.

My mother had been in town for only an hour and she'd already potentially tampered with a crime scene. It was going to be long two weeks. It really was good to see her, though, to be reminded of her smart but cringeworthy logic. She was trying to help me, even if I hoped I didn't need help.

I thought a moment. What if she hadn't come to town? Would I have run down to Lucy's room, grabbed Gril, and pointed out the stain?

I couldn't answer that question for sure, but I knew there

was a very good chance I wouldn't have. In fact, I might have just wiped it off, too.

"Look at me," I said. "Do you see any blood on me anywhere?"

Mill inspected me again, this time even more thoroughly. I had sweats over sweats, all under a thick coat. The parking lot wasn't the best place for a strip-down, but I knew there were no cameras nearby. I unzipped my coat and lifted up one layer of sweatshirt, exposing the bottom layer.

Mill looked closely. "Not a drop, not even something tiny, I don't think."

"This is what I wore last night. There was blood around the victim. If I'd . . . done anything, there would be more blood on me."

"Okay," Mill said doubtfully as I zipped up again. "Let's check your room, too."

She toed out her cigarette, but this time she picked up the butt herself.

We made our way back inside but stopped in the lobby just as Gril headed toward us. We couldn't hear Lucy anymore.

"How is she?" I asked.

"Upset. And stuck here. The ferry's not going back today"—he looked at Mill—"in case that was your plan."

"It wasn't. I hope to stay the full two weeks."

"Well, it looks like we'll need to keep Lucy here, too. I've contacted the authorities back in Juneau—only about Ned and Lucy—and there's nothing violent on her record, though she did have a firearm tucked into her jeans during her last robbery. She's going to remain in her room, but I'm not going to keep her locked up. She's not to leave the Benedict House without permission. Viola's going to put her to work. I don't have any other place for her, but you two could stay elsewhere."

"Do we have to?" I asked.

"No, but two fugitives from the law, here in the same house . . . I don't know."

Mill lifted her right hand. "Chief, I swear I won't cause any trouble. I'm just here to see my daughter. I will leave in a couple weeks or with the next ferry somehow. There's no reason for me to cause problems."

I hoped I hid another cringe. My mother promising not to cause trouble usually meant that she was well on her way to doing just that.

"All right." Gril paused. "I haven't given up on flying Lucy back over, but it's not looking good." He glanced down the hallway and then at us again. "I know Beth's identity is top secret, but let's continue to keep things as low-key as we can, all right? I do have a murder to investigate, and I'll need everyone out of my way as well as cooperative."

"Always." Mill's voice was so earnest I thought I should look down to keep my eyes from rolling.

Gril nodded and then made his way around us and out the door.

"What if we offered to help him?" Mill asked sincerely when he was gone.

"I have," I said, noticing how bizarre the question sounded coming from a mere civilian. It hadn't seemed so outrageous to me when I'd said it. "He doesn't want our help."

Mill nodded. "Let's check your room."

We did a thorough search. Mill, her face serious, her eyes sharp, zeroed in on the parts she thought important. The floor, the bed, including the bed frame, all the other doorknobs, and the sink and tub. My room was free of blood. There was no indication that I'd killed Ned Withers. There was no blood in my room. I hadn't even hurt myself when I'd fallen out of the bed—at least in a way that left a visible trail.

Finally Mill breathed a sigh of relief. So did I, but I tried not to let her see it.

"But there's a killer on the loose," Mill said, ramping up again. "I don't know enough about these people or this place to have any idea who it could be, other than his angry, abused wife or maybe Gril himself. Did he offer up any suspects?"

"No."

"I wish he would."

Mill never did like it when the police didn't include her.

"Hey, want to see where I work?" I asked, sensing I needed to give her something else to think about. "We can talk all you want in my office. No one can hear us there."

It took her a minute to further consider that she wasn't going to get any answers to questions that were none of her business anyway. Finally she stopped frowning. "Great idea, but I'm hungry. Is there a restaurant where I could buy you some lunch or an early dinner?"

My hunger had returned, too, with a vengeance. "I have just the place."

Eleven

The café was busy, the scents of fried food and the sound of raised voices filling the air when we walked in. It was warm and homey.

"Hey, Beth," the cook, Luther, said through the window of the wall that separated the kitchen from the dining area. "You two find some seats. Nancy will be over to get your order."

The only two seats available together were stools at the counter. The three other stools there were filled, those customers nodding at us as we sat. I didn't know any of them, but across the room saw Serena, a friend as well as the local knitting instructor and one of my self-defense classmates. She waved from a table in the corner, where she was eating with a couple of the men from the oil rig I'd seen at the knitting classes.

"This place is busy," Mill said.

"It's literally the only real sit-down restaurant in town. I eat most of my meals here. The cooks and waitstaff change up a lot, but Luther is great with homemade soup."

"Sign me up for that," Mill said.

Nancy took our orders, relaying them to a busy Luther. We both craved grilled cheese sandwiches and tomato soup. As we waited, we were curious enough about the conversations around us to listen closely. We weren't the only ones who'd been discussing murder. News spread quickly, and the gossip that filled the air was laced with concern and real fear.

Who would kill Ned?

What if we have a serial killer?

Is Gril aware of everyone coming over from Juneau— didn't the ferry get here today?

I could have answered the last one, but it would have been weird and would only have led to more questions.

Mill and I worked well together, particularly when it came to any sort of investigation. We'd shared many meals in small Missouri towns as we'd searched for answers as to where my father had gone, mostly when I was younger. Nevertheless, we were quickly able to fall back into our give-and-take, a form of silent communication that most people wouldn't pick up on. It was just short of reading each other's minds.

After the food arrived, while we both ate, we pretended to concentrate on our meals, but really, we were listening, cueing each other with tiny head nods and flicks of our fingers.

We picked up on some unsurprising tidbits. Ned was abusive to Claudia; he was an all-around asshole to most everyone else when he was being jealously protective of his wife. Ned was a bully. He'd also been what I'd come to call a town wanderer. It wasn't meant derogatorily. He didn't have a full-time job but helped out when someone, almost anyone, needed it. That could mean working just about anywhere—the airport, the library, the café, and so forth. Lots of people were on a bunch of different payrolls.

I'd helped Randy at the mercantile a couple times. I'd helped Benny at the bar. I'd even helped load frozen fish onto a tourist's airplane once. I didn't need the money, but it seemed almost contrary and wrong not to assist when it was obviously needed. I was a part-time wanderer.

Ned was paid, though a wanderer paycheck wasn't always reliable. I overheard that he didn't let Claudia work anywhere, though she actually wanted to—Mill and I sent each other small eye rolls at that one. Apparently, Claudia had briefly worked on one of the Glacier Bay tourist boats, but that hadn't lasted long. She'd even tried to sneak in a job at the small post office in town, but Ned found out and dragged her back home, a letter still clenched in her fist. The postmaster, Roxie, had to go out to their house to gather it.

"Where do they live? I don't even know," someone said. I listened closer for the answer.

"Out past the airport, two roads to the east."

Noted.

I thought I heard someone say something about Claudia and other men. Again, my listening skills came to attention—were they talking about Claudia and a few other men, or one in particular?

But that thread didn't get far before the door opened and the rumble of conversation came to a withering halt. The entrance was to our back, so Mill and I had to turn to see what was going on. It was Doug Vitner, the census man. Though I hadn't even noticed him before last night, it seemed I was one of the last. It wasn't just Benny who didn't want to say much when he was around. The conversations didn't resume.

"Howdy," Luther called from the back. "Find a seat if you can."

Vitner nodded. As he began to look around, the man sitting next to me dropped some bills on the counter and then spun the stool and stood. When his eyes landed on Vitner, he seemed to send the census man a suspicious look before he directed him to take the seat.

Surprisingly, Vitner nodded at me with a small smile of recognition, and then at the person on his other side as he sat and told Nancy he'd take some coffee as he looked at the menu.

"Hi," I said to him after he'd ordered.

Though I didn't want the census man to know anything about me, I couldn't deny the part of me that felt rude for not greeting him. Mill was much better at not feeling obligated to be friendly than I'd ever be.

"How're you doing?" he said with a huge sigh.

"I'm okay. You?"

"Oh." He sighed again. "I need to get out of this town. I thought I was in luck today, but now they're telling me the ferry isn't heading back over to Juneau. I'm stuck here for the foreseeable future. I'm not happy at all about it."

"There will be another break in the weather. Maybe not today, but in the next week or two," I offered.

"I'd like to get home." Vitner's gaze locked on me a long moment as if he were trying to remember how he knew me. A few seconds later, he lost whatever motivation had been spurring him on and turned his attention back to his coffee.

"Where's home?" Mill leaned forward and spoke around me.

He swallowed a gulp. "Seattle."

"Beautiful city," Mill said. "Family?"

"Nope." He smiled sadly. "Well, none that want to have anything to do with me."

"Oh. Sorry," Mill said.

He shook his head. "That was weird, what I just said. Apologies. I think I'm getting a little stir-crazy. Ignore me."

He seemed like a nice enough guy. I was working hard to find a reason not to like him, a reason that would validate Benny's treatment of him, but he seemed just fine. I still hoped he wouldn't ask any probing questions, but I felt a little sorry for him. The census was a good thing, even if I didn't want to participate. If pressed, I would lie to him, tell him my only job was at the *Petition*. I could give him my real name and it probably wouldn't lead to anything like Travis Walker finding me, but I'd rather not. I *was* trying to stay off the radar, after all.

"Your work is done, then?" I asked.

"I got what I need at least, and now"—he hunkered down a little—"there's been a murder. This place is nuts. I'd like to get out of here."

"At least we have a restaurant and a bar for some socializing," I said.

"I'm tired of that bar, too. I really don't know how you all do this."

"One day at a time, I suppose."

"I suppose."

A lull hit the conversation until I spoke again. "I, uh, heard something."

Mill cleared her throat at my ominous tone.

He looked at me, frowning. "What?"

"I heard that the man who was killed was angry that you stopped by and asked a bunch of questions."

Vitner fell into thought and then laughed once. "Oh, that's who was killed? Ned something. Of course—now I recognize the woman who came into the bar last night, even with the cut and black eye."

"Ned Withers."

"Right. He was a moron, but yes, he was upset when I started asking questions. Wasn't my fault he didn't understand what the census really was." Vitner pointed at something on the menu as Nancy peered at it. She nodded and turned to place the order.

"You don't give a spiel?" Mill asked. "I mean, when you introduce yourself?"

"I give a spiel," Vitner said. "Not my fault some people don't even understand that part."

Mill nodded in agreement. "Dumb people everywhere." She sat back a little to signal me to go on.

"And you're just trying to do your job."

"Damn straight."

"Was he a real ass to you?" I asked.

"Yep. His wife tried to ease the waters, though. I felt sorry for her. I quickly suspected they were hiding someone in the house. I hope for honesty, but I don't search premises. He was so shifty, though . . . Honestly, I just wanted to get my job done and get out of there, but he took it all as if I was prying, and then he behaved so suspiciously that I wondered if someone was being kept against their will. I just got up and made my way to the shed out back. When I saw the woman, she assured me she was there by her own choice. As I left, Ned was freaking out at everyone." He shook his head. "Maybe I should have made sure he didn't hurt anyone, but it all seemed like just the way they operated. Maybe if I'd told the police chief or something, maybe . . ."

"Maybe what?" I asked.

"It's hard for me to believe that my presence in their house had anything to do with that man's murder, but he was certainly upset. If he hit his wife because of . . . that, well then, maybe he deserved killing."

"Cheers to that!" Mill lifted her water in salute.

Nancy placed an order of toast on a plate in front of Vitner, but he didn't seem overly interested in the food.

"Damn. That might make me look guilty of something," he said. "But I had nothing to do with his murder. You know that, don't you?"

I jumped in my skin at his tone and the fact that he'd suddenly gotten a little too in my face.

People get funny when a murder happens. Not funny ha-ha, but funny off somehow. I've researched these sorts of things for my books. They say and do the strangest things when they think they might somehow be accused of involvement, even peripherally.

Good police officers know this; they know how to work around it. My grandfather called it the ability to separate the wheat from the chaff. He was extraordinarily good at it—one of the best. I'd seen Gril's knack for it, too, but I had no doubt that he would want to talk to Doug Vitner if he hadn't already. He'd see through him if there was anything to see through.

I suddenly suspected that even if the ferry were to head back to Juneau today, Vitner wouldn't be allowed to leave. None of us would, probably. Maybe not even Lucy and Claudia.

Or did Gril not suspect them of killing Ned? He should. It was yet another thing that made me wonder about his activities the night before. I was brought out of my reverie by Vitner.

He looked pointedly at me, moved even more into my space. "Right? You know that, don't you?"

It wasn't a rhetorical question; Vitner wanted an answer—something to make him feel better, less worried. His tone made me remember a similar moment in the van with Walker.

You are mine. You know that, don't you?

My mouth had been gagged. I'd been terrified in ways I could never have understood before the abduction. With my protective mother by my side and this stranger next to me, I experienced a brief instant of that terror, a short replay, but fortunately it passed quickly, leaving only some residual anger in its wake.

"Don't you?" Vitner said again.

I sensed Mill bristle next to me.

"I don't know you at all," I finally said.

It was the wrong answer for a man like Doug Vitner, but I wasn't in the mood to be bullied into appeasing him or anyone. I hoped I never would be again.

Suddenly he threw some bills on the counter, grabbed his toast off the plate, and left in a huff. He'd gone from pleasant to pugnacious in a flash. He had mentioned that he was tired of this place; maybe the isolation *was* getting to him.

"Don't mind me," I said quietly to Mill. "Just winning friends and influencing people."

"He's a fuckwad."

I sent her a smile only she could see. "Hey, I remembered something; remind me to tell you later."

"I'm not good at waiting for later. Eat up and let's get out of here."

We took a couple more hurried bites and dropped our own bills on the counter. Neither of us was interested in the gossip that resumed when Vitner was gone. Mill, ever the big tipper after her years as a waitress, left some extra for Nancy, who sent us a whistle and a thank-you as we left.

It was time for Mill to see the old hunting shed.

Twelve

It was probably because of the talk in the restaurant, all the buzz and speculation about Ned's murder, but both of us were on high alert as we walked to my truck. The winds were calm, and we saw no one else outside as we made our way under the now cloudy sky, but there were shadows everywhere. Though Mill was the toughest of the tough, she kept her eyes moving, searching for any threat.

Briefly I wondered about the weather. Even with a cloudy sky, it wasn't bad out. Was it worse by Juneau? Was that why the ferry wasn't returning? The planes not flying?

"Love this truck," Mill said when we closed the doors, both of them rattling.

"It's the best." It started right up. Not only did it have great tires, but the headlight lamps were so bright, they cut through the dusty gloom with authority.

Mill looked out the window as I drove us into the woods. Having her with me made me see my world with fresh eyes again. Huge trees covered in snow. A lot of nothing, really, but this nothing had become my everything, and though the natural world here was overwhelming and intimidating, it was also beautiful.

I watched as she moved her attention from out the window to her phone.

I'd been so glad to be away from my captor when I first got to Benedict that the primitive lifestyle had seemed a minor inconvenience. I'd learned to work with it, but this sort of backward living, with little internet and cell phone access, would be difficult for my very connected mother. Anchorage and Homer would both have been more plugged in.

"Did you get a new phone?"

"I did. No way to track it to me at all." She paused. "And it looks like there's no signal for me to use, either."

"It's almost impossible to get a signal out here."

Mill frowned but then shrugged and put the phone back into her jacket pocket. "That works."

"You waiting for a call?"

"Nope, just checking," she said.

This was a lie. She wasn't *just checking*. There was a reason she'd pulled out her phone. Briefly I studied her stoic profile. She knew I knew she'd lied, but she didn't care, felt no sense to explain further. I'd been through this before. She'd tell me eventually.

"This is it." I pulled to stop in front of the *Petition*, again seeing it as she might. Old, but kind of adorable.

"I think this is the first time in my life I would truly describe something as quaint. It looks like an old guy with a long gray beard could step outside and aim an antique gun our direction."

"It does," I agreed. "The inside is good, too. Since it's so small, it warms up quickly."

"Let's go in."

Mill loved the inside as well, but it was the entire package that she ultimately approved of: the tin roof, as well as the distance from everyone else, including the library, which was

close enough to see but far enough not to "need a fence"—
her favorite sort of neighbor. She brushed her fingers over one
of the typewriter's keys and made approving noises.

She lifted an eyebrow as I turned the lock, but she didn't
say anything. She made herself at home, taking the visitor's
seat and propping her feet up on the other side of my desk. She
declined a shot of the whiskey I kept in the drawer, more for
visitors than for me, but put on a pot of coffee and turned up
the furnace a notch.

"What did you remember?" she asked after we both held
warm mugs and I'd explained how the *Petition* had always,
since its inception, been written like the edition she'd come
across in Homer: light on news, heavy on calendar events.
Again, she commented that my writing voice still came
through loud and clear, making me glad I'd never included
my name on any edition, but also causing something else to
bother me. Chances were close to nil that Travis Walker would
somehow come across a copy, but a few days earlier I would
have thought the same for Mill. I couldn't quite let go of that
concern, but I could make myself move it to the back burner
for now.

"It came to me because of the way Vitner was behaving,
adamant that I *knew* he was innocent. Walker told me that I
was his and *didn't I know that* already," I said. "Same tone.
Ugh."

Mill pursed her lips and squinted at me over the mug. "I
see why you remembered it."

I nodded. "There's more. After I didn't answer Walker, he
said something to the effect of my being his forever, and this
is the part I wanted to tell you—since *practically the day I
was born*."

Mill nodded knowingly. "We know I remembered him
coming over to the house when you were a kid. Have you remembered any other times?"

"No, but I wondered if you did." I held my gaze, hoping there wasn't another lie coming.

Mill frowned and nodded, squinted again, but this time as if accessing something.

"What? You know more? Come on, Mill, I can handle it," I said.

Though I suspected that there was a bigger reason she'd come to Benedict than simply missing me, I suddenly wondered how big, perhaps life-altering, her reason would turn out to be. She'd been on the run. If she hadn't wanted to talk to me about something specific, she might have stayed in Anchorage or Homer. I hoped she didn't see me working hard to steel myself.

"It's about your dad, Beth," she finally said.

"What? Tell me. I can take anything, Mom. Is he dead?"

Mill shook her head. "I don't know, but . . . but he was in the middle of some terrible stuff, baby girl. I mean some drug stuff."

I was seven when he disappeared. Because I was so young, he would forever be the greatest dad in the history of all dads to me, the little girl who'd loved him so much. But he *had* been gone a long time.

"That probably shouldn't surprise us," I said. "We kind of suspected. I mean, it was a problem in our area of Missouri for a while. I remember Gramps fighting a bunch of drug problems."

Mill frowned and looked down at her folded hands. "There's more."

I took a deep breath. "You found him, didn't you?"

Mill looked up at me quickly. "No, no, that's not it. It's . . . it's about your grandfather."

Gramps was a man no one messed with, in life or in memory. I sat up straight. He'd been a father to me longer than my real father had been. I'd adored my grandfather above everyone else, probably including both my parents. I would never say that aloud to Mill, but it wouldn't be a surprise to her.

"I think he's the one responsible for Eddy leaving," Mill said with a sigh.

I had to let the words sink in a moment; they wouldn't go down easy. "What? How?"

"I am working on understanding exactly what happened, but I have something." She reached into her pocket and pulled out a crumpled time-worn piece of paper. "Stellan found it a while ago and finally gave it to me. Before all the shit hit the fan. I expect Gramps could just never bring himself to give it to us, and then he died."

"Stellan?"

Stellan was Milton's current police chief. He sat at the same desk my grandfather had worked behind. He was trying to help Detective Majors in any way he could. I'd talked to him on the phone a few months earlier. He had his local people working on keeping my identity a secret as well, though he didn't know where I was, either.

Mill nodded. "He had it for a few years, but for a long time he thought he should just leave well enough alone, leave Eddy's memory in the wind. But when all this new crap started boiling over, he couldn't help but wonder if things were all tied together somehow, so he handed it over. There's no obvious connection to your abductor in that note, but there's . . . some stuff that's not easy to accept. I wasn't going to tell you about it, but since we're face-to-face and in person and all. Here."

I took the paper reluctantly, almost not wanting to. But I couldn't have resisted. There was no point in delaying.

I unfolded and read.

Millicent and Beth, it began.

I recognized my grandfather's scratchy handwriting

immediately. I swallowed hard against the wave of emotion that washed through me and continued.

This is a letter to tell you I'm sorry. It's something I've wanted to say to you both for a long time, but I couldn't man up enough to do it. Frankly, I'm not even sure I'll be able to do it now, give you this letter. It's a chickenshit thing I've done, only made worse by my not 'fessing up to it.

Anyway.

Eddy was into some bad stuff. It broke my heart—for him, for me, but mostly for you two. He loved you so much, never think he didn't. He loved you with everything he was—which, unfortunately, wasn't quite enough good.

Lord, the man tried. He thought he worked so hard, when in fact he fell short all the time. Never could go that extra inch, let alone mile. Life was passing him by quickly. The mistakes and missteps were piling up.

He saw a shortcut, a way to put his bank accounts in the black and give his girls everything they could ever want. But Eddy, being Eddy, was so into those shortcuts that he never paid attention to the price he'd eventually have to pay. There are no shortcuts. People who actually grow up and mature do learn and understand that.

Eddy was never going to grow up. He got himself in the middle of drugs—selling them. His cleaning supply job was just a cover for the real work. He and some other men got in quick and deep. He came to me to bail him out of the trouble.

Here's the hardest part to tell you, my girls. I couldn't—wouldn't—help him or his fellow criminals. I'm sorry because I'm sure it was that decision that led to the inevitable—Eddy had to go, one way or another.

I tried my hardest to get rid of the others, too, but they were more sophisticated than I gave them credit for. I caused them enough trouble, though, that most of them just left. At least they're causing trouble for some other police chief somewhere.

For now.

Yes, I'm sorry for what I did to contribute to Eddy's disappearance, but only because of you two—and that's the reason I do everything I have ever done in the first place. I was scared for you. Now you're obsessed, Mill, and I can't do anything to change that.

I would if I could. I want you to know that. If I could deliver Eddy up, dead or alive, I would, but no matter how much I have tried, some of this ugliness got out of my control and I can't find him.

It is what it is now. I just hope you get over it—no, past it, Mill, and get on with life. Beth, you are the most precious of all, and whatever I do from this moment on, it will be to honor and take care of you. Mill, I wish you'd come back to yourself, but until you do, Beth is my first priority.

I'm sorry. So, so sorry.

Lovingly,
Gramps

I folded the note. I wasn't as rocked as I might have predicted.

I unfolded it again and looked at the date scribbled at the top of the letter. "Gramps wrote this when I was about twelve; Dad disappeared five years earlier. He never hinted at anything like this to me. Did he to you?"

"No, never. Well, he did tell me a time or two that I needed to move on, but no, nothing about the drugs."

"Did you sense Dad was into any of that?"

Mill frowned. "No. I sensed something was up, wasn't right sometimes, but never drugs. Your dad was a teetotaler."

I nodded.

"We never really had financial difficulties, Beth. We weren't rich, but we just never lived in ways that required lots of money. That's what I'm most bothered by in this letter. Sure, who doesn't want to make a fast and easy buck, but we were okay."

"Dad wanted more."

Mill shook her head. "I guess."

I looked at the note. "Do you think Gramps really couldn't find Dad?"

"I don't know for sure," Mill said. "But I don't think he would have written the letter that way if he had. I don't sense he was trying to fool anyone. I do think he *was* somehow more involved than he admits here in Dad's disappearance. Gramps was nothing if not proactive." Mill sat up, her feet going to the floor. "I'm not even mad at him. He did what he had to do; I get that more than anyone maybe. But the other people involved, Beth . . . I can only guess, but I bet that Walker was one."

"I agree, but not because I remember him telling me anything like that. It's just that all of it together . . . makes sense, I suppose."

"I've got Stellan working on rounding up any old paper-work that might tell us something more. Well, I *had* him working on it. Stellan would have handed me over to the St. Louis police in a heartbeat if I'd followed up. I can't contact him again, haven't been able to for months."

I looked at her, things clicking into place. "But I can."

"Yes, that might work." Mill's gaze leveled. "But that's not why I'm here. I could have asked you to contact Stellan over a phone call or an email. I really did want to see you."

I cocked my head and looked at her. She was concerned I'd think she didn't care about me.

In her strange, obsessive ways, she'd proved time and time again that she probably cared for me more than she should, but she also always had ulterior motives.

"I know," I said. "And I'm glad to see you."

Mill smiled. "Me too. Now, will you call Stellan?"

"I will." I fell into thought. "I did talk to him a few months ago and told him Walker's name, but he'd heard it already. He said he was going to see if he could find anything. We haven't spoken since. I didn't get an email from him, so I assumed he found nothing else, or he just talked to Detective Majors and they're not sharing with me. Or maybe since you disappeared, he's afraid to make contact with me."

"Maybe, but you know what happens when you assume?"

"You're right." I reached into my coat pocket and pulled out my phone.

I knew Stellan's number by heart; I used to be the one to answer it.

Thirteen

left a message with my number but knew that the chances of Stellan's catching me in a spot with cell phone coverage were slim. I also asked his secretary to email me with a time I could call back. Benedict communication required a few extra steps along the way.

However, from just that one phone call, Mill commented that I'd already involved too many people. When she'd asked me to call Stellan, she had wanted me just to talk to him right then, no one else. I couldn't stop her from stewing about it, so I didn't even try.

It was a good thing I didn't have any pressing writing deadlines because it looked like I was going to have to be my mother's host—and that would require some pretty constant attention. If I'd been in the throes of a deadline, she would have found a way to keep herself busy, but I still would have sensed her neediness. Mill did fine by herself, except for when she wasn't by herself.

"We'll talk to Stellan at some point. How about a tour of the area?" I suggested. I could have shown her the airport and Tochco's, but there wasn't much to explore with many of the so-called roads covered with snow.

Just as Mill frowned and shrugged at the idea, we heard a loud cranking sound from outside.

We exchanged raised eyebrows and went to see what was causing the ruckus.

We'd missed some activity. While we'd been inside the shed, one of the vans that was kept at the airport had somehow gotten stuck on the unpaved but much-used lane between the *Petition* and the library. It was frequently muddy during the summer, but now the snowpack had made it slippery and unwieldy. The van had gone off the side, its back end now sunk over a small berm that had come about naturally over time.

The noise had come from the tow truck that was now pulling the van up and over the berm. Elijah and I had first met yesterday, but now he seemed to be everywhere. He was currently outside his truck, working the mechanism that I knew only as a mechanical crank. I glanced toward the cab of the truck with a fleeting curiosity, wondering if Gus was there; there was no sign of him.

Elijah didn't notice us right away, but Doug Vitner did as he appeared from around the van, high-stepping to get out of the way of Elijah's work and through the snow. Mill and I hadn't put our coats back on, but at least I still had my cap in place. We stood next to each other with our arms crossed in front of ourselves as we observed. We looked exactly like the people he'd sat next to at the diner just an hour or so ago. Vitner did a surprised double take and then waved hesitantly.

I waved back. Mill didn't.

Elijah looked over at us, too, and waved and smiled. Mill and I both waved back that time.

Vitner started to walk toward us.

"Uh-oh," Mill said under her breath. "Let me handle this."

I wasn't sure what she was going to handle, and I wasn't

sure I was going to let her handle anything, but I was glad she was there.

"Hey," Vitner said as he approached. "Funny meeting you here."

"Yeah," Mill said.

"I was headed to the library and I went off the road, if that's what you can call it. Jesus, this place. Thank goodness there was a phone in the library." He looked at the shed. "You two live in that?"

I wasn't sure if he was asking professionally or just making conversation, but I suddenly understood what it was that Mill thought might need handling. I jumped in. "It's where we work."

"Oh. Well, that makes sense." He studied us. "Where do you live?"

There it was, a question I'd been dreading. In fact, I wondered again how I'd missed him all these months. Had we just not crossed paths, even in this place where there were so few paths to take? How had I not met Elijah nor been aware of Vitner? Even with my work and visits to the businesses downtown, I hadn't been out much since the real cold had set in. I hadn't even called Tex. Not only had I not been out much, I'd also drawn into myself more than usual. It hadn't been uncomfortable, but if it went on for months on end, I could understand how it could cause emotional havoc.

"Just visiting," Mill interjected. "We live in Homer."

"But you work here?" Vitner asked.

"When we're here," I said.

Vitner nodded casually. He didn't seem to be asking us for anything official. "You know, I heard there's a way to get to another town from here without a plane or ferry ride."

I wondered if he meant Brayn, where Tex lived, but I didn't want to share even that much with him, so I just nodded.

"It's called Flynn or something," he continued. "I was

supposed to get over there, too, but unless it's by dogsled, I'm not going to make it any farther than this crazy place. I can't even get to the library without going off the road." He threw up his hands in exasperation. There was no humor to his tone. He was fed up.

I remembered someone mentioning Flynn, or a place with a name like that, at one point, but I'd never been there. I didn't know how to get there even by dogsled. I was just relieved that Vitner seemed not to care in the least that he might have missed talking to me for his census duties.

"All done, Mr. Vitner," Elijah called from next to the truck. He sent Mill and me another smile and wave.

Vitner shook his head as he looked toward the van. "I was just going to the library to use the internet, but the airport is better. The road to it is easier." He turned and walked toward the van without a further goodbye.

He was correct. The small airport was at the end of one of the two paved roads. I looked toward Elijah's truck and inspected the blade on its front. He must have plowed the main roads earlier today. I wondered if Gril had talked to Elijah yet about anything suspicious he might have seen, but now wasn't the time to ask.

I realized how integral Elijah was to Benedict's shaky and small infrastructure, especially during the winter. I was glad I'd finally met him, and hoped I wouldn't need him.

"Let's get inside and warm up," I said.

"Didn't you tell me the special ops guy runs the library?" Mill asked.

"I did."

"Let's get warmed up, and then how about an introduction?" Mill asked.

"All right." I hoped she didn't hear the hesitation in my voice. I wasn't sure introducing the two of them was a wise idea, but I couldn't think of anything to divert her.

We hurried back into the shed, warmed up, and then bundled up before we hopped back into my truck and headed to the library. The tow truck, van, and two men were gone by that time, and my tires didn't have a problem navigating the way.

Orin had been badly injured a few months earlier. I'd been there when it happened, and I'd been terrified that he wouldn't survive. Not only had he survived, but he'd battled hard and was making himself stronger as he also fought debilitating back pain that came from earlier injuries. Every time I thought about those moments when I didn't know if he would live, panic tightened my chest.

"Orin smokes weed. In his office. It's for pain," I told Mill as we got out of my truck.

Though we were covered in coats again, I assessed that Mill needed better winter gear if she was going to stay for longer than even a day or two. A stop at the mercantile was in our near future.

"Good to know." She patted her pocket. "Maybe he and I can take a smoke break out back together."

"Why do you want to meet him?"

"I want to see if he can track down Walker, of course. I take it you haven't asked, right?"

We were just outside the library doors. I put my hand on her arm. "Mill, if anyone has figured out who I am, it's Orin, but he's never thrown it in my face."

She looked at me and leaned on the railing next to the stairs, crossing her arms in front of herself. "I can't let the opportunity pass. It's not every day you meet someone with special ops training—and if his expertise extends to computer stuff, well, I just can't not try. I'll keep it ambiguous."

"How?"

"Don't know yet, but I'll figure it out."

She would. Maybe.

"You'll like him," I said, swallowing some fear.

"You like him?"

"I do, very much. He's a good friend."

"Think of how good friends you can be if you're honest with him. I mean, sure, you can be friend*ly*, but honesty makes the real friendships. Ever thought of telling him?"

"Many times," I said. "I get what you're saying."

"Should we tell him today?" Mill smiled.

The cold was starting to burn my nose and cheeks uncomfortably. "No," I said automatically. "I'm just not there yet."

"Okay, okay, I understand. I know how to handle it appropriately. Let's go talk to the former special ops guy who smokes weed."

"He also looks like Willie Nelson."

"Of course he does."

As usual, the library was busy. Expanding upon Vitner's earlier observations, I gave Mill a quick explanation about the enviable internet access here and at the airport, and how people traveled back and forth just for the ability to use the connections.

We wove our way toward Orin's office, and I knocked.

"Enter."

We weren't met with a thick cloud of smoke, but there was some residual haze. Orin sat behind his desk, readers on the tip of his nose as he looked at his laptop screen. The room was decorated in an array of peace sign artwork. Mill looked around and gave a small coo of approval.

"Hello." Orin stood. He wouldn't have stood if it had just been me.

"This is my mom, Mill," I said. "Mom, this is Orin."

Orin removed the readers. I noticed that his eyes were unusually rimmed in red.

"Ah. A pleasure." Orin extended his hand.

Something wasn't right. "What's up?" I asked.

Orin nodded once, unsurprised that I'd tuned into his demeanor. "Close the door and have a seat. It's been a rough day."

"Would you rather I wait outside?" Mill asked.

Later I would remember that moment and be surprised she'd offered. She wasn't one to remove herself out of a sensitivity for others.

"No, it's all right," Orin said. "Please, make yourself comfortable."

Once the door was closed and we were all sitting, Mill and I waited for Orin to gather his thoughts.

He closed his laptop and folded his hands across the top of it. "The murder," he murmured simply, his eyes filling with tears.

He was the first person I'd come across who seemed genuinely sad about Ned. In fact, I hadn't much considered sadness, just fear that there was a killer among us.

"Oh, Orin! I'm so sorry. Did you know Ned?"

"Yes, but, well, I need to clarify some. I'm always sad for a loss of life, but I'd been trying to get Claudia to leave him. I was going to give her a job. I was going to let her rent a room from me, too, but we both knew that Ned would take that the wrong way—and there was nothing 'wrong' about it." He paused. Mill and I nodded as if we understood. "Anyway, I feel like I failed them both, or at least didn't do enough. I apologize for my emotion, but I really thought we could get her away from him, and then none of this would have had to happen."

"I'm so sorry," I said again. "You know she could have left on her own. I had no idea you were trying to help her, but it's not your fault."

"It's not," Mill added.

"Truly, I know that, but I'd sure like to understand how the worst came about."

"I can tell you what happened from my vantage point, if that would help."

"It might. Sure."

I went through the night's events at the bar and then the discovery made by Donner of Ned's body. I didn't share the middle-of-the-night activities that still left me uneasy. I didn't tell him about the blood on my doorknob, either. I did tell him about Lucy.

"I didn't know most of that," Orin said when I'd finished. "I didn't even know Ned had a sister, let alone one that was hiding at his place. Gril didn't tell me that Claudia had come to the bar injured. Damn."

"Did he ask you where you were last night?" Mill asked.

Orin and I looked at Mill; he didn't seem offended. "Yes. I was home alone. Got nothing to prove it, but I don't really think Gril suspects I had anything to do with the murder." Orin shrugged. "Maybe he does. But I didn't. I ran into Claudia at the mercantile last week, but she told me not to tell Ned that she'd left the house. He didn't like her to go anywhere alone. I told her the job was here, the room if she wanted it, but she was adamant that it wasn't going to work. Unfortunately, I kind of gave up then. I shouldn't have."

"No, you did the right thing," I said. "There was only so much anyone could do to help Claudia."

"Ned was a real piece of work," Mill added.

"He was a terrible guy," Orin said. "But I have no idea who would have murdered him, and so brutally. Despite the fact that he wasn't liked, no one I knew of would put themselves under suspicion for killing Ned."

"Ned wasn't worth it?" I asked.

Orin shook his head slowly. "I don't think so. Maybe if

Claudia had worked harder to get away from him, but you know us, Beth, we tend to mind our own business out here, maybe even too much. I know you've met good people in Benedict, but there are plenty of bad ones, too."

It was my turn to nod. When I took the time to think about the positive outcomes of my running away, the people I'd met were the best part. "I'm sorry, Orin," I said once again.

Orin smiled sadly.

"So, at one time you were special ops?" Mill asked.

She wasn't unsympathetic, but she had a goal in mind. I would explain that to Orin later.

Orin's eyes widened and he nodded. He got it—no explanation would be necessary. "Yes, that's correct."

"But that's all you can tell us about it, right?" Mill recrossed her legs.

"Afraid so." Orin smiled, a little less sadly this time.

Mill surprised me by her next question. I'd been preparing for her launch into wanting information about Travis Walker, but that's not where she went first.

"Have you met the census guy?" she asked. "His name is Doug Vitner."

"Once or twice."

"He hasn't done his census thing with you?"

"No, in fact he hasn't."

"Other than Ned and Claudia, who the hell has that man officially talked to? We've run into him a couple times just this morning and I've gotten the impression he's not just tired of being here in Benedict, he's tired of his job. But I wonder if he's really doing what he's supposed to be doing," Mill said.

"He's talked to a few folks. I've heard some of them mention him stopping by." Orin thought a moment. "He's probably not a welcome visitor. Lots of people are dodging him."

Mill nodded. "Do you think he's doing his job appropriately?"

"What do you mean?"

"From what I've seen, he's not a pleasant person. Is that because he's been turned away by so many people, or is that why he was sent here in the first place? When Beth and I talked to him briefly this morning, he seemed fine and then . . . on edge, easily irritated. He also told us he was bold enough to search Ned and Claudia's shed. I can't quite figure him out, but I wonder about him."

"Is there a way to confirm his credentials?" I asked Orin.

"Sure," he said. "You think he's not for real?"

"Mill's right. Something's off," I said. "I don't know exactly what."

All I'd picked up on was the fact that I didn't like him. Mill was hinting at something bigger, something I wasn't sure I could sense. But I knew her instincts were good.

"All right. Let's see what we can find."

He opened the laptop again, and his fingers flew over the keyboard.

Only a few moments later, he said, "Were you thinking he might be a fraud or something?"

"I just don't know," Mill said.

"He's legit, a bona fide census taker. Here's his ID." Orin swung the laptop around so we could see the screen, displaying Vitner's credentials alongside a frowning headshot.

Mill read aloud his birth date as well as the day he started working for the census. "He's been an employee for only a few months, which doesn't mean much, I suppose."

"Says he was trained in California," Orin added.

"At breakfast, he said he was from Seattle, behaved as if he wasn't close to family," Mill pointed out.

"That sounds like a little more than small talk." Orin turned the laptop around and started typing again.

"Believe it or not, it was a brief and less-than-friendly conversation," I said.

"I guess I can believe it." Orin typed. "Hmm. I can't find any Doug Vitner in Seattle. That seems odd."

"Maybe you need to go deeper," Mill suggested.

Orin lifted his eyebrows at her. "Not many people go deeper than I do."

"About that . . ." Mill sat up a little straighter.

"Yeah?" Orin said, though his attention had moved back to the screen.

Mill looked at me. I shrugged, but my breath caught in my throat. She was about to say my abductor's name out loud. I was as ready as I could be.

"If I gave you a name, is there any way you could search for that person?" Mill asked.

"Of course," Orin answered, though he appeared distracted.

"What?" I asked.

"Are you sure he said Seattle?"

"Yes," I said.

"No Doug Vitners anywhere in the state of Washington."

"Under the radar somehow?"

"No way to get under my radars, but maybe it was a misunderstanding or maybe he doesn't like to tell people where he's really from. Some people are like that." Orin seemed to purposely keep his gaze away from me. "I could probably get his home address via the census people, but I'd have to go through some firewalls I might not want to go through quite yet."

"I think we should tell Gril," I said. "Let's just call him, let him know what Vitner told us and what you didn't find. It might be nothing, but it's a discrepancy."

Orin thought a long moment but finally nodded. "All right."

As Orin dialed the police chief, Mill sent me a furtive wink. My anxiety ramped up again. Maybe her asking about Vitner was just greasing the wheels. It wasn't possible for me to understand all her methods. And maybe I was just tired of the roller coaster of emotions, but it now felt okay for her to do it, or as okay as it could feel.

If he hadn't already, Orin might put it together who I really was, even if Mill was cagey, but maybe that was okay now, too.

Maybe. I took one more deep breath as we waited for Orin to hang up the call.

I gripped the chair's armrests in anticipation.

And then nothing happened.

Gril didn't answer Orin's call. Orin left a concise message, stating that he didn't think he had urgent information to share but that it might be helpful. This was Benedict's version of emergency services. If there was no one there to answer, leaving a message was the only option. Of course, other numbers could then be called. Gril's cell, Donner's, then maybe even Viola's phone at the Benedict House.

Orin, still distracted by his task, searched for other Doug Vitners, but despite the lack of them in Washington, there were far too many, even in the western United States, to narrow the results down to the Vitner we knew.

Just as the conversation slowed and I was certain Mill would finally ask Orin about Travis Walker, a knock sounded on the door.

One of the patrons needed help finding a book. Library duty called for Orin, so we said we'd talk to him later. As we were leaving, he told us he'd be at the bar in an hour or so and asked if we'd be there, too.

"Something going on?" I asked.

"It's for Claudia. It's what we do," he said without further explanation.

"We'll be there," I said.

I hadn't heard about the get-together, didn't quite understand what he meant, but Mill and I wouldn't have missed it.

I looked at her as we stepped back outside. She plopped a cigarette into her mouth and struck a match. "You wish we'd just gotten it over with, huh?"

"How did you know?"

"Mother always knows." She pulled and then blew out. "We'll get it done. What now?"

"Hop in the truck. But only after you finish the smoke."

Mill puffed again and shook her head. "This world. No equal rights for smokers. I should start a campaign."

Nevertheless, she toed out the cigarette and picked up the butt before she got back in and buckled up.

Fourteen

The sun had completely set by the time we drove by the *Petition* shed. We couldn't see any stars through the thick cloud cover, but it felt like nighttime, though it wasn't even five o'clock in the afternoon. It was still cold, but not stormy.

"I can smoke at this bar, can't I?" Mill asked.

"I don't think so."

"Probably wouldn't be as serious as the other crimes I've committed lately."

"Might have worse consequences, though. Benny doesn't put up with much crap."

"Noted."

Even though the area around the library had better internet than the rest of the town, my phone rang so infrequently that I jumped when it sounded from my pocket.

I had to reach under my winter layers to grab it.

"It's Detective Majors," I said when I saw the caller ID.

Mill just shrugged and then looked away. It was her way of telling me it was my decision what I wanted to say to the detective about my mother's visit to Alaska. A part of me didn't want to answer the phone, so I wouldn't have to lie, but another, bigger part of me wanted to know if there was more news on finding Walker.

I stopped the truck for fear of losing the connection and flipped the burner open. "Hey, Detective."

"Beth, hello. My goodness, you sound so clear."

"I'm in a good pocket. How are you? What's up?"

Detective Majors sighed. "I'm fine, Beth. Sorry we haven't spoken for a while. I really do hope you're doing okay."

"I'm good." I looked out the windshield at the cold darkness, thinking I saw the glimmer of eyes out in the woods, maybe a bear or a moose. I pointed for Mill, but the animal never fully showed itself. "Do you have news?"

"No news about Walker. I'm sorry about that. I thought we had a line on something, maybe a possible sighting in Kansas, but it turned out to be nothing. We'll find him. We'll get him. He can't hide forever."

"I hope not," I said.

"But I do have some news—it's about your mother."

"Mill?"

In the seat next to me she glanced my direction but remained silent.

"Yes, we got word that someone in Juneau might have had an identification card in her name. The description of the woman matched your mother."

"Juneau? Really? When?" I wasn't sure if I was supposed to let on that Gril had told me as much or not. I hoped I'd picked the right fork in the lies.

"Just last week. I let your chief know; he didn't tell you?"

"Not yet." I'd have to let Gril know what I was supposed to know and when. My mother's being around tested my memory way too much. "He's been pretty busy, though."

"Well, he might not have wanted to worry you, and he said it was difficult to get back and forth to Juneau right now anyway."

"Yes, the weather slows down the ferry runs. Planes don't fly in the storms."

"I want you to be on the lookout, though. Your mother might be dangerous, Beth. I understand she might not be dangerous to you, but still . . . she's wanted for questioning."

"I know. I'll be careful, but I'm not sure how she could find me. I didn't tell her where I was."

"That's good, but she's particularly skilled."

"I hear you. I'll be careful. Thank you for letting me know."

"You're welcome. I'll stay in touch. I promise you, Beth, Walker will make a mistake. He's too arrogant not to."

I hoped she was right. "I know. Thank you again."

We ended the call.

"That seemed to go well," Mill said.

"As well as can be expected," I said. "Don't let me forget to tell Gril about that conversation. I don't think Detective Majors knew I was lying, but I can't be sure."

"Okay." She paused. "Hey, I'm sorry, girlie, to put you in any situation."

I smiled. It had been an almost lifelong situation. "Mill."

"I know, I know, but still."

"I'm happy to see you."

"For now."

"For now." I laughed.

"We'll see how you feel after twenty-four more hours," she said.

I didn't respond because it was such a typical Mill thing to say, but there was something more to her words than normal, something more ominous. I didn't dwell on it, but like her deeper curiosity about Vitner, it sparked my intuition.

I wondered what I was missing.

She still didn't know about the note that had been left on my desk, the one that listed Travis Walker's address. At that moment, as we idled between the library and the *Petition*, and as I suspected once again that there was something more to Mill's finding me in Benedict, I thought maybe I should share it with her. But I still didn't.

Knowing her, she'd tear the town down one cabin at a time, searching for the answer as to who had written the note. I didn't want that. I wasn't having extended flashbacks anymore, and her arrival had distracted me from that nagging mantra. Things were going well. There was no need to throw another wrench into it. Yet.

She was both a distraction and a source of strength. Maybe it was because she was my mother, but she'd never been a mothering person. She was fierce, and I needed a little of that. Even if she left suddenly, some of her fortitude might stick. I was wary because she was up to something, but I was also grateful she was here, at least temporarily.

I thought about the mantra: *You Rivers people never listen.*

It was good to feel some fight this time. You're wrong, Walker. I'm listening now, and I'm going to be ready for whatever comes next.

The mercantile was busier than usual, but we learned quickly that it was all because of Claudia.

Apparently, when a local person died in Benedict, a wake of sorts was automatically assumed to be taking place for the survivors of the deceased. Claudia's situation was particularly grim, bringing lots of folks into town to not only visit with her in the bar but buy things for her in the mercantile. Besides, the weather was acceptable, making the trip into a social—no matter how sad—event.

Attendees gave gifts to the survivor—items and money. It was as deep-seated a tradition as the spring Death Walk.

"Bunch of rubberneckers is what they are," Mill said quietly to me as we looked through a rack of coats. "Curious onlookers, want to see the grieving widow, want to understand the ugly murder."

"The killer will probably be there," I said.

"I'm sure the chief is counting on it." Mill hesitated. "I wonder if in this small community, the chief will look for the people who *don't* show up. I have just changed my mind about this. It could be fascinating."

"It's not snowing. No storm at the moment; nothing coming until later tonight, from what I could tell. The bar might be packed."

We bought Mill a new coat as well as some gloves and a hat. No matter that she wouldn't be visiting for long—even short-timers needed to be better protected than she was.

As I looked around at the other customers, all people who knew Claudia much better than I did, I decided we'd just slip her some cash. I introduced Mill to Randy, the man who ran the mercantile, as he rung us up. A line had formed, so there was no chance for conversation beyond asking if he was heading over to the bar, too. He wasn't sure.

"I'm going to run back to my room and grab some money for Claudia. You want to come with or go on without me?" I asked Mill as we stepped outside.

"I think I'll grab a pre-event smoke." Mill looked toward the end of the boardwalk. "See you there."

I felt a twinge of separation anxiety as we parted ways. *She'll be fine*, I told myself. *She won't get into any trouble. I'll rejoin her quickly.*

The lobby of the Benedict House was quiet and I didn't smell any food being prepared. I hadn't seen Viola for hours and suddenly felt like I needed to check on her.

I hurried to her door, passing the empty dining room and kitchen on the way, and knocked. There was no answer. I thought about checking upstairs, but stopped by Lucy's door next.

I knocked.

"What?" she said as she opened the door a moment later.

I had forgotten that Gril wasn't going to lock her in her room. I worked to hide the fact that I'd been startled.

"I'm looking for Viola. Do you know where she is?"

"Why would I know?"

"Gosh, Lucy, I'm not sure. Maybe she told you where she was going or maybe you saw her somewhere." I put my hands on my hips.

She didn't shrink back even a little. "I don't know where she is. I saw her about an hour ago when she brought me a sandwich made with stale bread. Yum. She told me I can't leave my room without her permission, but how am I supposed to get permission if she's not around for me to ask?"

I looked at her a long moment. "Do you need to leave your room for any reason?"

"*Just because* would be a good enough reason for me, but apparently not for everyone else."

"All right. *Really* sorry to bother you," I said as I turned to leave.

"Hey," she said, her tone suddenly pleading.

I told myself not to turn around, but I did anyway.

"Does anyone know what happened to my brother?" she asked as real tears pooled in her eyes.

I didn't feel sorry for her. In fact, I sensed that it was all manipulation. Still, I answered. "Not that I know of. Did you tell Gril everything you could to help with the investigation?"

"Of course, but there wasn't anything to tell."

"How long had you been hiding in Ned and Claudia's house?"

"Just a couple weeks. Came over on the last ferry."

"Did you see anything happen there that might be a clue?"

"Other than Claudia's a whiny bitch and my brother wasn't patient about it, no."

"You think Claudia could have killed Ned?"

"Sure." She shrugged. "I could see how she could get mad enough, and though she's not big, she's strong. But apparently she was in the bar with that woman who runs it all night."

Except for a smoke break, taken in the same place Mill was probably currently taking hers. Lucy didn't need to know that part.

Lucy and Claudia were about the same size—maybe five-five, trim but not skinny. In fact, I was about that size, too. We were a bunch of average-sized women who would all look about the same in our winter gear; the thought reminded me of my wet boots, but I didn't have enough information to dwell on it. No one had said they'd seen Ned's killer, but I stared at Lucy a long moment. Could she have killed her brother?

She'd been locked in her room the night of the murder, and Viola had been on watch. No one could have gotten past Viola, even if they could get a door unlocked.

"Anyone else you can think of?" I asked.

"I didn't see anyone else. I was in the shed in the back. Ned set up a heater, but I was cold all the time. That's all I know."

"Were you just on the run from Juneau? Is that why you came here?" I knew the answer, mostly.

"Yes. I didn't have anywhere else to hide."

I wanted to ask about her and Ned's parents, other family, but I didn't really need that much information, and it wasn't my business anyway.

I didn't want her to think I felt sorry for her, but there was some sympathy creeping in. It wasn't my most convenient trait—my ability to feel for criminals and the impossibility of some of their situations. My grandfather worked to get rid of it, but it hadn't disappeared. "I'm sorry about the situation."

She responded the way I expected her to—unpleasant and automatically defensive. She could tell I wasn't going to do anything to help her. "Yeah. Okay. What *is* your name? Why are you here?"

"Beth," I said. I didn't extend my hand. "I'm just a friend of Viola's."

She hesitated a moment. "Got it. Okay, then, since I can't go anywhere, I think I'll close the door now and try to find something to do with my time. Good luck finding Viola."

She closed the door but, surprisingly, didn't slam it.

I sighed before hurrying up the stairs to see if Viola was on the second floor. Those were usually the rooms the clients stayed in—they were just like my and Mill's rooms, but Viola didn't decorate them with fancy bedding and lamps. Everything in these rooms, when they were furnished, was strictly utilitarian.

Currently, all the beds upstairs were stripped bare, the doors propped wide open.

"Vi?" I called as I walked the length of the hallway.

There was no answer. I looked at the window at the far end. Not only was it shut and locked tight, it had been weatherproofed, insulated. A big sheet of plastic covered the entire opening on this side, sealed around the frame with numerous construction-sized staples.

I'd been up here just a few days before Ned's murder and the windows hadn't been weatherproofed. Had she done this the night Ned was killed?

I turned and headed back the other way, but stopped at the first room I came to. I went in and pulled the curtains wide, finding more plastic. Like the hallway window, the plastic was securely in place, sealed very well—a thorough job.

I checked all the other windows on the floor. They all were the same level of weatherproofed perfection. My grandfather would do the same thing to our windows during the windy and icy Missouri winters; even he couldn't have done a better job than someone had done on these.

It made sense that this was Viola's work, but how had she done it all by herself? This would explain the noises I'd heard—I could imagine the pop and thud of the industrial-sized stapler. I now knew why Viola had looked somewhat cold; just spending so much time near the drafty windows would make anyone cold.

I wished she would have asked me for help, but my shoulders relaxed as I understood the noises. There was nothing suspicious about what Viola had been up to. She probably couldn't sleep and thought she might as well get the task out of the way. This had been a small mystery, but it felt good to have something solved.

With a sense of relief still, I headed back down the stairs, sending Lucy's door a quick glance as I passed by on the way to my room. Hopefully, I'd find Viola at the bar.

A new wave of guilt ran through me as I looked at my doorknob. That stain—maybe blood—might have been important somehow.

Oh, Mill. I had no real choice but to shake it off.

I grabbed some cash I'd hidden in a bag taped to the back of the toilet—there were a limited number of hiding places in my room—and hurried back to the bar, where I hoped my mother wasn't causing too much trouble.

Unfortunately, you can't predict every kind of trouble that might be waiting around a corner.

Fifteen

"Tex?" I said as I came through the door, stutter-stepping so as not to run into him.

Though it wouldn't be easy to hide in the small bar, Tex was such a big guy that he'd be hard to miss in a stadium.

"Beth, hello." He'd been leaning against the wall right inside the door. He bounced himself off. "I've been waiting for you."

"You have?"

"Yes, Benny told me you'd be here soon."

I looked around the crowded space. Benny was behind the bar, but it seemed she hadn't noticed me come in. My mother and Viola were seated in a small booth, next to another booth where Claudia and Orin sat. Gril and Donner were at a table on the other side of the room, talking to Elijah as he showed them a piece of paper.

Everyone seemed to be well occupied and not caring in the least that I was talking to Tex.

There were others in the bar, too, but the only one I knew was Ruke, the man who'd taken Ned's body to one of the freezers somewhere. He was standing next to the bar, talking to Benny.

No one was looking in our direction, and likely no one

cared about two grown-ups who'd dated a few times saying hello to each other, but I was oddly uncomfortable.

I did acknowledge to myself that I might not have been uncomfortable if Mill hadn't been there. It was as if my old life was colliding with my Alaska life in ways I didn't want it to. The ramifications were unknown but suddenly seemed overwhelming.

That said, I couldn't help but smile at Tex. He was a good guy—in a big teddy bear way. He was a great dad to the daughters he'd adopted. We'd had five fun dates, all of them verging on romantic, but not quite getting that far.

Tonight he'd pulled his long hair back into a neat pony-tail, and his long beard had been recently trimmed.

I pushed away the discomfort and realized that if just see-ing him made me want to smile, maybe I should enjoy the moment.

"It's great to see you," I said.

"The circumstances are strange, I know. I hadn't heard about . . . the murder." He cleared his throat. "Anyway, I tried to call you at the Benedict House a few times but didn't reach anyone. I thought I'd take advantage of the decent weather and drive over to see if you're ignoring me on purpose or if I should keep trying to call."

I wasn't sure how to respond, so I simply took a differ-ent turn. I nodded toward Claudia—she was obviously sad, though she wasn't overwrought as she and Orin talked, and others stopped by their table to give her gifts. "Claudia is the wife of the man who was killed. I wasn't sure what this was going to be tonight, but it doesn't feel particularly somber. I don't know if people think there's a killer on the loose or that the victim was the only target—he wasn't the nicest of guys."

"Did he . . . do that to her face?"

"He did."

"I'm sorry for her, but she's not a suspect?" he asked, becoming serious.

"We're all suspects, I think, but there's nowhere for any of us to go, and not many places to put prisoners or suspects." A thought came to me and I glanced at Gril. I sure wanted a moment alone with him. "We're all on edge, but you can be scared for only so long before you just have to try to go about things as normally as possible." I paused, wondering if I could take my own advice. I looked at Tex a long moment and then said, "Want to meet my mom?"

Tex's eyes got big before he smiled, too. "Why, yes, I think I would very much enjoy meeting one of your parents, at a wake, right after a murder."

"Ideal timing, right?"

We made our way to the table. Viola greeted Tex and then excused herself. I introduced my mom to the closest thing to a boyfriend I'd had in a long time.

"Pleasure, Tex," Mill said, but she didn't hide her confusion. "Are you two . . . together?"

"We're friends," I said.

"Friends," Tex said as if he was testing out the word.

"Ah, I see." Mill tapped a cigarette out of the pack, popped it in between her lips, and continued. "Apparently I'm not allowed to smoke in here, but I can pretend."

"Sorry about that," I said.

"No problem." Mill studied Tex. "So, tell me about yourself."

Without skipping a beat, Tex shared the *Reader's Digest* version of his life in a nearby Tlingit village. I'd heard it all before, but it was no less interesting this time around. It was a life made of self-sufficiency but not neglect. He'd grown up in the tribe, his mother was still alive and doing well—and she apparently liked me a lot. My relationship with her had gotten off to a rocky start; I was glad we were in a better place now.

Tex had adopted two girls, though the legalities of the adoption were suspect because of the remote nature of this part of the world, which was naturally of interest to my mother.

She was completely judgmental about everyone, all the time, but she based her judgment upon things like hard work, equity, and honesty. I knew this and I didn't really care whether or not she liked Tex, but it was good to see that the two of them seemed to be *okay* with each other. Neither of them worked too hard to impress the other, but their conversation moved along easily. It was comfortable, which was something I wouldn't have predicted.

Tex stayed at the bar for a while—visiting with Mill and me for a bit before excusing himself to visit with others. The evening never became deeply sad or celebratory but felt . . . necessary. People came and went with specific tasks in mind: giving something to Claudia, having a drink, talking to a few friends, and then leaving before a storm hit again.

There were moments when Claudia seemed sadder than others. She never seemed happy. She cried a little. She thanked everyone. Her injuries were healing, but her bruises had that second-day look, when all the colors set in a little darker.

At one point, Orin stood from the table just as I was walking by. He didn't say anything but sent me a brief sad smile before he walked toward Gril's table. I took the moment to sit across from Claudia.

"I'm so sorry for everything, Claudia. I'm not sure I shared my name with you. I'm—"

She nodded. "I know who you are. Elizabeth something.

Thank you." She took a deep, almost shuddering breath and regarded her hands folded on the table in between us.

My own breath caught. It was a simple and common mistake, but her calling me the name I was hiding put me on alert. I told myself to calm down. "I go by Beth."

She seemed surprised by the correction, and I wondered at the tone of my voice. I cleared my throat.

"Beth. Right," she said.

She was so young, and would ultimately be better off without a man who was beating her, but that wasn't for me to determine.

"Do you need anything I can get for you?" I asked.

She shook her head but then looked up at me. "How's Lucy doing? Do you know?"

"She's staying in a room over at the Benedict House. I think she's okay, sad about her brother."

Claudia gave a laugh. "No, she's not. She hated him."

"I see." I paused. "Did you tell Gril?"

"Of course. I told him everything, even . . ."

"Even?"

"Nothing, really. I even told him about the jewelry that Lucy brought with her."

"Stuff she stole?"

"Yep." She looked at me, no visible grief in her eyes. She was wondering if she should continue talking—I'd seen the same sort of look when she'd first come into the bar after being beaten. I'd known then that she wasn't the kind to keep secrets to herself. "Ned took it from her, and that really pissed her off."

"I see. When did that happen?"

"Oh, it was all that night, after the census guy came by. Ned was upset anyway, then he took the jewelry, then he . . . hit me. I ran out of there after that."

Gril or Donner had seen or talked to Ned later on. At

least that had been the plan. I didn't know if they actually had. My eyes darted over to the table where Gril, Donner, Elijah, and now Orin sat, too. I still hoped to talk to Gril. I continued to look around the bar. Was there a killer with us? My eyes landed back on Claudia. Had she been considered at all?

I now understood Viola's actions better, but what had Gril and Donner been doing? I swallowed hard. I knew them. I trusted them. Was that enough? If they had somehow done something to Ned, should I let that be okay? Should I trust that they knew the right thing to do?

Claudia noticed my gaze and sat up straight, leveling her eyes on my inquisitive ones. Was I sensing some sort of challenge there? What would it be?

"Do you think that Lucy would have had it in her to kill her brother?" I asked.

"Oh, yeah," Claudia said. "She could kill anybody."

A chill ran up my spine. It was the result of my unwelcome and hazy but real suspicions about Gril and Donner mixing with what I sensed was the truth of her words.

I knew there *were* people who could kill anybody. Sociopaths, psychopaths, the people without empathy. If I'd had to make an appraisal of Lucy, it wouldn't have been along those lines. Had I read her tough-girl act incorrectly?

You Rivers people never listen.

I pushed Travis Walker and his words away.

Something in Claudia's eyes just then reminded me of things I'd seen in Lucy's, things I remembered from Walker's. A challenge mixed with a coldness that could never be thawed. I didn't want Claudia to know what I was noticing—or imagining—so I kept my gaze as sympathetic as possible.

I was given an opportunity to excuse myself as more people stopped by to offer their gifts and condolences. I slipped

Claudia the money before I stood. She nodded a thank-you at me before she turned her attention to the new visitors.

It was a weird night. But as evidenced by Tex's drive into town, we Benedict folks had to take advantage of whatever socializing we could. I kept trying to catch Gril for a private moment, but he was never alone.

The mood darkened when Doug Vitner joined us at the bar. He stood inside the doorway and scowled at the crowd inside. There seemed to be something different about him than before. Something else now shadowed his eyes, something more disturbing.

"What's everyone looking at?" he demanded.

Gril stood from the booth he'd been sharing with Donner and approached Vitner. We all strained to listen to their exchange.

"You doing okay?" Gril asked him.

"No, I'm not," he said. "I'd like to get out of this place, but since I can't, I came back to this damn bar again. Isn't a man allowed to have a drink without everyone looking at him like they want him killed, too?"

"No one wants you killed, Doug." Gril put his hand on his arm. "Hey, it can get rough around here during the winter. We all get a little stir-crazy. Why don't you come sit with Donner and me?"

Vitner pulled his arm away. "I don't need to be babysat."

Gril's demeanor changed. He became the lawman, squaring his shoulders and lowering his voice so we couldn't hear him when he leaned closer to Vitner.

Whatever he said did the trick, and Vitner obediently walked over to the booth where now only Donner waited. Gril looked toward Benny and sent her a silent communication. She nodded and got to work behind the bar.

"Who's that?" Tex asked as he moved next to me.

"The census man," I said.

"What? Really? I've never heard of a census person coming out here. That's new."

"You aren't aware of a census person ever coming here or to your village?"

"No, neither place."

"That's interesting." I noted to myself that it was something else I wanted to ask Gril about.

Mill came up on my other side. "I bet he's the killer."

"Um, maybe," I said.

"Who else would it be? I haven't been here long, but he's already first on my list." Mill squinted over toward the three men at the table. "Excuse me. I'm stepping outside for a smoke. It's unbelievable to me that we can't even smoke in bars anymore."

Mill made her way around me and toward the door. I noticed her give another suspicious gaze in Vitner's direction, but doubted anyone else did.

"I like your mom," Tex said when she left.

"She likes you."

"She reminds me of you."

"Really? I can honestly say that no one has ever said anything like that to me."

"In that neither of you want to talk about your past. I feel like I know you only about twenty percent, Beth. I'm an open book, but you and your mother aren't."

I nodded. "You are correct, and I'm sorry about that. We're extraordinarily private about our past, but there are good reasons."

Tex looked at me a long moment. "I figured that, and I respect it. I would like the answer to one very important question, though."

"Okay?"

"Should I keep calling or stop? I'm a grown-up, Beth. I can take either answer, though there is one I'd prefer."

"Oh, keep calling. And sorry I haven't tried to call you. I've thought about it. There's something about the winter isolation. I think even a phone call can feel like too much work."

"You're onto something," Tex said. "It's real. Don't let it get to you. Force yourself to get things done. Okay?"

I nodded. "My mom will be here for a couple weeks, probably, or until the next ferry back to Juneau. I'll be busy with her until she's gone, but after that, keep calling. I'll call you, too. Viola said I could use her phone."

"Good. I understand, and I'm glad. I like you. I enjoy your company, even with all the secrets you keep."

"I like you, too, Tex," I said.

I made no promise to tell him my secrets. I wasn't sure of anything regarding our potential future, except that I really did want him to keep calling. That part wasn't a lie. I wouldn't have lied about such a thing. I was a grown-up, too. Well, mostly, anyway.

Sixteen

Mill and I were the last ones left in the bar. When Tex took off, there was no kiss, but our hug lasted a moment longer than any of the others had.

I talked to a few people that I'd seen around, some I thought might recognize me, too. I wondered if Vitner had been doing his job. Had he been talking to people or was there a reason he made such an effort with Ned and Claudia? Had he inserted himself into their lives for a reason that wasn't about the census, something that might have led to murder?

My informal poll didn't give me much to go on. A few people nodded and said they talked to him, that it was a quick conversation. A few other said they hadn't heard from him. A vast majority of those I spoke with said they'd ignored him.

Maybe that was contributing to his strange behavior, too. Maybe he was just trying to do a job and was being met with lots of closed doors. That could mess with anyone's mood.

Or maybe Mill was right, and he was a killer. But why? What would be his motive? I figured out nothing new, and I never got to talk to Gril.

Mill and I helped Benny clean up, glad that Claudia was still planning on staying in the back room but now worried about Benny getting rest. We were happy to hear that Viola would have a room ready for Benny tonight along with the rest of us.

"You need to make her go back to her house," Mill said to Benny. "She needs to learn how to be alone. The sooner the better."

She wasn't wrong, but I still wished she hadn't offered her opinion.

Benny shrugged. "That's what Orin told me. He also said she could stay with him, too, but only if Gril approved."

"Does Claudia have other family, maybe in the lower forty-eight?" I asked.

Benny shook her head. "Not that she wants to live with. She'll probably stay right here, and forty years down the road, she'll realize she had a pretty good life in Benedict, particularly after her husband was killed."

Mill shrugged as she carried a couple of beer bottles to the recycling bin behind the bar.

Finally Benny sent us away, saying that she'd be at the Benedict House in a bit. She just wanted to make sure everything was in order before she left.

As we stepped outside, we were once again greeted by Gus—and the rest of his pack, too.

Elijah, his sled, and the dogs were on the main road in front of the downtown square. I'd seen Elijah in the bar but hadn't noticed the dogs earlier.

"Hey!" I called as we redirected and walked toward him. My voice carried in the wind, and he looked up a few seconds later.

"Beth, Mill, hello." He was standing on the sled. "Good timing. You said you wanted to meet the dogs." He stepped down on something attached to the sled—a brake, I assumed. It didn't look like a new sled, so if the one he'd been waiting for had arrived on the ferry, he wasn't using it yet.

The dogs had been standing, seemingly anxious, but at Elijah's command, they all sat.

"Have the dogs been out here the whole time?" I said as I looked over the eight ragtag mutts and Gus in the lead.

"Oh no. I went home a while ago and just brought them out. Thought I'd get them a bit more exercise before the snow hit again. They get antsy."

It was bitter cold, but the dogs didn't seem to mind. It still wasn't snowing yet, but even I could tell it was coming. I felt the chill, but I was enjoying meeting the animals too much to care for the time being. However, it was Mill's reaction that truly surprised me. She took long minutes with each dog, crouching and talking to them as she scratched behind their ears.

Growing up, I'd never had a pet. I'd never once seen my mother so enamored with animals as she was with these dogs. They were all some mix of husky, probably. Three of them were all brown, two black and white, and three completely dark-furred. Only Gus had the purebred look, with the smooth husky coat, pristine markings, and bright blue eyes.

Mill and I fell in love with them, and they immediately fell in love with my mother.

"I would love to learn about dogsledding," she told Elijah.

"Sure. Come on by my place anytime. If I'm not there, I'm getting someone out of a ditch or unstuck, but I'll always be back soon. I'd be happy to show you all I know."

I looked at my mother as she gazed at the dogs. She was besotted. I'd truly never seen anything like it.

"Thank you," she said, just as another big gust of wind knocked us a little sideways.

Elijah frowned up at the sky with what seemed like genuine regret. "We best be heading home now. See you both again soon."

We watched as he climbed aboard the sled and moved

the brake handle, reminding me of a shabby yet endearing Santa whose A-team was too busy to work tonight. I looked at Mill. Her gaze was still fixed on the retreating team.

"Wow," I said.

She looked back at me. "That was the most incredible thing I've ever experienced. I loved those animals immediately. I felt such a connection. Did you?"

"Maybe not as much as you, but sure."

"Wow," she repeated. There were real tears in her eyes.

"Mill?"

She shook her head. "Sorry. That made my night."

In all my life, during all the times we'd received bad news, even my stint in the hospital, I'd never seen her tear up. Not once. I was thrown, but she walked away before I could ask her anything else. And all tears were gone by the time we made it back up to the boardwalk.

Before tonight, I hadn't once closed down the bar. Exhaustion washed through me as we walked against the wind back to the Benedict House. The buildings blocked some of the gust, and the cold wasn't quite as biting.

"I like your guy," Mill said.

"He's not really my guy—yet. We'll see."

"Well, just enjoy his company."

She hadn't said the part I'd heard in my head: "while you can." I wasn't going to be in Benedict forever, or at least I didn't think so. Was a continued relationship fair to Tex when I knew almost certainly that it wouldn't be permanent?

"Sure, we'll see." I paused. "I'm so tired, I think I'm going to pass out."

"Me too." Suddenly Mill stopped walking and put her hand out in front of me, blocking my path.

"Hear something?" Mill turned her head and looked toward Ben.

I followed her gaze as I shook my head and listened hard.

Light from the bar window leaked out onto the downtown's front grounds but didn't quite reach the bear sculpture.

Then I heard it—crunching noises, as if someone was walking over the frozen snow. An animal could make that sound, though these steps sounded distinctly human, two-footed.

But nothing moved out in the gloom and it was difficult to tell from which direction the sounds were coming.

The town played host to three horses that roamed free. But they also had a home, a stable, a place where they were safe out of the weather. I hadn't seen the horses in a while, but I wondered if that's what we were hearing.

I took a step toward the edge of the boardwalk, the direction of Ben, and craned to listen hard. "Who's there?"

No one answered and the footsteps ceased. I looked all around, not liking the idea that someone might be watching us without our knowledge or deliberately not telling us they were there.

Quickly, panic tightened my chest, and my insides began to swirl.

"Beth," Mill said a moment later as she took hold of my arm, "you're going to hyperventilate. Look around. We're okay. We're almost there." She nodded toward the door to the Benedict House. "It's fine. It might just be an animal. If it's some asshole, they don't want to show themselves. It's not . . . what you think it is."

I didn't even realize that my breathing had sped up. Whatever was happening to me wasn't happening at the same level it had when I'd first come to Benedict, but that reaction of pure terror was still there. It was something evil that still had the ability to crawl its way under my skin and control me.

But Mill *was* there. She was right beside me, holding my

arm. Everything was fine. It was just a noise, something I'd probably heard a thousand times.

"Don't let him in, dollie. You don't have to let anyone in you don't want to. Push him away. He got three days; don't give him another minute."

She'd said something like that before, when I'd been in the hospital. It had made sense then, but only as a faraway, distant idea. Now when she said it, it felt more solid, like something I could sink my teeth into.

"Yes," I said. I looked at her, this time tears filling *my* eyes. "Yes."

"That's right. Good." Mill let go of my arm. "You're here. You're fine. You're safe."

"Mom." I blinked away the tears.

"Yep, that's me. I might not be very good at it, but I'm not going to stop trying."

I hiccupped. No, she wasn't the most maternal mother in the world, but she was literally on the run from the law because she was the most protective and perhaps the craziest mother in the world.

She could obsess and be vengeful like no other, but I was suddenly so glad she was there next to me, talking me down from whatever ledge some silly crunching noises in the snow had put me on.

"Let's get inside," Mill said. "I'm pooped."

Seventeen

B eth?" The voice was female and gentle, but I wasn't
sure who it belonged to—Mill or Viola.

"Come on, dollie, wake up." That was Mill.

I swam up from the depths and worked to open my heavy
eyelids. "I'm awake. I'm awake."

I sat up and blinked into alertness.

I was in the Benedict House's kitchen, on the floor. Mill
and Viola were at my sides.

"What's going on?" I said with a sleep-slur.

"We don't know. We were hoping you could tell us." Mill
had been on her knees; now she lowered herself all the way
to the floor as Viola rested back on her heels.

"How did I get in here?" I asked.

"I heard someone in the kitchen. When I came to explore,
I found you," Viola said.

"I heard something, too, and got here at the same time
Viola did," Mill said.

"Did I sleepwalk?" I asked.

"It appears that way," Viola said.

"I've never done that before." I hadn't considered that
waking up on the floor the night before might have been because I had been sleepwalking.

I looked at Mill, whose expression wasn't hiding her concern.

"I'm sorry. Did I cause any damage?" I inquired.

"No. It looks like you got some cheese out of the fridge, but that's it," Viola said.

"And I was noisy? I mean, how in the world did you hear me? It doesn't seem like that would be something that would get anyone's attention."

"Don't know." Viola shrugged. "You okay?"

Mill bit her bottom lip. "Yeah, I heard you, too, but you're right, I'm not sure how I could have. I know I heard something, though."

Viola picked up on Mill's doubt and stood. "I wonder if Beth is who we really heard. Give me a minute." She sped out of the kitchen.

"Want to get up?" Mill asked me. "Or do you need to sit another minute?"

I was cold. I hadn't put socks on, though I'd thought about doing so before going to bed. I had on only one layer of sweats, and while it wasn't frigid in the kitchen, it wasn't toasty warm, either.

"Did I eat some cheese?"

Mill leaned and grabbed the package of cheese on the floor. "I don't think you managed to eat any. No harm, no foul."

"Right, but . . ."

"I know." Mill nodded. "Do you remember anything? Did you dream anything?"

I shook my head.

"Heads-up, ladies!" Viola's loud voice came from down the hallway.

Mill and I stood, her hand protectively holding my arm, and made our way to the kitchen doorway.

Viola was buckling the holster around her waist as she

marched quickly toward us. "Lucy's gone. I need to head out and find her."

"What?" I said.

"We'll help," Mill added. "What can we do?"

"Stay out of my way," Viola commanded.

That wasn't my mother's style, but she did let Viola pass by. However, we were right behind her as she yanked open the front door and propelled herself out into the cold night.

It hadn't changed much since Mill and I had come inside. Surprisingly, it still wasn't storming. I had no sense of time except that it was somewhere in that vast expanse called the middle of the night.

Viola took one step toward Ben and looked around with sharp, critical eyes. "Goddammit."

"She can't be far," I said as I stepped back into the lobby to grab my boots.

They weren't there. Three other pairs were, but none of them were mine.

I stuck my bare feet into a pair of Viola's and clomped back outside. "My boots are gone," I said. "Lucy probably has them."

Viola nodded but didn't stop scanning.

Benny came up behind me, bleary-eyed. I'd forgotten she was staying in the Benedict House, too.

"What's going on?" she asked.

"Lucy's gone," I said.

"Shh," Viola said.

We quieted and listened hard, just as Mill and I had earlier. The wind blew some, enough to hum with a low-toned whistle through the nearby snow-covered trees, but there was another sound, too, something like a moaning. It could have been the wind, or not.

"Over there." Mill pointed toward Ben.

We hurried to the statue, and Viola grabbed a flashlight from her pocket; she aimed the light at the ground.

"Uuuhh."

"Lucy!" Viola exclaimed.

We descended on her quickly.

She was conscious but not fully with it. Her face was covered in blood, her lip swollen and cut. She lay near the same spot Ned's body had been found. The snow had already been stained in spots, giving the illusion that she'd bled a lot, but we were probably seeing Ned's blood more than Lucy's.

"We need to get her out of the cold," Benny said.

"Moving her could be dangerous," Mill said. "She might be hurt. No, screw it, you're right. We need to get her inside."

Mill and Benny did most of the work, lifting Lucy from the ground and carrying her, with one of her arms around each of their shoulders, into the Benedict House. She couldn't walk, and I couldn't help but notice that her feet, as they dragged over the ground, were inside my boots.

In short order, the dining room was transformed. Two tables were moved together, and Lucy was placed on top. I didn't know if we stopped there because it was closer than her room, or if she was too bloody to put on an already made bed.

"Coffee," Viola commanded.

Benny took on that duty.

"Bedding. Blankets, pillows," Viola barked.

I took that job, leaving Viola's boots by the door and running to my room.

The door was wide open—presumably from my cheese-foraging adventure—and even though there was now something much more urgent happening, a twinge of bother zipped through me at the thought of my nighttime wandering. I didn't remember any of it.

I grabbed my pillow and blankets and hurried back to the dining room.

Benny called Dr. Powder as the rest of us wrapped up Lucy and attended to the wounds we could find. The cut on her lip would need stitches, but there were some cuts on her cheek that weren't as deep.

She became fully aware a few minutes after we spent time rubbing her arms and legs, trying to get circulation back. My boots might have saved her toes from frostbite, but I was worried about a couple of her fingers and one of her ears. I wished Dr. Powder would hurry.

"What happened?" Viola asked Lucy when she was coherent.

"I . . ." She took a deep breath, her body quaking with an exhale.

"Drink." Mill handed her a cup of coffee.

Lucy nodded and brought the cup to her lips. When it touched the cut, she flinched but then managed a sip through the side of her mouth. She handed the cup back to Mill.

"I just stepped outside for a minute." Lucy looked at Viola. "I wanted some fresh air. I wasn't going anywhere. I've been in my room all day. I wasn't tired."

"Got it. But what happened?" Viola asked.

"I don't really know." She frowned. "Oh, I think I slipped and fell."

The air went out of the room.

"That was it? You fell?" Viola said.

"I . . . I think so."

I looked at the wounds on her face, trying to ascertain if the story seemed plausible. It did. Kind of. If she fell just the right way.

"What were you doing outside?" I asked.

"I told you. Just getting some air." She scowled, but then flinched at the pain it caused her. "I wasn't locked in my room."

"But you weren't supposed to leave without asking me first."

"Well ex-fucking-cuse me for not wanting to wake you up, bother you. I couldn't go anywhere anyway, just out for a minute of fresh air."

"No, but if we hadn't come out to find you, you might have died from exposure. Believe it or not, the rules are for your safety, too."

Lucy rolled her eyes but didn't respond. Instead she looked at Viola and said, "Am I going to need stitches? I won't look good with stitches."

"You are an idiot," Mill said to her, though there was something behind her words—was it admiration?

It might have been. Mill always did like a rebel.

Something suddenly struck me, and I blurted out another question. "Did someone ask you to come outside?"

"What?"

I shook my head, hoping to break loose the thread of a memory that had popped into it. Had I heard someone saying those words earlier tonight? Last night? *Come outside.*

As the moments ticked by and everyone watched me, the muddle in my mind didn't clear. The words rang, now in Travis Walker's voice.

Was I remembering or imagining? It was late. I was confused.

I blinked and looked at all the eyes watching me. "Nothing. I'm sorry. Nothing."

Mill squinted at me, but Viola turned back to Lucy. "You *are* an idiot," she said but with no hint of admiration. "And evidently you can't handle following the rules. We'll get you taken care of, but you've used up my patience."

"Sorry," Lucy spat. She caught Viola's dark expression and cleared her throat. "Really, I am sorry."

I stepped away and out into the hall. Mill followed close behind.

"You okay, dollie?" she asked.

I sighed and looked at her. "I had a strange memory, but I'm not sure where it came from. I think it's just because it's late . . . I don't know, but someone was saying to come outside. I don't know."

"Things are percolating?"

"Probably."

"What?"

"I . . . oh, I'm not sure. It's probably nothing. It's passing."

Mill nodded. "Well, I'll tell you this much—that little tart in there is lying, but I'm not sure about what exactly."

"And by *tart,* you mean Lucy?"

Mill nodded. "Viola will shoot it out of her or something."

"Or something," I said, looking at my mother and wondering again about her tone. Her words certainly weren't complimentary, but again, I thought I heard something else. A hint of camaraderie regarding Lucy?

We stood out there a few minutes. In the light of the hallway, away from the others for even that short amount of time, the haze cleared away even more.

Whatever earlier confusion I'd felt faded like a bad dream. Maybe it had just been the product of some late-night fear. Or the cheese.

"Dr. Powder will take care of her injuries," I said. "Should we head back to bed?"

Mill frowned as she looked at me and then back toward the dining room. "I'd like to see what happens next. You go to bed, but I'm not ready." She paused. "You're okay?"

"I'm fine."

"All right. I'll see you in the morning. I'm going back in there."

Mill turned and went back into the dining room. A moment later, I followed her.

Eighteen

Once again, Dr. Powder picked up Gril on the way in. The Benedict House was crowded. Lucy required a couple of stitches on her lip, but the concerns I'd had about frostbite were unwarranted. Once warmed up, she was back to her normal self.

A timeline was put together. Lucy said she'd gone outside at about four A.M. It was about six when Gril and Powder arrived, a little after five when I'd been found in the kitchen. Lucy had been outside probably for about an hour, long enough to cause damage, but she'd gotten lucky.

Once she was fed and fully caffeinated, she seemed to like the attention.

Lucy wasn't supposed to leave the Benedict House without permission, and Gril noticed that she'd been dressed for more than a quick trip for some fresh air. She claimed she wasn't meeting anyone or trying to run away.

"Where would I go? I don't fucking swim," she said in answer to Gril's questioning.

At that point, Benny left to check on Claudia and "do stuff around the bar that needed done," since it didn't look like there was any more chance of sleep that night. Mill and I were sent out into the hall, mostly to keep us out of the way.

We tried to listen to more of what was being said in there, but nothing was clear.

Gril came out of the dining room only a few minutes later, stopping short when he saw us. "You two okay?"

"We're fine," I said.

"Maybe get some rest. Head over to the *Petition*?"

"We will, but . . ."

"What, Beth?" He crossed his arms in front of himself.

"You took Vitner back to your house earlier tonight?"

"I did."

"Has there really never been a census person in town before?"

"Not that I'm aware of."

I swallowed. Gril was not in a good mood, but I couldn't stop myself from continuing. "Did you hear what Orin found?"

"That Vitner's got the qualifications, but he couldn't find any sign of him in Seattle?"

"Does that bother you?"

Gril bit his bottom lip as he looked at me. "Are you saying he's suspicious, Beth?"

"I am."

"You'll be happy to know that I don't disagree."

"So that's why the ferry didn't go back? Right? You held it here on purpose." It was the question I'd been wanting to ask.

"Weather is always a problem," he said easily.

"But not this time, right?"

"Beth, I'm not going to share my investigative tactics with you. Vitner's presence does bother me, though you need to know that he is struggling with the isolation. Some people do."

"Was he asleep when you left to come here?" I asked.

"Powder woke me up. He'd tried to call, but I didn't

hear the phone. He pounded on my door and got me out of bed. I . . . didn't make sure Vitner was there. That's where I was going. I'm heading back now. Why are you asking me this?"

"I'm not sure. Earlier, it might have even been last night, I thought I might have heard something in my sleep, someone saying to come outside. Tonight, I sleepwalked to the kitchen, though, so I don't know. I have no proof that I heard anything, no proof that Vitner has done anything at all. Something's just gotten under my skin and he comes to mind."

"I appreciate the information," Gril said flatly. "I will check on him now. You two be careful. I'm glad you're here, Mill. Stay with your daughter."

"Will do. Any chance you'd let me have a weapon?" Mill asked.

Gril barely bothered to take the time to glare at her before he made his way toward the front door.

"I guess that's a no," Mill said quietly when he was gone. She turned back to me. "Why were you asking him about the ferry?"

I looked around and lowered my voice, "Because I don't know what he was up to the night Ned was killed. If he kept the ferry here, I might feel some relief, like he thinks someone else killed Ned."

"Or he could just be using that as a ploy."

"I know."

"He didn't really answer, though."

"Not clearly, no." I paused. "Did I ever sleepwalk when I was a child?"

"Not once that I remember."

"Do you suppose I sleepwalked outside the night Ned was killed? Maybe that's why my boots were wet, why I woke up on the floor."

"Were you cold?"

"Yes, but . . . I'm not sure I was cold enough to have been outside."

Mill got a distant look in her eyes.

"What?" I asked.

"I'm processing. Why didn't Gril investigate out there?" she asked.

"What do you mean?"

"Did he spend one minute looking for footprints or a trace of someone else outside?"

"I don't know. Maybe when he first got here or when he left. We didn't see him come in or follow him out. He might be out there right now."

"No, he was in a hurry to get back to Vitner. Come on, let's look around."

I put my hand on her arm. "Get some better clothes on. Change your socks and put on your boots."

"I was just going to take a quick look."

"Gear up, Mill. I'll meet you by the door." I stepped around her and went into the dining room to gather my boots from where they'd been put after being pulled off Lucy's feet. She frowned at me as I took them from the room.

The snow had finally arrived, big speedy flakes dropping more than falling.

"Maybe Gril was planning to come back when it got light out," I said as we stood outside the Benedict House's front door, no sign of the police chief as the miserable weather swirled around us.

"Well, let's make sure," Mill said.

I couldn't think of a good argument against it, though I still wondered if he *had* searched and we'd missed it, or if it was something he was going to do when it was easier to see, or if it even mattered. I so wanted to think he hadn't done anything wrong.

"Let's not stay out here too long," I said.

"Long as it takes," Mill said, seemingly not noticing the less-than-ideal conditions.

I flipped the switch on a flashlight I'd grabbed from behind the front counter and aimed it out toward Ben, where we'd found Lucy.

"No, let's check the back," Mill suggested.

"Why?"

"Whatever went on out front has been compromised. All us gals tromped through here. We need some virgin snow."

Though snow was falling, the boardwalk was covered in only a light dusting.

"Okay, no footprints visible here on the boardwalk," I observed. "We can get to the back through a slot in between the main buildings."

"Rock and roll." Mill took off walking toward where I shined the light.

I followed her through the gap in the two building arms.

The Benedict House took up one whole block, and the other businesses made up the other. The space in between them wasn't big enough to be called an alley or even a walkway, but a person could fit through and make their way to the back of the buildings and toward some thick woods that began about thirty feet farther.

I aimed the flashlight downward as we walked sideways through the slot. "Nothing on the ground here. Not even much old snow. It's icy."

"Right. It is warmer here next to the buildings, though."

As we emerged at the back, I still had the light aimed low. "Look."

Obvious in the snow, even as more was quickly falling, footprints made a path heading away from us.

I hopscotched the light from the first print and then on down the others, all the way to the woods.

"I don't see any return prints," I said. "Someone walked to the woods, but then what?"

Mill crouched next to me and gazed out to the woods. "I think we'd better follow them and see where they lead."

"You don't think we should call Gril?"

"No, darlin', I don't. Not yet."

"I do."

"Let me see if I can change your mind. Take a close gander at that first print."

I did.

"Look familiar?" Mill said.

It took only a second for me to realize the prints were from my own boots. I put my foot next to the first one just to confirm. "So Lucy walked out this way? But didn't come back? That doesn't make sense."

Mill stood. "Maybe."

"What other . . . of course, you think I might have made these prints."

"I don't know what I think except that we should get our own understanding of all of this before we involve the law."

"Damn."

"Yeah. Maybe. Come on. I'll decide if we need to have a big old footprint destruction party out here."

I swallowed and nodded.

She was right, and she wasn't right—typical Mill. I didn't argue, though; I followed her and hoped we weren't making a big mistake, or another one, depending upon how you looked at it.

We followed the footprints all the way to the woods, where they disappeared abruptly. Too abruptly. It was as if the feet that had been inside them had either taken a backward path exactly the way they'd come or had been lifted off the ground.

Though there were a few trees in the area between the

building and the woods, the forest thickened substantially at the perimeter and the terrain changed. There really was no easy walk, not here, not at this spot. If whoever had been wearing my boots had gone farther into the woods, there's a good chance that the brush and old foliage, some still not covered by snow, would keep prints from being easily recognizable or hide them altogether.

"We don't want to go any deeper," I said.

"Well, we do, but we shouldn't," Mill clarified. "Even I'm intimidated by whatever all that is out there."

"It's dark and we don't want to surprise any wild animals."

"Bears hibernate, don't they?"

"Fun fact—not all of them do, particularly in this part of Alaska, where food might be readily available throughout the winter."

"Well, damn, another myth busted."

I aimed the light into the dense forest and didn't immediately spot any threat, but did think I saw a clearing of sorts. I had been out this way during the daytime, although I hadn't inspected this area closely.

Now, as I aimed the light, I wondered about something. Where the trees were thick, the snow wasn't falling as much—the trees were stopping some of it before it hit the ground. But in a snow globe type of illusion, I thought I saw a clearing on the other side where it was coming down hard.

"Uh, I've changed my mind. I need to go in there about thirty feet," I said to Mill.

"Got it. I'll be right behind you."

We trudged along. It wasn't easy, but we were well rewarded. Yes, there was a clearing of sorts, and it was obvious what it was used for. Sled tracks as well as a flurry of paw prints lined the middle of the long gap.

"It's coming down hard right here. A few more minutes and we might not see this much," I said.

"Can you tell if the sled marks and the paw prints are fresh?" Mill asked.

She'd probably expected me to be an expert in such things by now. To be fair, she would have been herself.

"I can't."

"I wish we had a way to take a picture or something." She patted her pockets but must not have grabbed her phone earlier.

"We'll just have to try to remember it," I said.

"You think that Elijah character is somehow involved in this?" Mill had to raise her voice because the wind suddenly picked up even more.

"I suspect there are lots of sleds around here, and this is a well-traveled corridor. Who knows if the boot prints and these tracks have anything to do with each other?"

"Mmm-hmm." Mill looked down the way. She wanted to follow it.

"We need to get back," I said.

Mill hesitated. "You're right. But let's be careful again. See if we can find anything else important over on the other side."

"Got it."

Once we were through the trees once more, I aimed the light back down.

"It would not surprise me if Lucy walked out here tonight and then walked backward in the prints just to fuck with any-one who might wonder," Mill said.

"We sure don't see any other boot prints."

"I know, and that's what I was hoping for, maybe count-ing on," Mill said.

"To prove she was meeting someone?"

Mill nodded toward the window to my room. "That, and to see if anyone was outside your window, talking to you. You said you might have heard something. . . ."

"Doesn't look like it."

"Nope, it sure doesn't."

"I don't know what that means about what I thought I might have heard."

Mill shrugged. "Too soon to answer that one, dollie. All right. Now, I can't decide if we should destroy these prints."

"Why would we need to?"

"Because I don't trust the police."

"But Lucy had my boots on tonight. If these boots were involved in any crime, they and I now have plausible deniability."

She smiled at me proudly. "Plausible deniability. That's my girl."

Mill set off back toward the Benedict House and I followed behind.

We didn't destroy the prints, but we didn't walk inside them, either. We weren't even all that careful, but we didn't see anything that might help us understand what had gone on out there. I wished I knew for certain that Lucy had been the one to make the prints, but short of asking her and then taking the leap to believe she was being honest, there was no way to be sure.

I might be ready to ask, but I certainly wasn't ready to trust her.

Nineteen

A re you sure?" Mill asked Lucy.

"I would never have done anything like that. I wouldn't explore. It's like I said, I just wanted some fresh air. Jesus, I was the one hurt, and you're coming in here sounding like you're accusing me of something." Lucy placed her finger gingerly next to the now-stitched-up cut on her lip.

"No one is accusing you of anything," Viola said. "They just asked if you went out back. You won't be in any trouble if you did. We just need to nail down the footprints they saw."

Lucy looked around the room at Viola, Mill, and me. Dr. Powder had left, and if Gril was coming back, he hadn't returned yet.

Mill had decided it was probably best to face these questions head on, maybe get some answers before the police got involved, even if we couldn't completely verify. I couldn't have stopped her from questioning Lucy even if I'd tried, and Viola didn't seem to care what Mill did.

The "prisoner" had been moved to her room, where she was sitting up in her bed, all her needs being met. She was working the sympathy pretty well.

My mother had been gentle—in her own way, which probably sounded phony to Lucy—but Viola stood tall behind her with her hand on her gun.

"I didn't walk back there," Lucy said after she looked away from Viola's gun again. "I swear."

"But you said you don't remember everything," Mill said.

"Are you kidding me? Do you honestly think I would have gone behind the buildings in the cold and dark? I'm not stupid, and that sounds scary as shit."

Viola quirked her eyebrow and Mill made a noise.

"Thanks, Lucy," I said as cordially as I could muster. "Would you let us know if you remember anything else?"

"Of course." She looked at the tray on her lap. "Any chance I could have more hot chocolate?"

Viola sighed. "Sure. I'll grab it for you."

With my eyes I asked Mill to leave the room, too. She understood, and though she didn't like to be left out, our silent code was at work again. Maybe my playing the extra-good cop would help some.

Lucy was a lot like Mill, though significantly younger. It would take some years of refining her hard edges before she could come off as tough.

This was only my mother's second day in town. So far she'd erased a potential bloody spot on my doorknob, debated hiding some footprints, and asked Gril for a weapon. I didn't know if we were headed toward solving crimes or committing them.

I would have bet that Lucy would have done the same.

I really needed to know who made those prints in the snow, because if it was me, I was now dealing with something that went beyond my amnesia. Why was I sleepwalking in the middle of an Alaskan winter? And what night had the prints actually been made?

I sat on the edge of her bed. She worked hard at keeping

irritation out of her eyes. We'd saved her, taken care of her. She didn't want to be friendly to us, but she knew she should. She owed us, but she was the type who didn't like owing anything to anyone.

"You feeling okay?" I asked.

"No. My mouth and head hurt, and my body is achy."

"But you're going to be fine."

"I hope so."

"About those footprints . . ."

"I told you, I didn't walk back there. I wouldn't!"

I nodded and smiled sympathetically at her. "I hear you." I looked at the door and then back at her. Lowering my voice, I said, "Viola scares the crap out of me. I get it."

"She doesn't scare me." Lucy's eyes glanced quickly toward the doorway, too.

I nodded. "I think something's been overlooked, Lucy, and I want you to know that I haven't forgotten."

"What?"

"You lost a brother, tragically. I'm sorry for your loss."

"Exactly. Everyone seems to forget I'm mostly the victim here. I mean, yeah, Ned was, too, but I'm still alive to feel it. And then I get locked up in this room. I tried to get two seconds of fresh air and everyone thinks I was up to something." A few real tears rolled down her cheek.

"I'm sorry."

She sniffed and wiped her arm under her nose. "Do you think it was Claudia?"

"What about Claudia?" I asked, surprised by the abrupt turn she'd taken.

"What if Claudia killed Ned?"

"Benny was with Claudia." I knew that Claudia had been outside for a smoke, but I still didn't bring that up. Besides, as I'd thought about it, I couldn't imagine that Claudia managed to kill Ned, have a smoke, and clean herself up enough to hide evidence of doing the deed. The timing didn't feel like it fit.

"I know, but boy, he sure got mad at her."

"Earlier the night he was killed?"

"I had to pull him off her. I bet she didn't tell anyone that part. I had to save her."

"I don't know what she's told the police, but she looked pretty beat up. You don't think she shared all the details?"

"I don't know. I just don't know her that well."

"Were you and Ned pretty close?" I asked.

Lucy deflated some as she sat back against the headboard. She looked over at the scrunchies still on the nightstand and grabbed one. A stack of bobby pins fell onto the floor. I reached for them and put them back where they'd been as Lucy pulled her hair into a ponytail.

"We used to be close," she said a long moment later. "I hadn't seen him in about five years. Our parents died when we were kids—him six and me four. We first went to the same foster home but were separated a few months later. They liked him, but they didn't like me. They sent me away."

"I'm sorry. That had to be rough."

"It wasn't easy. We saw each other for a while when we were in different houses, but things changed, and we just stopped making the effort, or our foster families did. It happens."

"Was this all in Juneau?"

Lucy nodded. "Ned and Claudia have only been over here for a few years."

"Why did you come over to Benedict? Well, I know you were on the run from the police, but may I ask why you didn't try somewhere else, go farther?"

"I came over because Ned was here and he would protect me. I don't know anyone else, pretty much in the entire world."

"So you took some things in Juneau?"

"Yes."

"What things?"

She glared at me, confirming my rapport-building instincts weren't stellar. She had no obligation to tell me anything, but I was hoping she'd feel a tiny bit of desire to.

"Jewelry," Lucy finally said.

"From a shop? From a person?"

"Jesus, Beth, what's the deal here? Why do you need to know?"

"I'm curious, is all." I shrugged and smiled.

"Well, that's it. Jewelry, from a shop. I didn't have a weapon, so it wasn't an armed robbery, but you know Mr. Police Chief here thinks I did. I don't know why, but I can't seem to convince him otherwise."

I nodded, remembering Gril had said the Juneau police told him that Lucy had a gun on her during the last robbery, though she hadn't used it. "Well, that's good. I bet that if you return the jewelry, fess up, your sentence might not be too bad."

"I don't have it anymore, so I can't do that."

"What did you do with it?"

"Ditched it in a garbage can."

Claudia had mentioned that Ned had some of it. I gauged that I wasn't going to get the full truth no matter what.

"Where?"

She shrugged. "I don't remember."

This wasn't getting us anywhere.

"Hey, I'm really sorry about you and Ned being separated when you were kids. That truly had to suck," I said.

"It did," she said, obviously happy to move on.

I looked at my feet. "Did you like my boots?"

"What? Sure. I don't know. They were just there and looked like the ones closest to my size."

"They're warm, though, huh?"

"I guess." She sat forward again. "I didn't wear them long enough that I remember. I slipped them on, went outside, and then fell. I don't remember noticing if they were warm."

I thought back to the moments I'd watched her toes dragging over the ground. The boots had laces, sturdy shoe-strings that wove around eye hooks. I remembered seeing the strings dragging, too. Lucy hadn't laced up the boots. I suddenly sensed that she just might not be lying about not walking far, because if she'd made those prints in the back, the boots would have had to have been laced. Her steps would have been too clunky otherwise.

However, that also meant that if I'd made the prints out back, I would have had to lace the boots up, too—as I was sleepwalking. If I had done that, I didn't remember a moment of it.

"Beth?" she prompted.

I snapped out of my thoughts. I didn't understand anything more than the need for lacing the boots, and that seemed like a wimpy, useless detail.

Being nice to Lucy wasn't leading me anywhere, nor was it enjoyable enough to want to continue.

"Thanks for your time, Lucy. I hope you feel better quickly." I stood.

She didn't seem disappointed when I left.

Twenty

I looked at Mill sitting on the edge of my bed, absently picking at a fingernail. She was disappointed I hadn't gotten anything important out of Lucy.

"Do you . . . like her?" I asked. "I mean, you don't seem to be bothered by her."

Mill frowned. "I guess I just don't dislike her as much as everyone else seems to. She's had a rough life."

"She's a thief." We knew that much for sure.

Mill shrugged. "Sometimes the backstory explains everything. Now, I can't say I need to know more of her backstory, but maybe she's just done things she feels need to be done. If anyone knows about that, it's me, I guess."

I nodded. "Hey, let's go to the *Petition*."

"Even with the storm?" Mill said, though she sounded more excited than critical of the idea.

"Even with. I have a call I want to make anyway. I don't want anyone to hear it."

"Now that sounds interesting." Mill smiled.

The trip wasn't easy, but my truck and its tires were up for the challenge.

At the *Petition,* Mill made herself at home as I cranked the heat and lifted the mini blinds over the window.

I grabbed my burner phone and punched in Dr. Genero's number. Disappointingly, she didn't answer. I left a message, attempting not to sound like I was worried. Apparently, I wasn't successful.

"Beth," Mill said when I folded the phone closed, "you okay?"

"I am. I really am." I paused. "I'm concerned about me sleepwalking and what might have happened when and if I did, but sure, I'm fine."

"Darlin', if you're sleepwalking, there are ways to keep you safe. You didn't kill anyone, don't worry about that. We can put a monitor on you at night, maybe on your bed. It will beep if you get up."

"That sounds fabulous," I said flatly. I wanted to believe her, that there was no way I could ever kill anyone. There wasn't any evidence that I had—well, except maybe for the now-removed blood on my doorknob.

"I know you're worried, but there are ways to help us understand what might be going on. That's all I'm saying. Viola will be happy to monitor you after I leave."

"I'm sure *she'll* love that."

"I bet we can just order something online. A buzzer, a bell, something that might electronically send messages. I don't know. Let's look."

"We can order anything online, Mill, but we don't get consistent deliveries out here. It will take a while."

Mill frowned. "Man, that's irritating."

"Not all the time."

"Okay, let's put a bell on your door in the meantime. We'll figure something out."

I might have had a clever comeback about the bell, but my phone buzzed. I grabbed it too quickly and flipped it open, almost dropping it.

"Dr. Genero?" I said as I put it to my ear with too much force.

"Beth, I'm sorry I missed your call. How are you?"

Dr. Genero was one of the country's foremost brain surgeons. She had immediately answered my calls more times than I could remember, and she always apologized when she had to ring me back. She never behaved as if she'd come from a surgery where she'd saved another life, as she had mine. She never acted like she was too busy to speak to me.

"I'm okay. Thanks." I felt calmed by her comforting tone. "How are you?"

"I am fine. What can I do for you? Start by telling me about your headaches. How have they been?"

"I haven't had any headaches for a good long time." I hadn't. "But I was wondering . . . Could the injury to my brain cause delayed reactions, maybe something like sleep-walking?"

"Ah. Well, like some of your other questions, that's a bit difficult to answer. As you know, almost anything is possible with head injuries, and I have no scan to see if you're healing appropriately, but let's pretend you are. What about the other things you've mentioned in the past? Flashbacks of both your time in the van as well as about your father?"

"Lately I haven't experienced much of either of those. It's eased off."

"Has something else happened? Something stressful?"

I thought hard. Mill's being there was a little stressful, but allegedly I'd walked in my sleep the night before she'd arrived, so neither that nor Ned's murder could be the cause. The winter hadn't bothered me too much yet, and I'd also experienced a level of comfort at knowing that we were cut off from the rest of the world. No one could get here easily.

Until two weeks ago and then with Mill's arrival—that is, when the ferry had in fact made it from Juneau.

"I'm experiencing a winter like I never have before. It's restrictive, but I don't think it bothers me."

"All right. Have you begun working with a therapist?"

"No. I thought I was doing better. . . ."

"Yes, but I still think therapy would be good for you. In fact, I found someone who might be able to help you online. Do you mind if I send you her information?"

"That would be fine," I said.

It wasn't that I was anti-therapy. I simply thought I could handle my issues on my own. Maybe I was wrong. I would at least consider any contact Dr. Genero sent.

"Good. Now, are you drinking much alcohol?" Dr. Genero asked.

"Very little. Once or twice a week." I suddenly craved one of Benny's Bloody Marys, but I didn't say that aloud.

"Good, that's something you should watch if you're sleep-walking. Would you be willing to try some relaxation exercises before bed? Maybe meditation?"

"Sure."

"Work on that. There is a chance your subconscious is trying to tell you something. Don't be afraid of the message. Listen for it and understand that memories can't hurt you. In fact they might be able to help, particularly if you can process them and move on. There are apps that can help with meditation, instructions online. Look things up, research. Also, if you are sleepwalking, it would be good to have someone to redirect you. Gently, without trying to wake you up. You need to be safe."

"I should wear a bell or a monitor?" I looked at Mill, who lifted her eyebrows.

"Again, I don't want you startled awake, but that's not a bad idea if it's the best way to communicate to someone who could be there to help. This is not my area of expertise, but I would always say that you need to keep in mind that those who are sleepwalking need to be treated gently."

"All right."

"Is there any chance you could get a scan?"

"No, not right now. Maybe in the spring."

"Well, if things get worse, if your headaches come back, you need to get to a doctor." Dr. Genero sighed. "I've told you that before, though, and you're probably tired of hearing it. I have to be honest with you, Beth, I think you're fine, but I always worry when I don't get in-person follow-ups, and my sense is that something is causing you stress. Is there any chance that the man who took you is in your near vicinity?"

"No, not at all," I said. "Well, not really; he's not here in person, at least."

"That's where therapy can help. Please look into it."

"I will."

"What else? Are you well otherwise?"

"I am. I've been working out, taking self-defense classes. I'm doing well." We hadn't had a class for three weeks because of the weather, and I'd been neglecting my personal training, but I'd get back to it. I felt a twinge of guilt and wondered if I should try to get to the stationary bike at the community center today or the next, even with Mill here.

"How's the writing?"

"I turned in a book a couple weeks ago. My editor hasn't finished with it yet, but she says she likes what she's read so far. Things really are going fine. But I sleepwalked into the kitchen last night, for some cheese apparently, and I might have walked outside the night before. It's cold where I am, so that's not wise."

"Might have?"

"I'm not sure about the night before, but the kitchen walk is confirmed."

"Maybe you were just hungry?"

I laughed once. "Maybe. I'm certainly hungry most of the time, but that's back to just a little above normal."

"A good appetite is a good sign."

"Well, if I didn't work out, it wouldn't be so fabulous, but yes, though it's mellowed some. When I got here, my appetite was that of a growing teenager." Again, I thought about the stationary bike I needed to reacquaint myself with.

"I do think that's all good news. At this time, monitor the sleepwalking. It might be temporary, but you need to be safe. And relaxation exercises. Also, get in touch with the online therapist. I'll send you the information the moment I get back to my computer."

"Thanks, Dr. Genero."

"You're welcome. Call me with anything else."

"Will do."

I closed the phone and stared at it in my hand for a long moment.

"You feel better?" Mill asked.

"I do, but I'm not sure I got any real answers. Sometimes just hearing her voice is reassuring."

"She's a great doctor. We were lucky to have her."

I put the phone on my desk and looked up at my mother. I'd heard emotion in her voice. With her knuckle, she wiped at the corner of her eye.

"*Mom* . . ." I said.

"Stop it. I'm your mother; I'm allowed to be emotional, grateful that you're okay."

"Well, sure, but . . ."

I thought hard. Until our time with Elijah's dogs, I was certain that I hadn't seen her display such a swell of emotion. Here was another tear. Was she just getting older?

The phone buzzed. I guessed it was Dr. Genero again, but it wasn't.

"It's Stellan," I said.

"Oh, good." Mill nodded and sat up straighter, all sign of tears gone.

"Stellan," I said as I answered. I was surprised by the good timing.

"I took a chance and you answered. How are you, Beth?"

"I'm great." I shrugged at Mill. "How's it going there?"

"Good. You know about your mom, right?" His voice was oddly clear. I hadn't noticed how far away Dr. Genero had sounded until comparing Stellan's voice, which sounded like he was in the same room with us. In the back of my mind, I had the notion that I shouldn't move a muscle, not even twitch, so I wouldn't lose the clarity.

"I do. She's still on the run?" I said. I turned the phone upside down so he wouldn't hear me gulp-swallow.

"She is, but some of the St. Louis folks thought she might be in Juneau, Alaska. Are you in Alaska?"

I didn't answer.

"Never mind. If you are, though, be aware, she might be trying to find you," he said into the silence.

"Got it."

Stellan paused a long moment. "I know your mother well enough to think two things—she doesn't make many mistakes, but when she does, it's because her emotions get the best of her. Don't get yourself caught in that crossfire."

"I won't." I could hear acrimony in his tone, but it would have been impossible to argue with his assessment even if she hadn't been in the room with me.

I waited. He'd called me even though I wanted information from him, but I could tell this call wouldn't be as easy as just asking. It sounded like his anger at my mother's activities in the Piggly Wiggly parking lot had been reignited with the sighting of her in Juneau.

Just when I was about to jump in with my question, his

tone softened. "I got your message, Beth, and I *have* been looking into more things from back then. I don't have much, but a little more."

"Thank you, Stellan. I know you have plenty to do. I appreciate the extra time you've put in." My words were genuine, but they did make me sound a little like a suck-up.

Mill rolled her eyes.

"You're welcome," Stellan said. "Look, I need to tell you about a letter I gave to your mom a while ago."

"It's okay, Stellan. She sent me an email, telling me about it. I know it was a tough decision for you to share it with her. Thank you."

"When did she send it to you?" he asked, his chair squeaking as he sat up and went into full cop mode.

I couldn't ask him to hold on a moment so I could confirm with Mill when she'd received the letter from him. I hoped my answer made sense.

"Right before . . . everything went down."

"Got it." Stellan sounded disappointed. "I hoped it was afterward. I'm not sure we could track her down by her email address, but at least I could write her a note, try to appeal to her good sense—if she has any left, that is. I've tried to send her notes, but I don't think she's read them."

"Yeah, me too. I haven't heard from her either. But this note, it's just taken me some time to process it, think about it. It was a big pill to swallow."

"I hear you." Stellan took a deep breath and then let it out. "Okay, it was the letter that took me in some different research directions. In your grandfather's day, this town was part of a drug traffic route. He was constantly having to deal with some sort of fallout."

I knew this. "Has that changed, gone away?"

"For the most part, yes. Roads changed; a better highway moved the main thoroughfares. It's in part the result of good police work, but not entirely. We're lucky that those roads came about, giving the dealers easier and different directions."

"And my father was involved?" I asked, hearing hesitation in my own voice.

Time had given some distance to my feelings about my father, and sometimes there came a point when you just wanted answers, to know the truth, no matter how ugly it was. But still, no one wants their daddy to be a bad guy.

My heart rate sped up in anticipation of Stellan's answer.

"Yes, Beth, he was. He was probably very involved. In fact, he might have headed up a local small group—only three men that I can figure, but still."

"And, let me guess who one of the men was," I said, my mouth dry.

"Yes. Walker. And though it's really hard to understand what happened, I think your father might have taken some money. That, along with some encouragement from your grandfather, being the impetus for him leaving."

"He might have *run off* with some money?" I asked.

Mill stared at me. She didn't move a muscle. I suspected she was dying for a cigarette.

"Something happened right before your father disappeared. There's a report here about a ruckus at a campground. Walker was there. So was another man—his name was Hugh Givens. Ever heard of him?"

"Hugh Givens?" I looked at Mill. With the smallest of movements, she shook her head once. "No, I don't think so, but it's been a long time. I'll try to remember."

"I'm trying to track him down now, too, but I don't have a line on him yet. Anyway, the police were called out to this campground, where Walker and Givens were bloodied and beaten. The two of them didn't want the police there, but some neighboring campers had called in the incident, which had sounded like heated fighting. Your grandfather went out himself. He wrote the report, but it's lacking—and his reports were usually so very thorough.

"It says that the men claimed they'd just gotten into fisti-cuffs between themselves and they were fine. There was no sign of alcohol or drugs there, but there were three sleeping bags at the site. There's nothing in the report that says your grandfather asked where the third person was, but he would have, he always would have."

"Yes, he would."

"Beth, the vehicle on site is described as the van you were kept in."

"Jesus."

"It was an old van back then, too, but from the description, it could be the same one. There were tire tracks from another car there as well. Believe it or not, there's no mention of the tracks in the report, but there are pictures of them inside the file. Again, a mistake your grandfather wouldn't have made. He deliberately left out any comments about the tracks, but dropped in the pictures—I bet it was all on purpose. He probably thought he'd try to understand the tracks later, on his own, just in case they were from your father's car. It's impossible to know, but I bet your grandfather wanted to take care of things himself. Anyway, these tire tracks are as clear as day in the picture. If you could just tell me what kind of car your father was driving back then, I might be able to see if they could have been on that model.

"I know there's a file on your father's disappearance. I opened it, too, Beth, and there's not one mention of your father's car."

"That's impossible. That would have been pertinent to the case—find the car, maybe find him."

"I know. It should be in there."

I looked at Mill. She was still as a statue. Did she know?

Stellan continued, "Do you remember what kind of car it was?"

"Not offhand. Give me a minute. It might come to me." I grabbed a pencil and a Post-it and scribbled *what car dad drove?*, passing the note to Mill. "What else, though?"

"There are some notes in here about the people who called the police, the neighboring campers. Your grandfather did talk to them. They said they heard lots of yelling, lots of cursing, and a car driving away in a hurry. They said they heard three distinct voices as well as someone yelling the name Rivers."

"That's in the report?"

"It is."

"Odd that he left that in, considering what's omitted."

Mill slid the Post-it back over to me.

"I couldn't agree more. There is one more thing you should know. This happened the day before your father disappeared," Stellan said.

"That seems to fit."

"Right. I don't know how to find out anything more about your grandfather's whereabouts directly after the incident at the campground, but the next report he worked on was about your father's disappearance. Other crimes were committed that day, but they were minor, and it seems your grandfather was not involved in investigating them."

"Oh!" I interjected. "I just remembered the car. It was an old Buick, maybe late seventies, blue."

In fact, Mill's note back to me read, *1977 Buick Skylark, baby blue, two-door, last odometer reading of 124,000. Back taillight was broken.*

I didn't share all the details; that would have been weird. Mill probably knew the locations of upholstery stains and cigarette burns, too.

"That's terrific. I'll look into it and let you know, but I bet it'll be a fit."

"Thanks, Stellan."

"You're welcome. I'll share whatever else I find, but I'm going to get to work on these tire tracks immediately."

"I appreciate that," I said. "Would you let me know if you hear from my mother?"

Mill rolled her eyes again.

"Sure. You do the same," he said.

"Of course."

We disconnected the call. I had to muster some courage to share the details of the police reports with my mother. If she'd known that my father's car wasn't noted in the report about his disappearance, she would have burned down the police station in admonition, even if my grandfather had been inside it.

This was going to be more tough news for her to process.

Twenty-one

Come on, Mill. I'll take you anywhere you want to go," I said as we stood out in the cold and now lightly falling snow. The sun had risen as much as it was going to, but it was still mostly dark because of the thick clouds. Everything was covered in a gloomy white—pretty enough, but it would have been prettier in full sun. I was grateful the snow had slowed some.

"I need to be alone, Beth. I need to smoke. It's easy to get back into town. I'll meet you there."

"It's unsafe," I said. "I got caught in a rainstorm right about here when I first arrived. I got lost and all turned around. The weather is dangerous."

"Beth, I'm going to be fine, unless you make me stay with you or ride with you right now. I need time alone. I need to process this. You should know that about me."

I did know that about her, but back in the lower forty-eight, she would just take off in her car, be gone for days, going who knew where, doing who knew what. She couldn't do that here.

"Take my truck. Just pick me up later. There are only two paved roads; stay on them."

Mill shook her head and then turned away. "I'm not taking your truck. I will meet you back downtown. Just leave me be a bit."

I watched as she pulled the cigarettes and lighter out of her pocket. She was moving quickly and it was completely irresponsible of me to let her go.

But that's what I did. I watched her march down the road, clouds of smoke mixing with foggy breath as she became a dark figure amid the freshly covered roads and trees.

I really hoped she wouldn't be attacked by a bear or that her anger wouldn't cause her to lash out at some wildlife. That would be one battle she couldn't win. Millicent Rivers in a fit of confused anger would stand as good a chance as anyone against a hungry bear or an agitated moose, but she'd still lose.

When she turned around a far bend and I couldn't see her anymore, I felt an urge to follow her.

But I didn't.

Instead, I gathered my things, hopped in my truck, and made my way to the library. I left the door to the *Petition* unlocked, something I hadn't done since moving to Benedict, just in case Mill came back this way and needed shelter. It was one of the hardest things I've ever done, harder even than letting her leave, and I obsessed over the decision until I went through the library doors.

The place was empty, but I'd seen Orin's truck out front. He'd be in his office. There was no strong smoke smell as I knocked.

"Come in."

"Hey," I said as I entered.

"Beth, I wondered who in the world would be out in this. How are you? Where's your mom?"

"I'm fine. She's doing some other things. How are you?"

"I'm fine, mostly."

"Understandable. What's up?"

"Just wish I could have done something to prevent everything that's happened. I heard about Ned's sister being hurt, too. I wish I knew what was going on."

"She's okay." I sat. "Did you hear *all* the details?"

"I don't know. Do tell."

"I will. I have quite a bit I'd like to share with you, though. You up for hearing a true story?"

Orin closed his laptop. "Always. Should we lock the door?"

I glanced over my shoulder. "No, it's okay."

"What's going on, Beth?"

And then I told him. First, what I knew about Lucy's exploration and fall. I hurried through that part so I wouldn't lose my courage to tell him what I'd really come over to share.

Then I told Orin why I was in Benedict. Who I was, what had happened to me—at least what I remembered. I told him about the flashbacks, the fear, my escape to Alaska. All of it.

He listened intently, appearing as though he was memorizing things—dates and names. When he asked questions for clarification, he didn't hesitate or stumble with any of the details I'd given. His mind was sharp, like a steel trap, it seemed.

Finally, when I was done, I asked, "Did you know who I was?"

"Not really," he said. "I suspected you weren't who you said you were, but that's a typical story for these parts. I am, however, pleased you trust me enough to tell me now." He smiled a little sadly. "I've read two of your books. They are wonderful."

"You don't need to say that."

Orin shrugged. "I know, but it's the truth. Beth, I'm sorry for what you've been through. Sounds terrible."

"It was."

"It explains some things, though. Your behavior, for one. I don't mean that in a bad way, but you tend to look over your shoulder, literally and figuratively, quite a bit. I'm probably the only one around here who would notice that and wonder about it, so don't think it's obvious."

"Huh. It's interesting to hear someone else's perspective."

"It's all good. I'm glad you're safe. I'm so glad you got away."

"Me too, but . . . well, it's not the reason I told you what I told you, but I do have some names I'd like to give you. Some people I'd like you to look for, using the skills or tools I know you must have. Would you be willing?"

"Absolutely. Other than Walker, who else?"

Still Orin didn't grab a pen and paper.

"Okay, well, here's another strange story: my father disappeared when I was younger."

"Wow, Beth, you have quite the history. Okay, tell me his story and his name."

I shared that part of my life, too. By the time I was done, I was tired, exhausted, and wondered how I'd packed so much into just over thirty years.

"When I put it all out there, it wears me out," I said.

"I'd say, and I can understand why the call with the police chief upset your mother. I didn't need to hear your explanation regarding her obsessive personality to notice that about her. This news is going to bother her quite a bit."

"Yes, but I do think my grandfather had his reasons for doing whatever he did. I think the St. Louis police are good too, doing their jobs well, but I need someone who can go deeper, Orin. If you're willing, at least. I have no doubt that you're able."

"I am able, and I'm willing. Okay, Dad's name is Edward Rivers."

Orin asked for some other information, including my

father's birthday and his social security number. I didn't know the number, though if Mill had been there, she probably could have recited it as accurately as she'd known about the car he'd driven. Again, Orin didn't write anything down.

I must have been giving him a strange look.

"Beth, do you know what an eidetic memory is?" he asked. "Photographic?"

"Sure. That's you?"

"That's me. It's part of why I was so valuable to our government for so many years." He flexed a skinny arm. "It wasn't my guns. Well, not these."

We laughed together. It hadn't really occurred to me that this Willie Nelson look-alike might not be the picture of physicality that some special ops people would display.

"I'm really smart on top of it," he added. "They were well able to look past my body type. They wanted me to cut my hair, but it wasn't going to happen. If they wanted my brain, I told them they had to have my hair, too. Okay, so the third guy you mentioned. You didn't say his name. Do you have it?"

"Hugh Givens." I hadn't written it down either, but when Stellan had said it, it had become ingrained into my mind—I was far from eidetic, but was at least able to keep some details straight.

Orin nodded. "Got it. Okay, I'll get to work. I'm afraid I can't ask you to wait or stay. I'll need privacy to do some deep dives."

"I can't thank you enough, Orin."

He smiled again. "It's good to know the real you, Beth. You might want to consider telling some others around here. I do think it would be a positive move, and I don't think it would jeopardize your safety. When you start sharing, you might be surprised by all the others who tell you their stories, too. We've got an interesting bunch in Benedict."

"I will think about it," I said, the idea both filling me with a new sense of freedom and scaring the crap out of me.

When I stood, Orin did too. He walked me out of his office and hugged me at the library's door, then turned and walked purposefully back toward his office.

I wasn't afraid of Orin, and it had been good to share, but once I was back in my truck, all I could think was that I wanted to tell my mother what I'd done. I had to find her.

Twenty-two

It shouldn't have been a surprise that I felt as if a huge weight had been lifted off my shoulders. I hadn't noticed the true heft of my secret, but I felt its absence. It wasn't completely gone, of course. Orin was right, there were more people I needed to tell. I didn't have to share everything with everyone, but it wouldn't hurt to talk to Viola, Donner, and of course, Tex.

With a reprieve in the weather, I made my way back toward the Benedict House, my mother on my mind. I looked but didn't see Mill anywhere along the route. Nor did I see the bloody remains of a wild animal attack—this was good news.

The sun had almost set, though, so my view was limited.

The only blood I saw was on the ground next to the sculpture of Ben, and those stains were disappearing under more snow. I didn't want to get close enough to investigate the vanishing spots.

I parked the truck and hurried inside the Benedict House. I really wanted to make sure Mill was okay, and I suddenly felt a need to talk to Viola—maybe now was the time to tell her everything, too. She had plenty on her plate, though; I'd have to see if the timing was right.

The warmth inside was welcome, and I heard voices coming from the dining room—loud, but not angry. I kicked off my boots and made my way toward them.

My eyes first landed on Mill. She was there. She was fine. Well, she was probably a little drunk, but she didn't look to be any worse for the wear. Seemingly she'd had no trouble getting back to the Benedict House.

Viola, Benny, and Claudia were all fine, too—Benny and Claudia maybe a little tipsy as well. Viola sat back in her chair, in a pose of observation rather than participation.

My mother had been drinking—what could possibly go wrong? She wasn't a big drinker, but when she drank, it was done like everything else she did, in a big way.

I sent Viola a tight, concerned smile, but she just nodded assuredly at me. She had this under control. Whatever this was.

"No, he wasn't the best husband, but he was my husband and I loved him. I really, really did." Claudia slurred some as she spoke. To punctuate her statement, she belatedly and clumsily pounded her fist on the table. Maybe she was beyond tipsy.

Benny, also sitting back in her chair, rolled her eyes at me.

"Bethie!" Mill said when she saw me.

"You okay, Mill?" I asked as I also sent a smile to Claudia.

"I'm great," Mill said. "Your host here has the best whiskey."

Viola shrugged. "Your mother was particularly wound up when she got back. This was her suggestion. No one argued."

"And Claudia seemed interested, too," Benny said. "We'd just come over to talk to Lucy."

"Lucy wasn't invited to the party?" I asked.

"No. When you're on the run from the law, you don't get to be invited," Viola said.

I looked at my mother, who sent me a sloppy wink that, surprisingly, no one else seemed to notice. Or maybe they just didn't consider what it might mean.

"I've ordered us a pizza. Are you hungry?" Viola asked.

"We have a pizza place in town?" I asked.

"No. We have a restaurant. Luther is working this evening and he has a pizza dough recipe to die for. Benny will go pick it up in a minute. In the meantime, Claudia was telling us about when the census man stopped by her house, how he angered Ned."

"Oh. Sorry to interrupt." I sat. I'd heard some of this from Lucy's vantage point. It would be good to hear the story from another person, even an inebriated one. I took a seat.

"He was so weird," Claudia said.

"He?" Viola prompted. "Which one?"

"The guy. He came into the house and was just rude. Plain old rude," Claudia said.

"Can you explain how he was rude, dear?" Viola asked.

Claudia poured herself another shot and downed it before she continued. "He came in and sat down. Right?"

We nodded and waited as she gathered her thoughts. Nothing she could say in this room, being under the influence as she clearly was, would convict her—or anyone else for that matter—of killing Ned. But I knew what Viola and Benny were doing—they were trying to get at *some* truth, something that might lead to finding a killer.

"He didn't even ask many questions, you know? And after only a couple, Ned didn't want to answer anyway. One of the first questions was if anyone else was living with us. Ned immediately got defensive because there was Lucy, hiding out in the shed and all, and he didn't understand that all he had to do was lie—or at least lie better than he was lying. Census guy—what's his name? Oh, yeah, Vitner. He got suspicious when Ned answered all funny, hemmed and hawed. He got up and started looking through the house. Ned yelled at him, got up and started limping around to chase him through the house and out to the back." Claudia paused, looking at me.

"That's definitely weird," I said, mostly just to let her know I was listening. "Mr. Vitner really got up and started looking?"

"Yeah," Claudia continued. "And when he saw the shed out the back window, he marched right out there and opened the door, saw Lucy, seemed all disappointed, shook his head, and then just closed the door."

"Disappointed?" I asked.

"Yepper-depper. Like he was looking for someone else, is what I thought."

"Did he say something when he saw her?" Benny asked.

"I don't know. Did you ask her?" Claudia said.

She'd told me that Vitner just made sure she was okay. I didn't think I'd gotten anything more specific.

"Did he make any notes after he saw her?" I asked.

Claudia pursed her lips. "I don't think so. I don't think he cared she was there."

None of what she'd said was reliable, but I was under the impression that he had in fact cared enough to question her safety.

I wanted to tell Viola that her methods didn't seem to be working well, but with a glance at her I realized she knew and didn't care. I'd read the situation wrong. She was just letting people blow off steam.

"I'll talk to Lucy," Viola said casually. "Get it from her viewpoint, but Gril probably has already."

"Can I come?" I stood up.

From what I knew, Claudia's story *did* match up with Lucy's, at least in the parts that it could, the parts they both could have witnessed, but there was one thing Claudia had said that piqued my curiosity to a whole new level. Vitner seemed *disappointed* to find Lucy? Did that mean he was looking for someone else? Who?

I really didn't think this was about me, or that Travis Walker had sent Vitner to town to search for me, but . . . well, I couldn't help but want to get some clarification.

"I was going to do it later," Viola said, as if she really wasn't going to do it ever.

"How about now?"

Viola lifted one eyebrow at me. "All righty, then. Let's go." She stood as well.

I followed her out of the room, but didn't miss Mill sending me a somewhat confused but approving raise of her shot glass.

Twenty-three

Lucy was up and out of bed, looking out her window. Her injuries were healing quickly. Viola hadn't announced we were entering her room. The door still wasn't locked, but it didn't look like Lucy was in any hurry to leave. I couldn't help but wonder if she was beginning to like it here. I'd seen it happen with others. It was a good place to be, even if you were a criminal—maybe particularly so.

However, when Lucy turned from the window and spotted us, she forced a frown to tug at her mouth, a wince to pull at the corners of her eyes. "What?"

"Beth here wants to talk to you," Viola said.

I had no idea I was taking the lead on this one.

"Okay." Lucy moved to her bed and sat, one foot under the other leg, the same way I often did.

We really were similar physically, which bothered me more than it probably needed to. I was reading too much into it. Nevertheless, I couldn't stop myself.

I stepped around Viola. I didn't feel intimidated, but despite being raised by Mill and spending time around an officer of the law for most of my childhood, I didn't naturally take charge.

I wasn't overly nice and polite, either, but even something approaching nice and polite wasn't going to work with Lucy. She'd pounce on anything less than demanding.

Inwardly I sighed, but outwardly I puffed up some. "I need to know what happened when the census man saw you."

"What? We talked about this, didn't we?"

"You did?" Viola said.

I nodded at her. "Just briefly." I looked at Lucy. "Tell me again exactly what happened."

"Like what? When he came into the shed, when he saw me?"

"Yes, exactly like that."

Viola stood next to me.

Lucy shrugged. "Not much to it. He burst open the door, I told him to fuck off, then he did, he left."

I cocked my head at her. "That's not exactly what you told me before."

She frowned. "Right. I know. Yes, he wanted to make sure I was okay, then I told him to fuck off."

"Lucy, was he concerned about you or not?" Viola asked.

She bit her bottom lip. "I don't know if he was truly concerned. It's hard to . . . Actually, maybe he was sorry to see me." She shrugged again.

"Disappointed?" Viola said.

"Yeah. That's it. It was as if maybe he was looking for someone, but I wasn't that person. It was weird. He wasn't an asshole and he did ask if I was okay, but you know how people sometimes droop a little when they don't get what they expect? He did that."

"Interesting," I said absently.

Lucy sat back on her bed and nodded. "Yep."

Maybe it was the combination of everything going on at once, but I suddenly understood why I'd needed to talk to her, to get answers, and it *did* have to do with me. Sure, maybe I was forcing something that wasn't there, but I needed to explore it.

The third man from my dad's gang. Hugh Givens. I'd just learned his name, his involvement, but either I was forcing pieces of a puzzle to fit together or it was just happening.

I needed a picture of Hugh Givens. In a way, everyone in Benedict did.

"Did he say anything to make you think he was looking for someone else, or was it just body language?" Viola asked.

Lucy shook her head. "Just shoulders. That's it."

"Could you hear any of his conversation with Ned and Claudia?" I asked.

Lucy scrunched up her face and shook her head. "Nah, but even from back in the shed I could tell Ned was losing his cool. He's loud. He was loud." She frowned at Viola. "You do know that's why he and Claudia moved out here, don't you?"

"What do you mean?" Viola asked.

"I've overheard you all talking about the winter and how rough it can be on some people. Ned is . . . was . . . always had violence problems. That's why they came out here. He fed Claudia some lines about freedom and living off the grid and how grand it would be. But he just wanted to go someplace where his assholeness wouldn't be so obvious."

"They didn't live off the grid," Viola said. "They had electricity."

"As close as you can get and still have electricity, then," Lucy said. "It's a great place to hide, both from yourself and everybody else." Lucy regarded Viola. "He was jealous, too. That's another reason Ned brought Claudia out here. He never did like when other men noticed her, and they noticed her plenty. She's pretty, right?"

Viola just looked at Lucy.

"And Claudia might have liked that extra attention," Lucy continued. "No, not *might* have. She did. She liked it. Come on, haven't you seen that?"

I hadn't, but I hadn't been around them enough to see much of anything, and though this wasn't why we'd come into Lucy's room, it was at least maybe something that should be considered.

"I'm not sure what us seeing that would mean," Viola retorted, probably mostly just to keep Lucy talking.

"Oh, come on! It would mean she just *might* have a boyfriend. Maybe more than one. Maybe that's why Ned was killed."

"Spill it, Lucy. Who was Claudia's boyfriend?" Viola took a step closer to the bed. I squelched the urge to do the same.

"I don't know!" Lucy threw her hands in the air. "I really don't. I know it's something they argued about around me, that's all I can tell you. Well, sort of. Insinuations were made, if you know what I mean. No names were mentioned. I thought by now all the rest of you would have picked up on that, but apparently not."

Viola looked at me.

I said, "Any other insinuations?"

Lucy took a breath in through her nose and let it out noisily. "I got nothin' else." She sighed yet again and looked at her fingernails.

Viola made a noise that I took for her signal that it was time to go.

After I waited a moment for Lucy to share more—a wasted moment, because she didn't even look up at me again—I turned and followed my landlord out of the room.

"That what you were looking for?" Viola said quietly after she relocked the door.

"Kind of, but the big revelation was that maybe Claudia had a boyfriend. That seems important."

"Right." Viola rolled her eyes in my direction as we set off back down the hallway.

I stopped walking. "Maybe just a revelation to me, then. Tell me more."

Reluctantly Viola stopped walking too. "Too many to name."

"That's no good." How had I missed this?

"I have no proof, but that's what Gril and Donner have spent most of their time doing, trying to track down the boyfriend or boyfriends."

"How's that going?"

"Slow. For a while she was pretty obvious about it, but she's been slyer lately. I tried to get her to talk right before you joined us today, but no luck so far."

We resumed walking as I processed this new and seemingly important information. This tidbit would surely lead to Ned's killer, right?

As I wrapped my head around it all, we stopped and stood side by side outside the dining room and peered in.

"Where's my mom?" I asked Benny. Claudia had her head down on the table, small snores buzzing through the air.

"Said she wasn't hungry. Bed. Probably where we all need to be," Benny said.

"Thanks." I hurried to my mother's room.

In truth, I'd been somewhat surprised to find her back at the Benedict House. Over the years, when she'd needed time to herself, it had always been a lot of time, not the short amount it would take for her to walk from the *Petition* to here. I was suddenly sure she'd left again, and the elements would win this time.

Without knocking or thinking her door might be locked, I opened it. I wasn't surprised in the least that the bed was made, that she wasn't anywhere else in the room. I made a noise in the back of my throat, but I held back yelling for help. I didn't think anyone else in the house was in any shape to help me anyway. I'd need to gear up and get out and look for her.

I hurried back to my room, fumbled to get that door unlocked, and then threw it open wide.

"Hey, dollie." Mill, taking up half my bed, struggled to get her eyes open. "Viola gave me a key. I'm going to sleep in here tonight. Let's see if we can get this sleepwalking thing under control." She patted the other side of the bed and then sunk her head back into the pillow.

Immediately, her snores were louder than Claudia's. I hadn't yet noticed that my heart was hammering in my chest, but as I watched my felonious mother fall back to a sleep so deep that I doubted my sleepwalking would wake her, it calmed back to normal rhythm.

At least something felt normal.

Twenty-four

, and I presumed Lucy, were the only people in the Benedict House not hung over the next morning. But Lucy wasn't invited to breakfast, so I couldn't confirm. It seemed that Viola had joined Benny and Claudia in drinking after Mill and I had gone to bed and the pizza had arrived.

I did the cooking this morning, but it was only bacon, eggs, and orange juice. It seemed enough for everyone, too much for Benny, who didn't want anything to eat and had complained a few times about the strong food smells. Viola had suggested she leave the dining room, but she couldn't seem to find the energy to remove herself.

"She talked in her sleep, but didn't walk?" Viola said to Mill.

They'd talked about the fact that Viola might need to watch me a little closer when Mill left. I wasn't happy they'd had the discussion without me, but it wasn't a hill I wanted to die on, so I didn't protest.

"That's right. She grumbled and mumbled but didn't make one move to get out of bed."

Mill and I had had this conversation in the middle of the night. I'd woken myself up and had been startled to find someone staring at me from the other pillow.

"Just me," she'd said.

Apparently, I'd barely even moved all night, falling asleep quickly and turning over only once.

I doubted Mill was awake watching me all night, but there was no indication that I'd sleepwalked anywhere, and even if she was asleep, too, Mill might have awakened if I'd tried to get out of the bed.

We heard the front door open. "Vi?" Gril called as we heard him come in.

"Back here," Viola announced. "Breakfast?"

He stood inside the entryway into the dining room. "We've got a problem."

Everyone stopped eating.

"Vitner is missing. The van is missing."

"What?" Mill asked with much more emotion than I would have expected.

In the confusion of the moment, I was sure I was the only one who noticed her alarm. Everyone else was doing their own processing, but I had my eyes on my mother, who sure seemed especially bothered for someone who wasn't from here, who was hung over, and who didn't particularly know the census man.

Had she had the idea of Vitner being Hugh Givens, too? We hadn't had a sober or non-hungover moment to discuss it, and any time I'd revisited the idea in my mind, it seemed pretty unsubstantial.

"He couldn't have gone far," Viola said.

"I agree, but we haven't found him or the van."

"He the killer?" Mill asked, seemingly back to a normal level of curiosity.

"Don't know."

"He sure acts like he's up to no good," Mill said.

"How long has he been missing?" Viola asked.

"Best we can determine, since yesterday night. The ferry

hasn't left port. No plane has taken off, but he had the van." He looked at me. "I grounded everything. I didn't even let Tex drive out of here before I checked his truck. Yes, I have suspicions about Vitner, but chances are he's just lost or stuck somewhere."

As I'd suspected, Gril had shut down all escape routes. I hoped that meant he and Donner weren't involved with Ned's murder, but now wasn't the time to dwell on that, either way.

"He's around, then," Viola said.

"We think he might need help, but . . . well, I'm worried about Lucy. That's why I'm here. I'd like to get her out of here."

"You think Vitner might hurt her?" I asked.

Claudia whimpered and put her fingers to her temples.

"You stick by Benny and Viola," Gril said to her. "But we don't think you're in any danger."

"But Lucy might be?" Viola asked.

"She's more an unknown part of the equation. Claudia's got constant company, and we know her. We really don't know Lucy or what she's truly been up to in Juneau."

"He's not with the census?" I interjected, remembering that Orin had confirmed to me that he in fact was.

Gril hesitated. There were too many people in this room, people who didn't need to know police business. But at least Viola should. "He's with the census, all right, but only for four months. Benedict wasn't even a real assignment until he requested it."

"Right," I said. Tex had basically said as much.

"His credentials are valid, but there was still something unusual about him being here. Why did he request this location? I'd like some answers that I haven't been able to get yet."

"Do you think he's hiding or lost?" Benny asked.

"I have no idea, but Donner and I are going to search. I

want you all to be aware and I want Lucy . . . protected. I want everyone protected."

"There's nowhere else safer for Lucy or Claudia to go. I'll just stay with them," Viola said.

"All right. In the same room if possible."

"Consider it done." Viola stood.

"I'll trade off with you," Benny said.

"Mill and I can help, too," I offered.

I wanted to talk privately with Gril. I wanted to tell him my shaky suspicions about Vitner potentially being Hugh Givens, but that would only delay the search for the man. As long as he was found, I could share my thoughts and maybe get the answer later.

Gril looked around the room. "Viola and Benny can take turns staying with Lucy. Claudia, stick close by them. Beth and Mill, just be careful. Either stay with everyone else, or maybe spend some time at the *Petition* today, but be aware. I don't know where he is or what he's up to, but I can't watch everybody at once, and there's still no way to get to Juneau."

I nodded. "Gril, if he's not Ned's killer, who else are you looking at?"

"I'm looking at every possible lead. Even if Vitner is the killer, it could have something to do with Ned specifically, or it could have been brought on by the isolation and the weather. It happens, sometimes more quickly than you might imagine. There could be another killer on the loose, though. Everyone needs to be extra careful, that's what I'm trying to say."

"I don't know who killed Ned. I wish I did. I'm afraid and I just want to go home," Claudia piped up.

"Home here or somewhere else?" Mill asked.

"Home here. This is the only home I have, and I want Ned to be there." Tears fell down Claudia's cheeks.

No one had an answer for that.

"I have to get to work." Gril's eyes locked on Viola's. "Are you all going to be okay?"

Just as in any good Western, Viola stood proudly and patted the gun at her side. "Right as rain."

"Good. I'll check in later." Gril turned and hurried away again.

Viola left next, thumping back to Lucy's room.

I wished I could have stopped myself from asking Claudia the question that was burning in my mind. It was none of my business, even if a murder had occurred, but I couldn't help myself.

"Who are your boyfriends, Claudia?" I demanded.

Mill's gaze snapped over to the young woman and Benny sat back in her chair, crossing her arms in front of herself. Even she didn't mind that I'd asked.

"I don't know what you're talking about," Claudia said.

"Sure you do. If you won't tell me, I sure hope you've told Gril, because if you are being smart at all, you will realize that if you truly don't know who killed your husband and there is a boyfriend out there, you are definitely next on his list." I didn't actually believe that, but I was willing to try to scare her. Better I try than the police, my own rattled mind concluded.

Claudia's eyes changed. I didn't know her, but at that moment I realized that she'd been faking . . . something. Whatever innocence that had come through before now visually transformed into something more hateful.

"All right. Yes, I told him. I told Gril about . . . him."

"Who?" Benny asked. "Which one?"

"I don't need to tell you. If I did the right thing, if I told the proper authorities, why does anyone here need to know?"

"Because I need to know," Benny said. "I've been taking care of you, Claudia—and this isn't the first time. You owe me. Who?"

"Elijah. Okay? Elijah."

"Elijah?" Benny said.

"The tow-truck driver?" I said.

Mill smirked and shook her head. "You just never know until you know, and then you need to verify again."

"He's . . . not young," I said. It was a completely inappropriate comment, but it was also true. And there was nothing about him that I could have pointed to as a reason he might have turned Claudia's head. She was young and adorable—again, probably an inappropriate way to look at this, but I couldn't help myself.

"No, but he's a good man," Claudia said.

"Daddy issues," Mill muttered unkindly.

I didn't argue. "Do you think he kill Ned?"

"No. I mean, I don't think so. I know Gril already talked to him, but I haven't had a chance to see him at all. Even last night at the bar, we didn't get to *really* talk."

I looked at Benny.

"I had no idea they were seeing each other," she answered the question in my eyes. "But I don't think that Claudia has been around him since Ned was killed."

"Are there others?" I asked.

Claudia sat up straight as if she was going to protest, but then she deflated a little. "Not for a long time, maybe about six months."

"Oh, god, she broke someone's heart," Mill said.

"Claudia, does Gril know about *all* your boyfriends, ever since you and Ned moved here? He needs to know about every single one," I said.

"Well, not all of them, but I told him about Jeff, too. The one from six months ago. And he's gone. He left Benedict."

"Are you sure he left?" I asked. There was a lot of wide openness out there. If someone could survive, they could hide quite well in the wild, and for a long time.

She nodded. "I got a letter from him last week, postmarked from Seattle." She hurried to add, "I showed it to Gril."

"Jeff who?" Benny asked, crossing her arms even more tightly in front of her body.

"Jeff Donald."

"Who is that?" Benny asked.

"He worked on the bay's tourist boat last season. He was a captain," she said proudly.

I tried not to roll my eyes, but Mill didn't hold back.

I'd yet to meet anyone who worked on one of the large ships that took tourists around Glacier Bay.

"Is that normal?" I asked Benny. "Do people leave after the season?"

"Sure. Sometimes."

I turned my gaze back to Claudia. "Here's the thing: yes, maybe Jeff left and went back to Seattle, but that's also where Vitner says he's from."

"I . . . I didn't know that."

"I'm not sure that matters, Beth," Benny added. "Lots of folks come up here from Seattle. It's an easy back-and-forth."

"But does Gril really and truly know all of this?" I asked. "And are there more?"

"Any others, Claudia?" Benny asked.

Claudia cowered. "Not really. I swear. Yes, Gril knows everything. You guys, I didn't want Ned killed. He was my husband. Sure, we got mad at each other sometimes, but we also took care of each other. I'm going to miss him." Real tears pooled in her eyes again. Or I thought they were real. It was impossible to know how much she could fake.

"You're from Seattle too, right?" Benny said.

Claudia sniffed and used her paper napkin to wipe under her nose. "Yeah. Gril knows. Gril knows everything."

I looked at Benny. "Surely he's made the Seattle connection."

"I can't imagine he wouldn't, but maybe not." Benny shrugged.

I looked at Mill. "You done eating?"

"Yes, ma'am."

"We have to go."

Without a word, she followed me out of the dining room.

Twenty-five

There wasn't much we could do. We weren't equipped in any way to search for Doug Vitner or the van. I wouldn't even try, though my truck and its tires could probably handle some of the job.

We could have stayed in the Benedict House all day with the others, but there wasn't much we could do to protect them, either. Viola and Benny were the armed ones. They'd be protecting us, and maybe it was better for them to have two fewer people to look out for.

I could have worked on my book. Mill would have sat quietly inside the shed as I pulled out some paper and threaded it through the typewriter. But writing with someone else in the room wasn't ideal. Besides, I had way too much on my mind to get anything done.

I decided we could try to talk to Orin. As we got in the truck, I told Mill that I'd shared with him who I was.

She was not surprised and seemed pleased. "Good. You need someone like him on your side."

"I do?" It was rhetorical. I knew exactly what she meant. "Sure, why not?"

But I sensed there was more. "Mill, I feel pretty safe here."

"Oh, I know, and that's what worries me. I know you think you're hiding, and you are, most definitely, but having good people with good skills on your side never hurts."

"That's true." I paused as I pulled into a spot in front of the library. "Do you think I should leave? Move someplace else?"

"I've been thinking plenty about that one, and I just don't know, Beth. Do you want to start over again, or is it better to keep building your team, your support system, here? It's a good strong team, by the way."

"Glad you think so." I was.

"I can't stay forever, dollie, you know that, too, but I'm not sure I'm much good here anyway. As soon as I think it's okay, I'll go back to hunting for Walker."

"And Dad."

She hesitated. "Yes."

"One is going to probably lead you to the other, right?"

"I'm beginning to think so."

"Well then, I hope you find them both. But no more shooting, okay? Just . . . I don't know. Please, no more shooting. They aren't worth your freedom."

"Have I ever lied to you?"

"Yes."

"Okay, well, this isn't a lie. I can't make any promises about what I'll do when I find either of them, but I will do my best to restrain myself. That's the best I can give you."

"I'll take it." I paused. "What happened back there?"

"Where?"

"In the dining room just now. You seemed awfully concerned about Vitner missing."

"Because I think he's the killer," she answered quickly.

And just like that, mere moments after she claimed she wasn't lying, she'd did exactly that. Her answer had been a prepared one. She'd seen me notice her reaction, and she'd been ready. I wasn't willing to challenge her on it just yet, though. I needed more information.

"Okay," I said.

We hopped out of the truck and hurried into the library. It was even more crowded than usual—the weather had remained calm—and we had to turn sideways to make our way around some chairs. I had to say hello to a few people before we could get to Orin's door. I didn't introduce Mill to anyone, but no one seemed offended.

"Enter," Orin said when we knocked.

I pushed the door open, glad the scent was down again today, and led Mill inside, closing the door tightly behind us.

"Hey," I said.

"I've been trying to call you."

"Sorry, I didn't notice a call." I hadn't, but I hadn't checked my phone for a long time.

"It's okay. I'm so glad you're here, though. I have information." Orin took a moment to smile and nod at Mill. She did the same, but neither of them needed a longer preamble.

"You know Vitner is missing?" I said.

"I do, and the van is, too. I know Gril is worried, but I'm not too concerned yet. The van will give him shelter and he can't go far.

I nodded. That made sense, but Gril's concern was very real; I didn't emphasize that with Orin. "Mill and I know about its being strange that Vitner is here, that we've never had a census person. Did you talk to someone with the census?"

"Yes. Vitner's a wild card, but he's also done everything appropriately. He passed all the background stuff you must pass to become a census taker. He did everything right, and then he asked specifically to come here, to Benedict. That might seem strange, but it wasn't inappropriate."

"And they just let him?" I asked. "Why wouldn't they send him someplace where they are used to sending people?"

Orin shrugged. "Don't really know, but he convinced them somehow. The woman I talked to at the census said in his file notes that he's a 'very pleasant guy and should do a great job.'"

"Maybe he has," I said.

"I don't know if he's a killer or not, Beth, but he wanted to come here specifically, and from what I've heard, now he can't wait to get away."

"He burst into the shed Lucy was staying in at Ned and Claudia's house. He seemed disappointed to find her. He's here looking for someone, is my guess. Who?" I asked.

"That's interesting." Orin fell into thought. "Okay, if we go in that direction, he's set himself up perfectly to search house to house for someone, being welcomed inside."

"Had he come to you?"

"Yes, but there wasn't much to say. I live alone. I've even thought back, wondering if he'd asked me about anyone else, maybe Ned and Claudia, but he didn't. He was all business. He was friendly but not overly so. I have nothing. He did nothing to set off any alarms with me."

"Do you know about Claudia's boyfriends?"

"I've heard rumors."

"Elijah Wyatt is the latest, apparently."

"Elijah?" Orin said. "That is a surprise."

"He lives back behind Tochco's, right?"

"You think Elijah might be involved?" Orin sat back in his chair. "I can't imagine."

"I don't have any idea, but it seems like a difficult pill for you to swallow."

"Elijah is one of the kindest men I've ever met, that's all I know." He bit his lip as he looked back and forth between me and Mill. "I'm sure he and I have had many friendly conversations, but probably never deep ones. He's such a good guy. I simply can't imagine him doing harm to anyone."

"Do you think he could be in harm's way?" Mill asked.

"Because of an affair with Claudia? Only from Ned—and I get where you're going. Maybe Ned did attack or confront Elijah and maybe Elijah had no choice but to defend himself, retaliate. I sure hope that's not what happened, but anything at all is possible."

"That wouldn't involve Vitner," I said.

"Vitner's probably stuck or lost somewhere, but if he has the van, he has shelter," Orin said.

"If he's stuck, who'll get him unstuck? Elijah," I added.

"Two men, both possibly high on Gril's suspect list, coming together—but not necessarily for any other reason."

"Unless we're missing something," Mill offered.

"There's always that possibility," Orin said doubtfully. A long few moments later, he shook his head. "But I just don't know." Orin's gaze swung back to Mill again before returning to me. "I have more information for you, though. It's big, and that's why I've been trying to reach you."

"How big?" I sat up some.

"Really big." Orin templed his fingers and rested his chin on them. "So big that I might worry how you will take it."

"Okay."

"Spill it," Mill said, using her unkindly tone again.

I shot her a quick look. "Mill."

"It's okay." Orin held up a hand. "I know you guys have been through some stuff. I can understand wanting to know everything that's out there. But this is big. It's about Edward Rivers. I have some very solid information on what happened to him."

Suddenly Mill stood up and stormed out of the room. I

couldn't have been more surprised if my dad had walked *into* the tiny office and told us the search for him was over, *Here I am!* Mill had spent her life looking for him, and now, when it seemed there was a real answer only a few heartbeats away, she left.

I understood being nervous and scared to know the truth, but I wouldn't think she'd run away—until she had all the facts, at least.

Leaving places in a huff was kind of her signature move, though.

For a long moment I sat, my mouth open, and wondered what I should do. Finally I stood and said, "I'm sorry" to Orin.

He nodded as I hurried to find Mill.

She'd left a string of surprised library patrons in her wake. Folks with books or laptops in front of them looked at me as if they wondered if I was going to bluster through with the same flair my mother must have just displayed.

I tried to move carefully, but I was in a hurry. I burst through the door and saw she'd already made it halfway to the *Petition*.

"Mill! Mom!" I hurried after her in the dusky light. It was cold out, but at least it wasn't currently snowing or raining. "Wait!"

She didn't wait, but she did slow down enough that I could catch up.

"I know, this might be hard," I said breathlessly as I reached her.

"I had to get out of there, Beth. I wasn't ready. I didn't know he was going to tell us something big about Eddy. I thought he was only working on Walker. I need to get my head around that first. I have to get my head around it," she repeated.

"I understand, but aren't you also curious?"

"Of course. I just need . . . time."

"How much?"

Mill stopped walking and threw her hands on her hips. She was breathing heavily, too, and a foggy cloud filled the air between us. "What?"

"How much time do you need, because I'd really like to hear what Orin has to say. The sooner the better."

She was taller than me, by about four inches. In all our wildest dreams, neither of us could have predicted that there would come a day when we'd be standing outside in a remote part of Alaska, trying to figure out what to do next.

"Well," she began, but then she smiled. And then she laughed. "I'm . . . not sure."

She laughed some more, and then I caught it, too. Our shared laughter didn't turn maniacal, but we both had to bend over and hold on to our stomachs for a minute or so. No one was around. I didn't think anyone heard us. If someone from the library was looking out the window, they knew we didn't require assistance.

The laughter made the best release, but we weren't simply letting go of some of the pain my father's disappearance had put us through. It was much more than that, and we both knew it. There was also a long history of Mill's leaving me behind to search for my dad. Even if I felt that my grandfather had more than compensated for Mill's poor parenting skills, there had been resentment, and some of that was still there. A few belly laughs didn't make it disappear, but it felt good to take everything that had mixed together and let it out some.

Some.

Feeling the residual ache in my stomach as I wiped cold tears from around my eyes, I said, "We can go back in now or later. You tell me. I won't go without you."

"I appreciate that. I'm ready. Let's go back."

Arm in arm, we made our way back to the library in Benedict, Alaska, maybe the last place on the planet we'd have predicted we'd learn the fate of my father.

But sometimes you just can't see it coming.

Twenty-six

Orin closed the library. He shooed everyone out, told them to go to the airport, even though it wasn't quite lunchtime. He instructed that they should call before coming back, that he'd reopen the library that afternoon, but he wasn't sure what time.

I appreciated his efforts, though the patrons didn't like it. By the surprised expressions, I wondered if Orin had ever done such a thing. I wanted to tell him it wasn't necessary, but considering Mill's unpredictable behavior, maybe it was.

With everyone gone, we could move out to the main part of the library, amid the books. The bigger space felt somehow comforting. In fact I noticed, though I didn't point it out, that if we looked closely enough, we could see a few of my books on a nearby shelf.

Orin brought his laptop out to a table. He made sure, for the second time, that no one was in either of the bathrooms and that the front door was locked before he sat in a chair on the other side of the table from Mill and me.

His attention to detail made me nervous, and I felt the release from the laughter replaced by a cold tension. My hands turned icy and my stomach flipped nauseatingly.

"Look, I appreciate that Beth shared who she is with me.

I'm embarrassed I didn't put it all together," Orin said. "I've made oaths and vows and signed legal documents that prohibit me from telling you too much about myself. But I will say that I have contacts that even you two would be surprised by. I did work for the government, and the rumors and conspiracies are true: the government does know much more than any of us who've been there are allowed to tell."

"Well, that doesn't surprise me in the least," Mill said.

Orin nodded, cleared his throat. "Very few people have the connections I do. I could get in trouble for telling you even that much, so I'd appreciate it if you kept it to yourselves."

"Of course," I said.

Mill nodded, her eyes locked on Orin's. It seemed to be a good enough response for him.

"First, I have the information from when Edward left Milton. That was easy to access. There were a few articles about his disappearance. Do you all remember that?"

Mill nodded.

"Not particularly," I said. "But I know the gist. You don't need to go over them in detail."

"Okay, I also have some stuff from Mill's searches, the times when she was caught by the police. You never got into too much trouble."

"Not until recently," Mill responded.

Orin cringed. "Right, but let's not talk about that right now. I need to keep pretending that I don't know about that trouble. It's much bigger than your other trouble, and I have a duty to report you to the authorities. I'm not going to. Ever, and that's a decision I'll live with."

"Thank you," Mill said.

"Gril knows," I said helpfully.

Orin's eyebrows lifted. "Ah, that's good. I might need to use that, though I'd never throw Gril under the bus, either. Anyway, with that prelude, I'll say that I actually found where Edward went when he left Milton, and who he went with. Are you ready to know?"

"Call him Eddy." Mill pulled her cigarettes out of her pocket and held one between her fingers. She didn't light it and didn't bother asking if she could.

"We're ready." I hoped we truly were. "Did he leave with Travis Walker?"

Orin shook his head. "No, Beth, not Travis. But I know where he went, too. That might be less interesting than the other part, though, believe it or not. I'll get there, but I think it's best to go in order. Edward, Eddy, left with a man named Hugh Givens. They went to Mexico."

"That was a name the Milton police chief recently mentioned," I said.

"Stellan Graystone?"

"Yes."

"I didn't talk to him, but I looked up the name. Did he tell you that Eddy left with Hugh?"

"He found an old report that talked about some trouble my dad had with Hugh and Travis Walker, but not that Dad and Hugh left together."

Orin nodded. "Right. Yes, they were quite the trio. I'm still unearthing some of their drug-dealing activity, but you do know that much, right? They were selling drugs. They weren't good at it, but they were lucky sometimes." Orin cleared his throat.

"Okay," I said.

"I've suspected it for years," Mill added. "I mean, I know more than I've shared with Beth, and this is still not a surprise."

"Okay. I have gone so far as to track the route Eddy and Hugh took to get to Mexico. I think the problem was that no one knew at first that Eddy went with Hugh. They used

Hugh's credit card, for fuck's sake. If the police had known the connection . . ."

"The police knew," Mill said. "They just kept it to themselves, or my father-in-law kept it to himself—something like that."

"Right."

"If he hadn't . . . well, he thought he was helping."

"I'm sure."

No matter what Orin said, how much he shared with us, he didn't have the whole story. It was impossible for him to know all the nuances of my family's history. Still, he was smart enough to connect some dots quickly.

"Okay," Orin continued. "I've put together a timeline. It's long, and it goes beyond when they stopped using the credit cards. Here's where my contacts really become helpful. Though they moved the cash down in Mexico, there are some other clues. Names on official papers. Here's what I've got."

Orin opened a folder he'd set on the table in front of him. "Again, it's long."

He handed us each a couple of sheets of paper.

I immediately saw how the credit card that Hugh and my dad had used was run at a gas station in southern Missouri, followed by a drugstore and then a shoe store that I'd never heard of.

"They got to Mexico in three days. Why'd it take them so long?" Mill asked, having scrutinized the first two pages much more quickly than I could have managed.

"I wondered the same thing, but if I were to put myself in their place, I'd think they were afraid to stay home but scared to run, too. They had a hard time committing to a plan, maybe. I can't find that Hugh had any family. I would bet it was difficult for Eddy to leave the two of you behind."

Mill simmered for a moment, grabbing the cigarette she'd

put on the table and turning it in her fingers like a small ba-
ton. "I suspect it was." She paused. "I got a call the night
he left. It was just a hang-up. No caller ID back then. Any
chance you could check pay phone records on the route from
that night?"

Orin smiled. "I'm not sure even I can do that, but I'll try.
Pay phone records are probably long gone by now."

"I'd just like to know. All these years, I've suspected it
was Eddy, and that he couldn't bring himself to say anything,
but that he was struggling with what he was doing. Maybe
it was wishful thinking, but if I can get the phone records, it
might give me some peace of mind. You know, that he actually was thinking about the people he was leaving behind."

"I can sure check."

"Thank you." Mill's attention went back to her packet.

I looked at mine.

Dad and Hugh stopped at bars all along the route in
Texas. Since my father wasn't much of a drinker, maybe
Hugh was, or maybe it was truly just another way to prolong
the escape, give themselves a chance to be sure or to change
their minds.

I turned the page.

It seemed that Dad and Hugh finally stopped in a small
village about fifty miles over the Mexican border. They spent
a good six months there. Though there was no credit card use,
it's almost impossible to hide everything from people like
Orin.

He had managed to track them through public records. It
seemed Hugh leased a bar, though a hut from which alcohol
could be served would be a more appropriate description.
Hugh's name was on the papers, but Dad hadn't gone completely dark. He'd signed his name to a few vendors' dotted
lines.

Two years later the two moved on, but Hugh's name

turned up again a short time later in Rocky Point, Mexico, a tourist area on the water. It looked like another restaurant/bar was leased there, but Dad's name showed up only twice—three years apart. From what we could tell, it looked like Hugh might still be operating that establishment, but there was no other official paperwork with his name.

"I don't think I knew Hugh," Mill said. "Do you have a picture?"

I looked at her. I'd heard something in her tone. Was she lying about knowing Hugh?

"I'm working on it," Orin said. "I have a contact down there. I talked to her this morning. She said that the bar closes down this time of year for renovations and cleaning. The manager wasn't on the premises, and she's not sure when he'll be. It seems he's been smart about keeping photos of himself off the web, and her description of him wasn't helpful. I'll get something."

Mill nodded and then turned her attention back to the papers. I decided I must have been mistaken about her tone.

"Where's my dad?" I asked as I flipped to the second page.

"Last I can tell, Cabo." Orin leaned forward and pointed at a line item. "His name shows up on some employment documents from a sort of flea market there. He registered a stall. But that was a long, long time ago, about fifteen years now. I contacted the people who run the market, but they aren't familiar with your father's name. I know some Spanish, but the conversation might not have been a good back-and-forth. They said they'd ask around for Eddy, but from what I can tell, he might not be there. I'm not done searching."

"Dad was in Cabo?" I said, more to myself than anyone else. I looked at Mill. "Did you have any other hang-up calls over the years? Anything happen that might make you think he was trying to get in touch?"

"I wish. For a long time, every time the phone rang or a car stopped in front of the house—shoot, even slowed down a little—I practically jumped out of my skin to see if it was him. All that went away after a while, but a small part of me still has hope. It's my normal, and I doubt it will ever change."

It's strange to go from darkness one moment to enlightenment the next. That's what learning is about, of course, but when the darkness has been so all-encompassing, a part of you as permanent as a limb, it can be discombobulating when the light is flipped on.

But it's never quite as transforming as you might predict it will be. With the new information on the pages that Orin had given us, you might think that everything would now be different. Freer. But I was still me, Mill was still Mill.

Honestly, it was a bit of a letdown.

I imagined a life in Cabo San Lucas. It was nothing like small-town Missouri. I was often grateful for the life I'd lived, the one that had led me to the place I was right at this moment. No matter the bad stuff.

When I envisioned my dad there in a sunny resort community, I had an urge to laugh and then punch him in the gut. What the hell? Even if he was afraid of the law, afraid of his own father, he had a family, and you aren't supposed to abandon your family, your wife and child, are you?

If you're any sort of good man, you don't. Was my father simply not a good man? I experienced the humanization of my mother years ago. Her warts and all have been exposed for as long as I can remember.

But I'd turned my dad into . . . either a hero or a martyr, depending on the day, maybe, the memory. The nostalgia.

Now it seemed he wasn't either of those. He was—maybe is—just a dude.

Orin seemed to key in on my thoughts. "Beth, this isn't the whole story. There's more to learn. I'm not done."

I nodded. My mind wandered to Cabo again, sunsets, drinks with umbrellas. The beach.

"I've never even been to Mexico," I said.

Mill laughed. "Me neither. And now's probably not the time for me to get a passport."

"No, probably not," I said.

"Do you think he's still alive? He would only be in his late fifties," I asked Orin.

"I don't know yet, and I don't want to make any promises. But I will definitely try to find out."

"You said you also know about Travis Walker?" Mill said.

I hadn't forgotten, but just as Mill ran away to avoid hearing about my dad, a part of me didn't want to know this next part. I'd stay in that chair and listen, though, try to process.

Orin bit his lip. "I do. I can track him from the day Eddy disappeared until about ten years ago, and I'll get those ten years, too. I know that's what will help the police find where he is now."

"You can track him since way back then?" Mill asked.

"I can. He didn't hide. I don't know why, but he didn't. He left Milton, but he didn't go far. It appears he stayed in Missouri, mostly, with a short stint in California."

I remembered Detective Majors telling me about a California author that had been stalked. I wondered again if the two stories were tied together, but I didn't mention it.

"Was he in lots of trouble with the law?" I asked.

"Some, but not as much as you might predict considering what he did to you."

Detective Majors had shown me an old booking photo for Travis. It hadn't occurred to me to ask her about the extent of his criminal behavior. Every conversation we'd had always felt so limited—by time, distance, and the possible loss of the connection. I knew Travis had been in trouble, but I'd never seen a rap sheet.

"I can't find much in the way of his earning an honest living, though, so there are lots of blank spots—and I suspect he had or has plenty of cash from his drug-dealing days. There's much more to learn," Orin said.

"I'm working with a detective in Missouri. May I put her in touch with you?" I asked.

Orin frowned. "Beth, I'm sorry to say this, but I can't work with law enforcement personnel that I . . . don't have a connection with. I've signed things. However, go ahead and send her whatever I'm giving you. If you want to tell her my name, feel free to do so, but I won't talk to her and there's simply no way she'll be able to compel me to do so."

I nodded. "Can I tell her that?"

"Yes, in fact, I would recommend that you lay that groundwork. Tell her what you know about me and tell her you can't know more. If she wants to use the information, she may. It's up to her, but even if she tries to subpoena me, it will be quashed quickly. That's just the way it works, I'm afraid."

"She'd be an idiot not to use the information," Mill said.

"She's not an idiot," I said.

"We'll see," Mill added.

She wasn't an idiot. But I truly didn't know how good she was. How was I supposed to compare her progress to what Orin had found? Had she found out more than she'd told me? Frequently I thought that was the case. She was working hard, that much I knew for certain, but was she working smart?

I looked back and forth at Mill and Orin. Now I wished I'd mentioned to Mill the note I'd found on my desk, the one that listed Travis Walker's name and an address. She wasn't going to like that I'd kept it from her, but it suddenly felt like something Orin should be aware of.

"Orin, I got a note on my desk a few months back. For a while, I thought it was from you or maybe Gril, but he says it wasn't him. And if you really didn't know who I was, you wouldn't have given it to me."

I reached for my bag and rummaged inside it. I'd put the note in a Ziploc and secured it in a zippered pocket.

"It goes nowhere," I continued. "Not even an empty lot. Nowhere."

I handed the Ziploc to Orin, but Mill grabbed it first. She looked at it and back up at me. "What the hell?"

"Mill, it's not a real place. There's not even a Rose Avenue in Milton."

"But it means something," Mill said. "Why didn't you tell me?"

"It seemed like too much, but now you know." I took it from her and gave it to Orin. I gave her a look that hopefully told her she could be mad at me later.

She turned her attention to Orin, too. "This must mean something."

Orin inspected the address and then started typing on his keyboard. Then he looked up at me. "Yeah, it's not real, but I'm with Mill, and we need to know who wrote it. I don't recognize the writing. I'd like to know who left this for you."

"Me too," I said. "I don't know how to figure it out. I did tell Detective Majors. She wanted me to send her a copy, but I never did. I told her what it said, but it didn't seem to mean much to her, or maybe it was just delivered to me too far away from her to be worried about it."

Orin grabbed his cell phone from a drawer and snapped a picture. "Do you have an email address?"

"I do."

"I'll email it to you and then you can forward it to her."

"Thanks. Burner phones don't have quite the same capabilities as smartphones." I smiled and then jotted down my email address for Orin. When I was finished, I looked up at him. "What? You look bothered."

"I am."

It wasn't that I'd put the note on the back burner; I just didn't know how to go about searching for whoever left it without giving away who I was. I'd forced myself not to think about it too much. But it had most certainly bothered me when I'd found it on my desk, next to another note from Tex. He'd stopped by the *Petition* to say hello and I hadn't been there, so he'd left a note with a greeting. His handwriting was nothing like the handwriting used on the one listing the address. During our second date, I'd asked him if he'd noticed the other note or seen anyone else at the shed the day he'd been there. He hadn't.

"My friend Tex left a note the same day. He didn't see anyone else, and the writing isn't the same."

"Tex Southern?"

"Yes."

"You're *friends*?" Orin smiled, the concern he'd just shown diminished by a twinkle in his eyes.

"Yes. Friends."

"Someone here knows who she is," Mill interjected.

"We don't know that for sure, but it's sounding more like it," Orin said.

"What other explanation could there be?" Mill asked.

"I'm not sure yet," Orin said.

There's something strange about fear. It comes and goes and can easily be replaced by other terror, at least temporarily. I'd noticed that as the small plane I took to Benedict landed that first day. For those few moments of what felt like free fall, though the aircraft was actually operating normally, I forgot about being taken from my home, held for three days in a van, and then needing brain surgery as a result of my escape.

Now it was suddenly as if I'd submerged myself in a tub of old bathwater. I knew this old Travis Walker fear that suddenly zipped through me. I didn't like it—I hated it—but its familiarity made it somewhat less threatening. Somewhat.

"I should have left town," I muttered. "Back when I could. Back before the weather got bad."

"You didn't and you're fine, Beth," Orin said. "You're fine."

"I'm here now, too," Mill added.

I heard some remnants of irritation in her voice. I suspected she thought I should have left, too.

"Sorry," I said, meaning a different sort of sorry for each of them.

Orin's attention went back to the note. "Look, this has to mean something. Even if it just means that someone here knows who you are, I'd like to figure it out. I would bet they don't mean you any harm or you would know by now."

"You remember Ellen?" I asked Orin.

"The woman who was at the Benedict House for a while?"

"Yes. She figured out who I was. Before she left, I asked her if she'd written it, but she said she hadn't. She was a junkie, though she was clean by the time she went back to Anchorage. Still, junkies lie." I paused. "But I truly don't think it was her."

"She would have given you an address for your kidnapper?" Orin said.

I shrugged. "I know—it doesn't fit."

"I'll work on it," Orin said. "I'll figure out who wrote it."

"You will?"

"I will."

He seemed so confident. I wished I'd talked to him much sooner.

It was a lot, maybe too much in this short meeting.

We sat together for a long few minutes, going over the notes again, repeating the same questions. Orin was patient and didn't act like he was trying to hide any additional bad news. Mill behaved like she suspected him of holding on to some, but before long, she seemed to settle into knowing that we could trust Orin, and that trusting him was a smart thing to do.

He didn't rush us away, but I sensed he would like to re-open the library. We thanked him and said we'd take whatever other information he wanted to send. He saw us to the door.

Mill and I stood on the stoop for a minute, both of us still processing. It would take us time, and we'd work through things in different ways, but Mill turned to me and forced a smile. I thought she was going to be angry at me again, but she wasn't.

"That was helpful" was all she said.

"It was. Let's go get something to eat."

"Good idea."

Twenty-seven

How about a quick detour before food?" Mill asked when we got into the truck.

"Sure."

"Let's go visit Elijah Wyatt."

"Why, because you're interested in his dogs or because he's rumored to be Claudia's boyfriend?"

"Both."

I hesitated. "You're not going to tell him he's too old for Claudia, are you?"

"No. That's none of my business, dollie."

I looked over at her. Her tone was critical and clipped, despite her words.

She went on. "I can't believe Orin was right here in your backyard—woods—this whole time. Holy moly, what a wonderful resource. I could rule the world if Orin answered all my questions."

"Well, I'm not sure he'd let it go that far."

"No, probably not, but goodness, he's something." She sighed. "Listen, nothing bad has come from that note, but I'm glad that Gril and now Orin know about it. I wish you'd told me, but I couldn't have done anything anyway, I guess."

"It's not a real address."

"You know that's not the point. Someone was telling you they know who you are, and that kind of sneaky doesn't sit right with me." She held up a finger when I glanced over at her. "However, it's all good so far. All I want to say is that I'm torn now. You might want to leave Benedict, but now you have Orin in the loop. I don't know what the answer is, but shit, Beth, just be careful."

"I am. Always."

"Good. Okay," she said with finality. She was done talking about it. For now.

I pulled around Tochco's and came to a stop next to a barn attached to a small cabin.

We got out of the car and made our way to the front door of the house. I knocked, but no one answered.

"Let's check the barn," Mill said, leading the way without waiting for me to reply.

I hurried to follow her, opening my mouth to say something as she opened the barn door, but she was inside before I could suggest that we not trespass.

Once I rejoined her, I encountered the version of my mother that had surprised me earlier.

The barn was heated comfortably, but not too warm. The dogs were all inside their own individual stalls, replete with fresh hay and blankets. Each stall held a full bowl of water and an empty bowl for food, I presumed. The place smelled of the animals, but not in an unclean way. All indications were that these animals' needs were well attended to.

On the other side of the stalls, three sleds were stored—I still didn't spot a new one. Mill hadn't made it as far as the sleds, because she couldn't get enough of the dogs. She leaned over the half doors of each stall, petting and talking to each animal. I followed behind and found myself doing the same. I recognized Gus, of course, but I had to check the tags on the other collars.

Being with those dogs did something to my mother's soul. It softened her, made her more human. I'd never witnessed anything like it before.

It had the same effect on me, but I didn't think my changes were so visible. My mother's smile became friendlier, her eyes less harsh.

"What's the deal?" I asked after we'd greeted all the dogs. "I didn't know you liked dogs so much."

"I love them so much that I would never have one because I know I couldn't stay home and take care of it. It wouldn't be fair. I had them when I was a child and I've missed them."

"How did I not know this?"

Mill shrugged and then smiled at Gus again. "Too much other shit going on, I suppose."

"I suppose."

I looked around. There'd been no sign of Elijah. "I didn't see his truck outside. Maybe he's helping someone."

"Maybe he's helping Vitner," Mill said, her smile disappearing, her tone turning harsh again.

"You don't like Vitner."

"Not even a little bit. It's simple. I suspect he killed Ned. I think he must have come here specifically for that reason. He's not stupid, though. He used the census to get here. It took some smarts to think that through."

"But to kill Ned? Why?"

Mill frowned, but her fingers kept scratching behind Gus's ears. "That's a quandary, but I'm going to get it figured out. I promise."

"I'm sure." I was.

We inspected some old Iditarod calendars pinned to one of the walls and then looked at the sleds.

"This is the bed. Where you store stuff." Mill pointed to the space in front of where the sledder stood. She crouched and pointed at the blades. "These are the runners. The brushbow is the front bumper, and here's the brake. You step on it."

"How in the world do you know all of this?"

"I asked Viola. She knows all about sledding."

"She does?"

"Yep. She used to have dogs, too."

"Boy, I have missed a lot."

"You've had other shit to worry about." Mill smiled as she stood.

"Do you want to move here and have your own dog team?" I asked, only slightly facetiously.

"I would love nothing more, but I'm on the run from the law. I doubt this group could get me away fast enough." Mill smiled sadly at the dogs, all of them wanting more of our attention.

As she walked back toward them, I wished she could move to Alaska and have a dog team, even if it meant we'd have to be around each other all the time. I felt bad that she couldn't. I was sad she was on the run from the law because of me—well, in a roundabout way, at least.

A desk took up a dark corner where there were no dogs or sledding items. Even if Mill hadn't been with me, I probably would have done a cursory snoop. But she was with me, so our explorations went a little deeper.

Boldly, Mill even flipped on the desk lamp before she rifled through folders full of papers. I took it as a good sign that she didn't dig too thoroughly. I witnessed a moment of conscience when she frowned, seeming to recognize that invoices and other personal documents really weren't any of her business.

She did, however, become momentarily fascinated by a small book, maybe three inches by three inches, a thick, full-color novelty booklet with pictures of dogs from years of Iditarods. She thumbed through it quickly and then stuck it in her pocket.

"Mill. You can't take that."

"You didn't see a thing," she said before she turned on her heel and went back to the dogs for one more round of petting.

We were there a long time, but Elijah never showed up. I was fairly confident that he was fine, but I wondered some. There was no way to find out, and we'd even worn out our welcome with the dogs; most of them curled up to rest.

As we stood by the door a moment, Mill said, "Well, there's no picture of Claudia in here. No sign that they are together in any way. I'm not going to break into his main house today, but it might be necessary at some point."

I held back an admonition. It wouldn't do any good to voice it anyway. I had to keep hoping the ferry would take her away from Benedict before she got herself into trouble here, too.

"Let's go eat," I said.

With one last glance toward the dogs, she led the way back out to my truck.

We decided to stop by the bar to check in with Benny. We found her and Claudia working, and Viola and Lucy sitting together at a table.

Mill and I made our way to their table.

The first thing we heard Lucy say to Viola was "Is the plan to starve me to death?"

I told Viola I'd handle it. I called the café next door and ordered a bunch of cheeseburgers and fries, enough that everyone in the bar could eat.

Lucy was on her second burger when she and Mill started talking about—of all things—hockey. Viola didn't seem interested; she stood and moved to the bar a few steps away to talk to Benny.

My mother, a lifelong St. Louis Blues fan, and Lucy, a lifelong Chicago Blackhawks fan, were rivals, but their common love for the game rose above their hatred for each other's teams.

Having finished one cheeseburger, I grabbed the platter and took it to Viola. "Hungry?" I inquired.

"Sure," she said after a moment's thought.

"May I join you?"

Viola glanced around me at the back table. "They bugging you?"

"So much."

"All right, have a seat. But every time that door opens, be prepared to get out of my way. If Vitner comes in, I have to grab him quickly."

I swallowed the urge to ask her if she wanted my help and nodded as I sat down on the stool next to her. "Gril and Donner find anything?"

Viola chewed as she shook her head. "Nope." She swallowed. "But I haven't talked to them for a couple hours, so who knows now."

"What are your thoughts about Elijah Wyatt and Claudia?" I asked.

She put the cheeseburger down. "Beth, it's different out here. I'm not saying we should condone anything harmful, but they are two consenting adults. The bad part is that Claudia was cheating on her husband, but she is of age."

I nodded. "Honestly, the age difference doesn't bother me. Much. Even the cheating doesn't surprise me. I was just wondering if you think Elijah could have killed Ned."

Viola shrugged. "At the right moment, anyone could have killed Ned. He wasn't a likable guy."

But I heard the doubt in her voice.

She frowned and shook her head as she continued. "But, no, I don't think Elijah could kill anyone, unless he was left with no choice. People with no choice do crazy things."

"Where, other than the obvious places I know about, could Vitner have gone?"

"Brayn, maybe, where your fella lives."

I didn't correct her.

She went on. "There's another village up north, Flynn, but it's pretty hard to get there right now. Shoot, he could've gone into the ocean even. Who knows?"

"I haven't asked you yet. Did he interview you for the census?"

"Yes."

"So you had to tell him about me?"

"Well, technically, legally, I was supposed to, but I didn't."

"Why not?"

"Because I figured I liked you better than I liked him, so he and the census can pound sand for all I care. Not overly patriotic of me or anything, but I'm pretty good at sensing when I need to just shut up."

It wasn't the way it was supposed to be done, but I was grateful. "Thank you."

"You're welcome."

The door opened and Viola went on alert. She swung the stool around and put her hand on the gun. I tensed as the crowd turned.

Ruke came through the door and nodded at all of us who were paying attention. He caught Viola's eye and made a bee-line to our table. "Don't understand what's going on, but Gril wants me to bring you, Claudia, and Lucy to his office."

"Is he there?" Viola said as she stood.

"He is."

Viola bit her bottom lip. "It would be better to have everyone at the Benedict House. Warmer, too."

Ruke shrugged. "Gril wants everyone there."

"Let me call him." Viola moved around Ruke to use Benny's landline in the back.

When Viola left the bar, I had a clear view of the table, where Lucy was now by herself. I looked around for Mill and had the faint sense that the door had opened and closed behind Ruke a couple of times in the few moments he was talking to Viola.

Had Mill left?

No, certainly not. Where would she go? Why would she leave without telling me?

I looked around again, forcing myself to take my time and really look closely. She wasn't here.

I hurried to Lucy. "Where's my mom?"

"You didn't see her leave?"

"No. What do you mean, leave?"

"Vamoose out the door. What else could I mean?"

I scanned the small bar again. No, she wouldn't do that.

Of course she would.

I hurried to the door and threw myself outside. I heard Lucy call my name but didn't turn back around.

In all my life, I had never stepped into such a cold darkness.

"Mill?" I called toward the Benedict House.

Light fixtures were hung above the house's front door as well as on the wall next to the small parking lot, but none of them was lit. Had Viola forgotten to flip a switch, or had they just not come on?

"Mill!" I stepped along the boardwalk and then cut the corner toward the Benedict House.

There was no sign of my mother outside, but I didn't think about looking at footprints or for any evidence other than Mill herself.

I opened the door and hurried inside, still calling for her.

I ran to her room. Her door still wasn't locked, but there was no sign of her. My door was locked, of course, but I managed to get it open without too much fumbling. She wasn't in there, either. I ran to the kitchen and dining room, but still nothing.

Where would she go?

"Shit," I muttered. I should have talked to Lucy, asked her more questions, waited for what she had to say to me.

I jetted back over to the bar, but of course she had gone with Viola, Claudia, and Ruke, back to the police cabin. Gratitude washed over me when I noticed that at least Benny was still there.

"Beth, what's wrong?" she asked when she saw my wild eyes.

"My mom?"

"Viola said you two left together."

"No!"

"She's around, Beth," Benny said with very little confidence.

"Where's Lucy? She was talking to Lucy."

"Went with Vi. Look, they're just over at Gril's office. I think. Want me to call over there?" Benny put the dishcloth she'd been holding down on the bar and made a move to go to the back room.

"No," I said as I turned the other direction. "I'll just go."

The last words I heard as the door closed me behind were "Are you sure . . ."

I wasn't sure about anything, except that my mother was up to something. In fact, a certainty was taking shape in the back of my mind, and it had to do with why she was here in the first place. There were bigger reasons for her finding me in Alaska.

For Mill, there were always bigger reasons. I knew that.

I just should have remembered it sooner.

Twenty-eight

The facial expressions I saw when I burst through the doors of the police station were a combination of expectation and disappointment.

A quick glance told me that the people *not* there were Donner and Mill. Gril, Viola, Claudia, Lucy, and even Ruke were sitting in chairs in the common space where Donner had his desk.

"Beth?" Viola asked.

"Does anyone know where my mother is?"

Viola and Gril shared a look.

"No, I thought she was with you," Gril said.

I made a beeline to Lucy. "You guys were talking. What did you discuss?"

"Nothing," she said. "Hockey."

"Come on, Lucy. I need to know. There was more, right?" I tried not to sound like I wanted to grab her and shake the answers out of her.

Viola added, "Lucy, spill it."

Lucy clicked her tongue and sighed heavily. "Well, I guess she grilled me for a while. Things about Juneau. She asked me if Claudia had ever talked about you."

"Had she?" I pushed when she went silent.

Lucy glanced at Claudia. "Sure, kind of. She told me about the girl in town with the scar on her head. No big deal." Lucy twisted her mouth and glared at me as Claudia started to squirm in the chair next to her.

I ignored Claudia for a second. "What, Lucy? What else?"

"Your mother asked me what name Claudia called you."

"Okay. And what name was it?"

"Claudia called you Elizabeth. That's it. That's all there was to it."

I finally turned my attention to Claudia. "Why did you call me Elizabeth?"

"Because your name is Beth," she said. "That's it! God, so you don't go by your full name. Why are you so weirded out about this?"

Gril and I exchanged a quick look. He had a murder to investigate, which was much more important than my personal business. Still, the glimmer in his eyes told me he knew there might be something important about someone calling me by my pseudonym, even if he couldn't make it a priority at the moment. I wouldn't have bothered him with it if Mill hadn't disappeared.

"My mother is missing now, too. I don't understand what's going on, but I suspect she's after Vitner. I can't understand why her conversation with Lucy would have spurred her to that, but it's my best guess."

In fact, though I couldn't have offered proof, I was suddenly certain that was exactly the reason she'd come to Benedict—for him, not for me at all.

Gril, his mouth in a serious line, nodded once. He'd already put those pieces together.

The door to the station opened again. We all turned.

"Hey," Donner said as he put up a gloved hand, "I have nothing new."

"Beth's mom is missing now, too. Any chance you saw her out there?" Gril asked.

"No. Missing? I don't understand."

I sat down in a chair as a wave of desperation swept over me. I had suspicions, but I truly didn't understand anything. I felt lost, unmoored.

"We'll find her," Gril said.

"Yeah, she hasn't gotten far," Viola said.

"It's so dark," I muttered. "Cold."

"We're used to dark and cold," Viola said.

I blinked as I looked around. Everyone, even Lucy and Claudia, was interested in what I was about to say. They didn't know why Mill had run off, even if they had in part compelled her to.

"I don't know what's going on, but I'm sure you'll find my mother with Vitner, or him with her, or something. She's after him." I didn't speak the other words that ran through my mind. *He's after me.*

Gril stood and looked at Donner. "Let's go."

There were no other options. We had to get others involved. Two people missing so recently after a murder was terrifying to everyone, especially law enforcement. Gril called Brayn, asking for help, and Tex, along with others, arrived about an hour later.

"I'm going with you," I told Tex.

"Beth, I got this," Tex said. "This is what I do."

It *was* what he did. He was a qualified and trained member of official search-and-rescue teams. He could track. He knew exactly what to do.

"You'll slow him down," Donner said matter-of-factly.

"But it's my mom."

"I understand," Tex said. "We'll find her."

No matter how confident he sounded, I knew how it

actually went. I knew thousands of people a year went missing in Alaska. It was a place where people could get swallowed up and never spit back out.

"I promise I won't slow you down," I said.

Tex and Donner exchanged a look. They were the two furriest men I'd ever known, all beard and intelligent eyes. Tex had grown up here; this remote land infused the blood running through his veins. Donner had come here after losing his family in a fire, but he was no less an Alaskan than Tex or Ruke.

"All right," Tex said. "At least it's not terrible out there at the moment. We'll be okay."

"Beth, Tex will be at his best without having to watch out for you," Gril said.

I heard him. I heard them all, and I understood what they were saying, but there was simply no way I could not go. I couldn't wait around for an answer. Even before I'd been kidnapped, I hadn't been good at waiting. It might have killed me to do it now.

"If I don't go with him, I'll go by myself," I said.

Gril lifted an eyebrow. "Fine. Go with Tex."

I was subjected to a new level of gearing up before we set out. I put on more layers than I'd ever worn, including three pairs of thin but warm socks under my boots. Tex frowned at the boots, telling me they were fine for everything I might need them for in Alaska, except for this. I told him I would be okay, that I would keep up. He wore better boots, as well as a backpack that held tools we might need. I was sure he hoped I'd give up and go home before too long.

I followed behind him, my steps double time to his. Though it wasn't easy to breathe normally, I needed to talk to him. "Tex, there's something I need to tell you."

"Now?" He kept marching, his eyes looking everywhere but at me behind him.

"You said I'm secretive. I'm about to spill all my secrets."

"As much as I appreciate that, Beth, could it wait?"

"I don't think so. It might be important."

"Okay, can you talk and walk?"

"I can."

The woods were more uninviting than I'd ever experienced. Briefly, I wondered what Gril would have done if I'd set out on my own. He would have tried to stop me, of course, but short of being locked up, I couldn't have been kept from the search for Mill.

For the first time in my life, I thought I might finally understand my mother as I never could before, in ways I didn't think my grandfather ever managed to grasp.

If the need she felt to search for my father was even half as strong as the need I felt to search for her, she couldn't have denied it, no matter that she had a child at home to care for. I was going to find my mother or die trying.

Tex had also, with Gril's permission, holstered a gun over his shoulder. Gril asked Tex if he knew how to use it. In response, Tex demonstrated his ability to load and unload the weapon as if it were an extension of his own hands.

Tex was a large human being, as well as agile. Though none of our dates had included a hike in any woods, and as unfeminist as it might sound, just being near his gigantic and confident strength made me feel safe.

As I relied on him to lead the way, I told him who I was. This time around wasn't as easy as it had been with Orin. Then it felt as if I was sharing a new secret, bringing an object out in the sun to shine. This time, with the panic over my missing mother still strong, it felt like maybe I was overdoing it, telling too many people, maybe blinding with too much light, but I did it anyway. It seemed pertinent to whatever my mother was doing in these woods. It would be unfair for Tex not to know, even if the ramifications were unclear.

As I finished, we stepped out into a clearing and the half-moon moved from behind a cloud. Tex stopped walking and sent me a sad smile. The moon shadowed his eyes, but I could see his mouth, even through the thick beard.

"What?" I said.

"I've read one of your books. You have a sick mind."

I couldn't help but laugh. "I think I must."

"Oh, you do."

We looked at each other a long time. Despite the moonlight, there was nothing romantic about the moment.

"Beth," Tex finally said, "you're safe with me. You know that, don't you?"

"I feel safe with you."

"If someone was to try to hurt you, I would stop them, in whatever way it took."

"I appreciate that."

"I'm glad you told me who you are. It . . . clears up some things."

"My sick mind explains me better?"

"No, your secretiveness. I understand your need to hide, but sometimes we hide too hard, too well. It's good that Gril knows who you are. I'm glad you trust me, too."

"I do."

"Not at this exact moment, but I think we need to tell Donner and Viola."

"Why? And *we*?"

"Or just you."

"Why?"

"I don't want to scare you more, but with that note appearing on your desk, it's clear that someone here knows who you are, and you need as many people on your side as possible."

"All right, that *definitely* scares me."

"Again, don't mean to, and we might find your mother

quickly and your story won't matter, but I understand why you wanted me to know; it gives me a better heads-up, takes away some possible surprises."

"Okay," I said. I didn't really have any argument in me anyway, though the break in the hike helped me catch my breath.

"Come on, I have an idea," Tex said.

He set out again, turning to lead us toward a wider path under more trees.

"Where are we going?"

"There's a road over here. It leads to an old hunting shed."

"Like the *Petition*?"

"Not exactly."

We moved through the trees. Once we emerged in another clearing of sorts, we found the road he'd mentioned.

Tire tracks moved down the middle of it.

"How did you know?" I asked, almost breathless again.

"Process of elimination. Lucky guess, I don't know. Vitner has the van. I'm not sure we'll find your mother, but we might find him at the end of this road, in the shed." He hesitated. "The tracks are a tell and it's not far. Let's go back and let Gril know."

"No! Stop worrying about me. I'll be fine. You've got a gun."

Tex shook his head. "I don't know."

"I told you my story for two reasons, Tex. One, I'm so freaked out about my mother that I needed to aim my thoughts somewhere else. But I also wanted to give you some background that in some way I can't understand yet might help us find her. We're not going backward now. We're going to search. Besides, these tracks might be from Gril or Donner. They might have checked down here already. Let's at least get closer."

"Stay behind me, Beth," he finally said.

"I promise," I quipped.

Though we'd traveled over snowy ground, it had been mostly flat. Now we were going to have to somehow traverse a slope whose end we couldn't quite see. We had a small flashlight, but Tex said he needed more. He took off the backpack and reached inside it, pulling out another light the size of a toaster. He flipped it on and aimed it downward.

"That's a steep road," I said as he made a noise at the back of his throat that probably meant the same thing.

"Will you wait here?"

I looked down the slope. Even with my dedication to the mission, my commitment faltered some. That hill was *steep*.

"No, I won't wait," I finally said, though I had to work to keep my tone firm.

"Hold on to my arm. My boots will grip fine. Yours will probably do okay, but I don't want you to fall." Tex crooked his arm in the most utilitarian way.

"I don't want to make you fall, too."

"Beth, really?"

He probably weighed at least a hundred more pounds than I did, and was close to a foot taller.

"Right." I took his arm.

He walked surely down the incline. I kept up only because holding on to his arm propelled me along. Another day, another cold, dark night, this could have been turned into something fun. It might make a good sixth date. Someday.

Once he seemed to understand the direction the road fell and turned, Tex flipped off the giant lantern and clipped it to his belt. He turned on the smaller one again.

"Don't want to announce us?" I asked.

"Exactly. Explain again how knowing your story might have to do with why your mother ran off," Tex asked quietly. "Can you give me anything specific?"

"I think Lucy must have said something that made her think Vitner has something to do with the man who kidnapped me, knew him years ago. It's the best thing I can come up with, but I sense I'm missing some obvious things."

"She thinks he's the man named Hugh Givens?"

"Yes, but I still need a picture from Orin. I can't be sure."

"What would she do to Vitner if she found him?"

Kill him, probably. "I don't know."

"You don't?"

"Whatever, it wouldn't be good. She's lived a lot of years in search of someone who she just learned might have been on the beach in Mexico since he left us. She can't accept that someone thought it was okay to kidnap me—I can't, either, for that matter—but we just learned some new stuff about my father, and all these things seem to be tied together. She just learned about the note left on my desk. She's angry. Maybe more than she's ever been before."

"Orin is the librarian, the one who got hurt?"

"Yes. He's better, and he's a good friend. I should have trusted him with my story earlier, but I didn't."

"All things have their time."

"Yeah, but . . . well, sometimes it feels like time doesn't move *on* quickly enough."

"And then all of a sudden it feels like it went way too fast."

I nodded, but I didn't think he was paying attention.

"Shh." He stopped walking, so I did, too.

The noises we heard could have been anything at all; they weren't immediately distinctive. A few long seconds later, though, there was no doubt they were groans, but weren't coming from close by.

I remained as silent as a church mouse as we listened hard.

"It's coming from the direction of the shed, but maybe on its other side," Tex said quietly.

We'd come to a flatter part of the road. I let go of Tex's arm as he took off with long brisk steps. I kept up, but just barely, glad when he slowed again.

He switched back to the big lantern, lighting up the night and the woods with a far-reaching glow. In the middle distance, amid another copse of trees, we spotted a darkened shed. Again, we hurried in that direction, but stopped a good twenty feet from the building. Tex's arm flew out to keep me behind him.

Until we were upon it, we hadn't seen the van at the side of the shed, its nose aimed downward in the snow. Its front doors were open wide, but no light came from the inside.

"I think we'd better check inside them both," I said.

"I'll do it. Stand over there, behind the tree." Tex gave me a push as he swung his arm again.

He didn't seem to notice his own strength, but I stumbled a little before hiding myself.

Tex trudged toward the van, unsnapping the chest holster as he made his way. "Hello, I'm with the police. Anyone there?"

No one answered. The silence was heavy with something I couldn't pinpoint, but it made my limbs shake.

Carefully Tex shone the light in the front of the van. And then in the back.

"No one in the van," he said.

"We heard moaning, though," I said, but it did seem farther away than it had taken us to get here.

"I know. Stay there. I'm going to check the shed."

I didn't announce that I was going with him, but I did anyway. He was too focused on the task at hand to admonish me.

This shed was nothing like the shed that housed the *Petition*. This one was made of wood planks aged with time and weather. It was half the size of mine, and wasn't reinforced with a tin roof, but, for whatever reason, the roof had held up well, and the inside did offer some shelter.

However, no one was inside, and it was hard to tell if

anyone had been there recently. Blankets and bottles of water sat in one corner, but the water was frozen. Maybe someone had just left the stuff there in case someone else who needed them happened by.

"Vitner had the van. He must have been here at some point," I observed.

"Hello? Anyone here?" Tex called as he stepped back outside.

No one answered, not even the wind.

"I'm going to see if the keys are in the van," he said.

I wasn't sure why he wanted to—that van wasn't getting out of there without Elijah's tow truck—but I followed him as he made his way to the open driver's door.

Tex wedged his way onto the seat and reached for the key. I heard him turn it, but we were met with silence, not even clicks from a dying battery.

Tex moved out of the van and then around to its other side. I followed and watched as he aimed the giant light again. "Snowmobile tracks."

A trail marked with the tracks stretched before us. It wasn't long before it seemed to disappear into another gathering of trees, or maybe just into some thickened darkness. I also saw footprints, and maybe paw prints.

I studied the snow even harder and took a step toward a print. "Look." I put my boot near it. My own print was smaller than the one I'd found, but the tread was identical. "This could be my mom's boot."

"She got them at the mercantile?"

"Yes."

"Lots of those kinds around here."

"Well, these could be hers. They look like her size."

"There are bigger prints, too, probably men's."

"Which man or men?" I said, though I'd narrowed down the selection to Elijah or Vitner.

"That's the question. I need to follow the tracks for as long as I can. You going to be able to stay with me?"

"Yes."

The giant lantern led the way. Tex's urgency ramped up, and so did his speed, but no matter how strong or in shape you were, trudging through the wintery forest couldn't be quick. We came upon an intersection of sorts. The snowmobile tracks went one way, but the boot prints took off the other way, into the woods.

I suddenly thought I recognized something. "This is the way to Dr. Powder's office."

Tex bit his bottom lip and pondered which way we should go. There was something to the boot prints that made them seem like the right choice—perhaps those prints would be easier to catch up with. Someone had gone into the woods when the other option of riding a sled seemed so much easier.

"Damn. Let's hurry." Tex took off.

"What? Why?" I said as I caught up to him. But the answer came to me. "Oh, you think someone might have needed medical help?"

"It's a possibility."

"And Vitner and Elijah probably knew the doctor and his wife were down here."

A worst-case scenario played through my mind. I was suddenly worried about the sweet, wise doctor who'd cared for me without asking too many questions.

I grabbed the lantern from Tex's hands as we came around the final curve before the house. I aimed the light toward the misfit house. Made of bricks in a Victorian style, it looked nothing like most of the other wood cabins around Benedict.

The front door was wide open and light spilled out.

"Oh no, that's not right," I said. I took a frantic step forward, then promptly slipped and fell flat on my face.

"You okay?" Tex said as he reached to help me.

I was in that place where the pain hadn't hit yet. "I'm fine. Let's get in there."

"Hang on." He helped me up. "Beth, hang on! We need to make sure you didn't hurt yourself."

"I am fine. Let go," I said, now between teeth gritted not from pain but from anger at him for holding my arms so tightly. I thought I might throw up on this man I'd liked so much a few minutes earlier.

Tex let go. "Beth, I'm sorry. Hang on. Just give me twenty seconds to make sure you're not hurt, and then we'll get in there. Okay? I'm truly sorry."

I breathed two times out of my nose, like a bull.

"Beth, please."

My emotions ran the gamut. I was panicked and scared, but Tex Southern would never hurt me—I knew this. I nodded.

He shined the light in my eyes and then did a quick check on the movement of my limbs. "Good. You're fine. Again, I'm sorry. Now, please, stay here."

I opened my mouth to protest, but Tex didn't wait to hear what I had to say. He hurried into the house, gun drawn.

He took the big light with him, which left me in a darkness so deep I thought it might hide me forever. "Oh, please, let them be okay," I muttered, listening for gunfire, a noise that would surely ruin me.

A long few minutes later, maybe an eternity, I heard Tex's voice. "Beth! Come on in."

I didn't even know I was crying, but I sniffed away the tears as I hurried into the house.

And into a bloody mess.

Twenty-nine

Oh, Doc," I said as I gently touched the cut on his head.

"Beth, I'm fine," he said with a crooked smile. "Lynny's okay too."

They were okay, but they were also hurt and bloody.

The doctor and his wife had become the patients. Tex knew enough first aid to get them taken care of, with my assistance. They didn't need stitches and it didn't seem either of them had concussions, but Dr. Powder had cut his head, more from being startled by the intruder, as we learned, than from being intentionally hurt by him. Head cuts bleed a lot.

"That man, he's . . . horrible. The doctor would have taken care of him, if only he'd asked. That's what doctors do," Lynny said with her deep southern drawl.

"Can you guys tell us what happened, in the order it happened?" Tex asked after their wounds had been attended to and I'd handed Dr. Powder and Lynny cups of warm coffee that had apparently been brewed right before the violence had begun.

We'd gotten bits and pieces of the story as we'd worked, but Gril would want to know the sequence of events, as precisely as possible. He'd want his own accounting, too, but Tex was right to ask. The sooner we got the story from them, the more accurate it would be.

Dr. Powder nodded. "We were just listening to some Barry Manilow when someone knocked on the door. We're used to that sort of thing."

"It's fine. All hours of the day and night are fine," Lynny said. She frowned at her husband before she continued. "I opened the door, and the man, pressing a wound in his side, pushed past me. Knocked me over."

She lifted her foot and turned her ankle slowly. She didn't wince, which I took as a good sign.

"When Lynny screamed and fell, I stood up from my stool—I was back here in the exam room going over some notes from today—to hurry to her, but I slipped and fell, too, hit my head on the corner of my own damn exam table. Not hard, but enough to cut it. Anyway, I gathered myself up and came out to find her and Mr. Vitner. I went to Lynny on the floor, but I should have gone to Vitner first. He was definitely bleeding badly. I couldn't help myself, though. I had to make sure she was okay."

"And I'm fine," Lynny said, her drawl stretching out the words as she put her hand over his.

We hadn't even noticed the pools and trail of blood outside until after we'd taken care of the Powders and did a cursory glance out the front door before shutting and locking it.

Inside, though, Vitner had left a red trail all the way through and to the back of the house. On his way, he'd grabbed some gauze and other supplies. Dr. Powder had tried to stop him, tried to tell him he would take care of him, but Vitner wouldn't listen.

"He just ran off with everything," Lynny said. "He didn't say a word."

"Doc, was he alone? Was there anyone else with him?" I asked.

"No one that we saw. We don't even know how he got wounded. If someone hurt him or if he did it to himself. He was bleeding from his side, that's it."

"I should go after him now," Tex said.

"It's too late," Lynny offered.

"I can follow the blood pretty easily."

Lynny eyed Tex's gun, now reholstered on his chest. "Young man, I don't know what's going on out there, but unless you really do feel prepared to use that, you should stay right where you are and let law enforcement officials take care of things."

I looked at Tex. He was prepared—but only if it was necessary.

"I'll try to call Gril again," I offered.

I made my way to the phone in the front room that also served as a reception area for patients. We'd done some cleanup, but there was still blood everywhere. The tangy metallic scent filled the small space. I unlocked and opened the front door for some air while I called Gril.

I stepped back outside, keeping close to the door but taking a better look around. I glanced out toward the woods, moving my gaze down the walkway. "Was he stabbed or shot right here?" I muttered quietly.

I squinted into the darkness, but without a better light, I couldn't tell how far the trail went, and I wasn't walking out there alone. I glanced down at the ground around me again. Tex, Vitner, and I had left plenty of footprints everywhere, but one pair seemed to be aimed in a different direction, away from the puddle, and headed around the side of the house.

The footprints looked exactly like mine, but bigger. I hadn't gone that way.

"Mill," I said.

I imagined what might have happened. Right here, on the stoop, Mill had somehow hurt Vitner, and then she ran off.

"Mill!" I called in the direction the prints had gone. "Mom!"

My voice fell flat quickly, muffled by the woods and the clouds above.

If she was out there, she wasn't answering.

"He's gone," I added loudly, hoping that might bring her out. "I'll take care of you. It'll be okay."

She didn't emerge. I sensed she wasn't there. I sensed that no one was there. Where had everyone gone?

I shut and locked the door again and went to the phone.

When Gril made it to the Powders', he wasn't particularly happy about anything we had found out, but he was grateful that the doctor and Lynny were okay.

Donner had come with him, but then gone with Tex back out into the woods to see if they could find Mill or Vitner or both. I was forbidden from joining them. Firmly.

Gril and I made sure Dr. Powder and Lynny would be comfortable for the rest of the night, and he took me back to the Benedict House.

"I should be out there helping look for her," I said to Gril, not hiding my resentment as he parked in front of the Benedict House.

The panic that had propelled me earlier was now a low buzz in my ears and chest. I was still sick to my stomach with worry, but this emotion was now mixed with the adrenaline buzz and a big wave of exhaustion.

"Beth," Gril said, "your mother has disappeared for stretches of time before, right?"

"Yes, but not in the wilds of Alaska."

Gril paused and scrubbed his hand over his scruffy chin. It was not a good night in Benedict, Alaska, and the police chief was feeling the brunt of it. "She's not going to change," he finally said.

"I know that. . . ."

"She is who she is, and you can neither save her nor

be responsible for her. She's a grown woman. You are her daughter, not her keeper. You can either let her drive you crazy or accept that she's . . . not like you. Her mistakes are hers. I do not want to be patronizing, but you have to let go at least that much."

I suddenly remembered a similar conversation I'd had with my grandfather. *"Mill is . . . just Mill,"* he'd said with *a shrug.*

Gril went on. "Of course you're worried, but you gotta know that if anyone will be okay, it's your mother, and your concern might only cloud your ability to somehow key in on where she might be."

"You want me to think clearly?"

"Kind of. I want you to take care of you. I want you to know that your mother has made her own bed, time and time again—and she's never really lain in it. She will someday, or . . ."

"She'll die trying."

"Well, that's a bit on the nose, but yeah. We'll search. You'll do your part. But do your best to keep your concern under control—because you are never, ever going to be able to *control* her. Try not to let other fears come into this. I know you've struggled, but you've also come so far. Your mother has always done what she deemed the right thing to do, even when the rest of the world might disagree with her definition of it."

"I'll try." I took a deep breath but didn't feel much better. "What can I do to help now?"

"Nothing. Stay out of my way. Well, if your mother comes back, tie her to something until I can take her in."

"Gril, you gotta realize that I don't know what she's up to," I said. "I don't know why she's here, but it's not just to see me."

"Explain," he said curtly.

"I don't know what set her off, caused her to run away. She was talking to Lucy, who told her that Claudia called me Elizabeth. She had only recently learned about the note with the address left on my desk. She didn't like that I hadn't told her, but I don't know if that's what bothered her the most. Orin found a lot of information about my dad, which doesn't seem important to any of this, but maybe it is. Someone else here knows who I am—someone left the note. Does she think that person is tied to Vitner? I don't know. I know she thinks Vitner killed Ned. I can't understand what she's putting together."

"Do you think she's taking it upon herself to bring Vitner to justice?" he said incredulously.

"I don't know, but it wouldn't surprise me, Gril. I'm sorry."

Gril nodded. "How in the world did she find you?"

"She knew I was in Alaska. She said she saw a copy of the *Petition* in Homer and knew I had written the copy."

"Really?"

"Yep."

"That doesn't ring true, Beth. There's not much in the paper but local events. There's no way to 'hear' your voice."

It had seemed farfetched when she'd first told me, but I'd shrugged it off, thinking that if anyone could do such a thing, Mill could.

"I just don't know," I finally said.

"Me neither, but thanks for the information. I need to get back to work. I'm going to run you inside, talk to Vi first."

Gril escorted me into the Benedict House, where Viola was waiting in the dining room. Benny, Claudia, and Lucy were all locked in their own rooms. Gril would head back out for a while, but he would be back and he and Viola would take turns keeping watch tonight.

Gril nodded at me. "Get some rest, Beth. You think you can?"

"I hope so."

He left the dining room, saying he'd return in a couple of hours.

"Want me to help you watch?" I asked Viola.

"No, but I want you to wear this to bed." Viola reached into her pocket and pulled out a bracelet, strung with small bells.

I slipped it on my wrist and jingled the bells. "They're pretty quiet."

"They are the best I could do for now. If you get out of bed, whoever is in here will hear you. I don't want you going anywhere. It'll work. For now."

I hugged Viola, which wasn't as poorly received as I might have predicted. Neither of us were touchy-feely, but she hugged me back. A little bit.

As I made my way to my room, my mind was tired and wired. My body was sluggish and electrified at the same time. I was trying to process Gril's advice, but it wasn't easy.

Exhaustion won, though, and I was able to sleep. However, even as I drifted off, I couldn't let go of a question. *Could my mother really have known my voice well enough to know I'd written the* Petition *she'd found?*

And if the answer was no, what did *that* mean?

Thirty

I woke up the next day not having any idea where I was, though once I put it all together, I knew I was where I was supposed to be. I was in Alaska, in my room at the Benedict House, despite the sense of discombobulation washing through me.

I glanced at the bracelet on my wrist—still there. For my peace of mind, I'd not only propped my desk chair under the doorknob but had also placed a shoe on the chair. It was still there.

I hadn't fallen out of bed, either.

Good news on all those fronts.

However, as far as I knew, my mother was still missing.

I got out of bed, splashed some water on my face, put on a cap, and made my way toward the dining room. No one was there, but Viola called from her office. "That you, Beth? I'm down here."

"Anything new?" I asked as I stood in her doorway.

"Not a lot. No sign of your mom or Vitner yet. Orin left a message last night, and he wants you to call him when he gets in today—a couple hours from now. You can use my phone."

"No, I'll go to the library. So, any leads on where Mill and Vitner *might* be?"

"Nothing, Beth. I'm sorry." Viola frowned. "Why don't

you stick around here, though. I think it would be better than heading out there for now."

I nodded, but my insides were dancing. My skin felt like it didn't fit. Now that I was fully awake, the anxiety was coming back full force. I wanted to say something to Viola that would help her understand, but I also didn't want to worry her any more than I had. As I was coming up with the right words, I put my hands into the pockets of my jeans. I felt something in the right one.

I pulled out the metal object and looked at it in my hand. "A bobby pin?"

"Looks like it," Viola said.

"Why would I have a bobby pin in my pocket?"

"I don't know, Beth, but isn't that what bobby pins do, disappear when you need them and show up again when you don't?"

"I don't own any," I said.

But I had. Back before the brain surgery and the hospital bathroom haircut, I did use bobby pins every now and then on my long brown locks. Now I barely even combed or brushed my stark white hair, more often opting to just throw on a cap of some sort, as I had done this morning.

I'd come to Alaska with very little and had purchased most everything else from the mercantile. I hadn't purchased bobby pins, but I'd seen some recently.

Where had that been?

Lucy's room.

Okay, so what?

"Beth?" Viola said.

"No," I said to myself as I looked at the pin in my hand. "It can't be that."

"Beth? What's up?"

I looked at Viola again. "Can I talk to Lucy?"

"Why? Because you think that's hers?"

"I don't know if it's hers or not, but somehow this got into my pocket. I picked some up from the floor in her room the other day. There's a chance I somehow kept it. We were talking. Maybe I just absent-mindedly . . ."

"Okay. How about I just give it to her later?" Viola extended her hand.

I shook my head. "I'd really like to talk to her and . . . Viola, could she have unlocked her door from the inside using one of these?"

Viola's eyebrows came together. Neither of us could know the ramifications of Lucy's escaping her room the times she'd been locked inside, but she had been in there the night Ned was killed. A bobby pin didn't a murder suspect make, but it required some exploration.

Viola moved past me and marched down the hallway. I followed right behind her.

Without knocking, Viola unlocked and pushed open the door. Lucy was fast asleep, her eyes popping open as we burst inside.

"God, what now?"

"This yours?" I asked as I extended the pin.

She looked at it. "What? How would I know? They all look alike to me."

Viola and I looked at the scrunchies and pins on the side table. The pins were exactly like the one in my hand, but that didn't mean much of anything. I hadn't counted them.

"Ugh," Lucy said as she lay back down and pulled the covers over her head. "Go away, you weirdos. Let me at least get some sleep. God!"

I looked at Viola.

"I'll close the door and lock it from the outside," Viola said to me. "You see if you can jimmy the lock."

"What?" Lucy threw the covers back and sat up again. "You're kidding me."

I nodded at Viola. She went through and then closed the door. I heard her lock the bolt in place.

I went to my knees and stuck the pin into the keyhole. The doors were from the same period my grandfather's house had been built, with keyholes one could peer through.

As I worked, I heard Lucy come up behind me, but I didn't look at her.

"You are the worst detectives ever," she said.

I continued to ignore her.

"You probably used the bobby pin to unlock your own door so you could get out and, what, steal some cheese?" she added.

"My door doesn't lock from the outside like yours does."

"Huh," she said. "Well then, I don't have a clue."

I heard the waver in her voice, but when I glanced up to catch the expression on her face, she was already heading back to bed. She plopped down on it and looked at me with impatience but no guilt, no fear of getting caught. Had she managed to normalize her features, or had I just imagined her sound like she'd been figured out?

I turned back to the keyhole. A few seconds later, I had the lock tripped and the door swung open. It was easy.

Viola came back inside and looked at Lucy. "Is that what you did?"

"It would never have even occurred to me!" Lucy pounded the bed with her hand. "Seriously, what is wrong with everyone around here? I'm the victim, remember." She pointed at the stitches on her lip.

Neither Viola nor I answered.

Finally Viola grabbed the other bobby pins from the nightstand and glared at Lucy. "Stay in here."

Lucy opened her mouth to offer what was probably another smart-alecky comment, but she saw the look on Viola's face. She closed her mouth and rolled her eyes only a little as she nodded once.

Viola locked the door again as we left.

"Do you think she escaped and maybe killed Ned?" I whispered, no matter that I'd almost convinced myself that Vitner had been the killer.

"I have no idea, Beth, but I *can* tell you that she asked me for the hair things the first night she was here—specifically for bobby pins—and I haven't seen her wear one once."

"That might not mean anything."

"It might not."

But it might mean something.

My wet boots. Viola being upstairs that night, working on the windows.

The blood on my doorknob.

I wasn't ready to bring that blood into the conversation, but I sure did wonder who'd put it there, and I hadn't imagined how wet and cold my boots had been. I knew I hadn't.

I also knew I couldn't have killed Ned. There was no way. I'm not a killer. I could maybe have killed my kidnapper, given the opportunity, but no one else.

I didn't think so, at least.

"Viola, I need to get out of here. I'm going to the *Petition*. I'll go see or call Orin from there," I said as we made it to the dining room.

"Want Benny to go with you?" Viola nodded toward the door I assumed Benny was still sleeping behind.

That sounded like a perfect idea, but I wouldn't take away Viola's help. "No. I'll be okay. I'll have phone coverage from there. Call me if you hear anything."

"Will do. Watch your ass, Beth."

"Oh, I will."

Thirty-one

I could have told Viola that one of the reasons I wanted to go to the *Petition* was because I thought that my mother might try to find me there. There would be fewer people watching that building than the downtown area. But my landlord probably already figured that out.

Even with everything else going on, all I really cared about was that my mother was okay. I hoped she hadn't hurt someone again, but I wanted her alive and in one piece, even if it meant handing that one piece over to Gril so Mill could answer for the crimes she'd committed.

It wouldn't be that easy, though. We all knew that.

There was no sign of her when I first arrived, checking all around the outside for more telltale boot prints or even blood. Neither were visible.

I pulled my key out but found that the door was already unlocked. Panic zipped through me as I pushed it open, hoping she was inside. She wasn't, and I remembered quickly that I'd been the one to leave the office unlocked two days earlier when Mill had run off, in case she'd come back on her own and needed shelter. I hadn't returned to relock it.

From the open doorway, I turned and looked out into the woods. The sun was up, even if I couldn't see it. It wasn't completely dark out there, but it wasn't light enough to erase shadows, either.

"Mill! It's just me here. Come on out!" I called.

There was no response, and once more I sensed she wasn't in hearing range.

Where had she gone?

I closed the door and turned the bolt. I cranked up the furnace and twisted the mini blinds over the one small window. I glanced out toward the library. There were no vehicles out front. It was too early for patrons, but sometimes not too early for Orin. I wondered where he was and why he wanted to talk to me.

I grabbed the burner phone and dialed the library's landline. It went to voice mail.

After leaving a message, I pondered who to call next, what to do. I looked out the window again. I didn't need to be concerned about Orin, but it was highly unusual that he wasn't there this early. Not unheard of, though. I was projecting danger, doing some disaster thinking, because of what he'd gone through a few months earlier.

Still, it might not hurt to run over there and make sure.

As I was gearing up again, I set my phone on the desk. It rang, dancing a short way before I could catch it in my anxious hands.

"Hello. Yes. Hello."

"Beth. Hey, it's Stellan," the police chief said from the other end of the line.

"Hey," I said, calming my voice to almost normal. I cleared my throat. "What's up?"

"I got a picture of Hugh Givens. Remember him?"

"Sure, the third man who sold drugs with my dad and Travis Walker." And the one I suspected was currently posing as a census man.

"Yes, ma'am. I thought I'd email it to you if you want."

"I do. Thanks."

"Anything else going on? Have you heard from your mother?"

"I haven't." I hoped something hadn't trickled down to the lower forty-eight about her presence in Benedict.

"That's good," he said. "Better that way."

"I cannot disagree." We both paused a moment. "Have *you* heard anything else?"

"Not a thing, Beth. I talked to Detective Majors yesterday, shared all of this with her. They thought they had a line on Walker, but it dried up."

"So they still have nothing?"

"As far as I can tell. And I'm still waiting to hear back about the tire tracks."

Mill's words rang through my head. *If you want a job done right, you've got to rightly do it yourself.*

I didn't much care about the tire tracks, but tears filled my eyes. I hoped I'd get to hear Mill mess up a few more clichés. I covered the speaker with my hand and took a deep breath, letting it out before I continued. "Well, I'm sure they'll find him."

"They will. We will." Stellan paused again. "You want to take a look at the picture while we're on the phone together?"

"Sure." I turned in my chair. I'd been in such a hurry to get out of the Benedict House that I'd left my laptop in my room. "Shoot, Stellan. My internet is out. Once it's up and running, I'll take a look. I'll let you know if he's familiar.

"I can text."

My burner phone couldn't download a picture. I'd tried. "It's okay. Email's good."

"Thanks, Beth."

"Thank you. I appreciate all you're doing for me."

"All right then. I'll talk to you later," Stellan said warily. He must have heard the hesitation in my voice.

I hung up before either of us could say more. I wanted my laptop. I'd cruise by the library and then head back downtown.

I wasn't on my A-game. I needed to get myself together. I'd never forgotten my laptop before.

I left the shed, but once again didn't lock the door.

There was no sign of distress at the library. I saw old tire tracks here and there in the snow, but nothing that sparked suspicion about anything going sideways either inside or near the building. I even looked in the windows, confirming that all was fine inside. It was scheduled to open in about an hour. I'd come back or keep an eye out for Orin from the *Petition*.

But I had to get my computer.

I wrote all my first drafts on my typewriter, but used my laptop for final copies as well as correspondence with the important people in my life—agent, editor, Dr. Genero, Detective Majors, Stellan, and Mill. Though my world had shrunk, I still felt disconnected from it when I didn't have access to my email.

Somewhat absent-mindedly, I steered the truck back toward the Benedict House. As I came to the spot where the rough path turns into paved road, my mantra, all but gone for at least a few days, came back full force.

You Rivers people never listen.

Suddenly, all my focus was once more on that single sentence.

There was no one around—not a vehicle, person, or wild animal in sight. I pulled the truck over and parked, closing my eyes and trying to push away all the other mental noise. I wanted to hear Travis Walker say those words, see his lips move in my mind's eye.

Now, I wanted to remember.

I needed to remember. I knew I could do it. I just needed to relax and focus. Not easy tasks, but I'd been working on them.

A few deep breaths later, I found a place in my mind where I could be both in that van and safe here in Alaska. It was a thin line between the two, but I'd worked hard to create that line and it was at least solid.

The sun was shining through the van's front window. Bright. And hot. Yes, so very hot and humid. There was no air-conditioning, and I hadn't stopped sweating since Travis had grabbed me on that humid summer day.

Music came from tinny speakers somewhere. Oldies. The only stations we ever listened to were talk radio and oldies music—stuff from the 1950s and 1960s. There was no FM radio in the van, no place for a CD or an old cassette or eight-track. Just an AM radio.

The song was something like "Big Girls Don't Cry"— "cry-yi-yi," I remembered the male falsetto coming through the speakers, Travis singing along, pretending to serenade me with a side-eye as he held an invisible microphone.

He turned off the radio. "You cry, don't you, Elizabeth Fairchild?"

I had cried. I'd cried a lot since he'd grabbed me three days earlier. I had to take a moment to think about that—had I really been in this van for three days? Tied up, gagged, exposed to as many indignities as possible.

I wouldn't look directly at him anymore, but I could see him in my peripheral vision. He was trying to get my attention, induce me to look over. The last time I'd fallen for his verbal jabbing, he'd cackled and said, "Made you look, made you look."

No more. I was done. I just wanted to hurry up and die now. If he wasn't going to kill me, I would look for the first opportunity to kill myself, or both of us, which would be ideal, of course.

Something was happening up ahead with the traffic. We were on a two-lane highway and it seemed the cars were slowing. Travis was too busy goading me to immediately notice. I didn't want anyone else to get hurt, but an accident might do me the favor I'd been wishing for. I remained as stoic as I could.

"Mother!" Travis suddenly yelled as he stomped hard on the brake, the van rocking as it slowed.

He'd saved us from hitting a truck. My hopes frayed again as we continued down the highway slowly, the traffic never coming to a complete stop.

"You know, you are mine, all mine," Travis said as we tooled along. "You will be mine forever and ever. Do you hear me? Are you listening to me?"

I did hear him and wanted to throw up, but I'd done that before, too, and all it did was make everything even more unbearable. I forced myself to keep the acid in my stomach, because that's all that was left in there.

"Mine, all mi-yi-yine, mine, mine, mine," he sang.

And I snapped. At this moment, in Alaska, as I closed my eyes inside my truck sitting at probably one of the quietest intersections in the world, I remembered the sensation.

Something surged through me. If I believed in a higher being, I'd have to say that's what it was, but since I didn't, I had to chalk it up to something deep in my gut that awakened.

A fury fueled by fear and hatred twisted like a cyclone inside me. I felt it spin in my chest and then reach out to the rest of me, to the tips of my fingers and toes. I'd never felt anything like it, such strength, such power.

Travis continued to sing as I sat forward some and then rocked back, bringing my legs up. I was tied at the ankles and secured around my middle and the entire seat, but I could still move, I could still swing around. Why I hadn't done it before, I wasn't sure, but now it seemed like the thing to do. The only thing to do.

I angled my legs just right so that I could rabbit-kick Travis in the side. I'd moved so quickly that he hadn't processed what I was doing, and now I remembered the surprise on his face. In the midst of the recollection I laughed aloud at the idea that I'd gotten some sort of drop on him. Then I went back to the memory.

The van swerved and skidded along the road before it flew off and over the berm, somehow landing upright.

In the flight over the side, I turned myself the other way. As Travis was yelling when we stopped, I kicked the door, springing it wide open. He had me tied with some fabric around the seat, but it was no match for the tornado of power in me. I yanked once, feeling the breath come out of me, but then I yanked again, with enough strength to cut myself in half.

Instead, I sprang free of the fabric. I propelled myself out of that van, landing sideways on the downhill slope of the berm. I hit my head hard as I rolled but kept moving farther away from the van.

When I stopped rolling, I managed a look up. Other cars were stopping, people rushing out of them to come to my aid.

Travis was leaning out the passenger side. "You are mine, Beth, but you *Rivers* people never listen, do you?"

And then he was gone. He shut the door I'd kicked open and climbed back over to the driver's seat, and somehow got the engine restarted. Travis got the hell out of there right before my world went black.

I opened my eyes in the here and now again. Tears were streaming down my face. I'd done it. I'd gotten away from him. Me, on my own. I knew I'd escaped, but until that moment I hadn't remembered the details—I'd done what I needed to do. The sense of freedom and pride that came with that memory was so gigantic I wasn't sure it could be contained even in Alaska.

I realized something else, too. He'd said those parting words to tell me two things: he knew my family, and he knew who I was.

Again, this was not exactly news now, but somehow it took away the mantra's power. I understood it. Not only that, but I realized that Travis had spoken those words to me because I'd fought back.

And I'd won.

Thirty-two

sniffed and wiped away the tears with the backs of my gloved hands. Winning was good.

No traffic came from any direction. I still wanted my laptop, so I shifted to drive, pulled back on the road, and let my tires get a good grip before pushing down hard on the accelerator.

Just as I was revving to a reasonable speed, a team of dogs leading a sled came from a break in the woods up ahead. The dogs pulled out and onto the main road. This was the first time I'd really seen anything like it, during the daytime at least, and on a paved road. It was a spectacular sight—the primitiveness of the ride mixed with the power of the dogs. I felt like it was something everyone should get to see.

"Elijah," I said aloud.

I was far enough away that I wasn't any threat to him or the dogs, but now I wanted to talk to him. I sped up a little and then—even though it felt rude—I honked. Just a tap on the horn.

The driver was dressed in thick winter gear, but I could see him turn his head slightly before he steered the dogs to the side of the road. I pulled next to him and waved, hopefully telling him I was friendly.

It's not easy coming to a complete stop in these road conditions, either in a truck or with a team of dogs, but we both managed it.

I hopped out of the vehicle and hurried around to him. "Eli . . ."

"Can I help you?" the man asked. Though he was fully covered, including goggles over his eyes, I knew immediately that he wasn't who I thought he was. This man was thinner, younger probably.

"Oh. I'm so sorry. I thought you were Elijah Wyatt. I wanted to talk to him."

Understanding relaxed the irritated set of the man's shoulders. "Someone need a tow?"

I just went with it and nodded. "How can I get ahold of him?"

"Everyone just calls Tochco's." He hesitated. "Are you the new girl with the scar?"

"I've been here a while, but yep, that's me," I said with a shrug.

"I'm Grant. Good to meet you." He looked down the road. "If you can't reach Elijah, it means he's probably out working the dogs. We sometimes travel the same routes, but I haven't seen him today. There's a track of sorts directly east of the airport. He might be there. If you can get a signal, call the airport, ask if the Harvingtons have seen him." He looked up at the clouds. "I heard they might be flying today, but who knows."

I was always amazed by how quickly news spread in a place with little phone and internet access. Did everyone already know that travel was potentially possible today? Maybe important things just found their own legs.

"Thanks. I'm really sorry to bother you," I said. I was cringing inwardly at myself. I'd just pulled over a dogsled. I looked at the dogs, all sitting patiently as they panted. There were a few more purebred huskies in this group than in Elijah's. "Your dogs are beautiful."

"Thank you."

"Elijah's dogs are wonderful, too, but they aren't quite so . . . husky. Except for Gus, I suppose."

"Except for Gus, yes." Grant laughed. "Elijah's not from around here. I tease him all the time that he put together Alaska's only Missouri hillbilly team."

"What?" I said as I felt my blood both curdle and freeze.

"He's from some small town in Missouri. It's okay, he makes fun of it himself."

"Right. Do you know what town?"

Grant shook his head. "If he told me, I don't remember."

"How long has he been here in Benedict?" I asked, somehow managing to keep my voice fairly even.

"Maybe fifteen years, I think." Grant looked at me expectantly.

He wanted to go, but he didn't want to be rude. I was so stunned that I had to force myself to speak polite words. "Thanks, Grant. Nice to meet you and apologies for stopping you."

"It's okay. If this is your first winter, you'll get used to us. There are quite a few teams around. Sometimes it's the only way to get anywhere this time of year."

"Good to know. Thanks." I nodded and then watched as he restarted the dogs. I waved as they rode away, though Grant didn't have a rearview mirror and couldn't have seen me.

I needed a few moments to talk myself down from whatever this was. Elijah's being from Missouri didn't necessarily mean anything. I was looking and listening too hard for clues or answers. There were probably other people in Benedict who'd come from small Missouri towns. The fact that I hadn't met them yet didn't matter.

My concern about my mother poked away this new discovery, though. Did everything, whatever all this was, mean something together? I looked around. Once the team was out of sight, I was alone again.

I put my hands up around my mouth. "Mill!" I turned and yelled the other direction, too.

Not surprisingly, there was no answer. I still wanted that damn laptop, but I was going to make a detour first. I steered the truck to the home behind Toscho's.

The small parking lot in front of the store was overflowing, trucks and other vehicles parked willy-nilly around the building. It wasn't easy to get back to Elijah's house and barn, but I managed.

His tow truck was there—something Mill and I hadn't seen when we'd been spying earlier.

"Elijah," I said as I knocked on his front door.

I wasn't afraid of him, but with my new knowledge I thought I should be careful, be aware. There were so many vehicles around that if I screamed, someone would probably hear.

I looked in a window to the side of the front door, seeing only a small but comfortable living room with a couch, a chair, a coffee table, and some end tables with lamps. Books were everywhere, which, as such a sight always did, made me curious about what he liked to read.

I hoped I wasn't one of his favorites.

I made my way into the barn. The dogs were there—except for Gus, I realized as I greeted each animal, though much more quickly than the first time. They were happy for the attention but calmed when I walked back to the desk.

I put my hands on my hips and bit my bottom lip. Time for more snooping. I wished Mill and I had done more earlier. Mom was usually right about this stuff.

Instead of just a cursory glance over the items on the desk, I dove deep, opening drawers and rifling through files. I found lots of invoices for the tow-truck business, as well as files for the dogs, each labeled with a dog's name and a picture. I recognized some of the animals but figured that others had passed on.

It wasn't until I reached to the back of one of the drawers that I found anything helpful. A piece of paper was stuck to the roof of the drawer.

It was a photo of Claudia and Elijah at the bar, smiling as their heads touched. I tried not to be too judgmental, but Elijah looked much more like her father than her close friend. The picture was in color, but just printed on a regular piece of paper. Written underneath the photo were the words *me and my boo*.

My breath rushed out of my lungs as I recognized the writing. It was the exact same writing used on the note with Travis Walker's address, the note that had been left on my desk next to Tex's.

Until that moment, I didn't realize how distinctively angled the letters were, and the way all the *a*'s ended with curlicues. It was a perfect match.

Claudia seemed more likely to use the word *boo,* but it could have been Elijah. I looked through the paperwork on top of and inside his desk again. I saw some examples of his handwriting, but so many of his papers had been filled out using a computer. As certain as I was that the handwriting on the two notes was the same, I couldn't know exactly who'd written them, Claudia or Elijah.

My conversation with Grant echoed in the back of my mind. A small Missouri town. The Missouri hillbilly team . . .

Did Elijah know who I was? And if he did, why would he want to taunt me?

I needed to get out of there. I put the picture back and then moved around the desk. I said a goodbye to the dogs as I hurried to the door. I fully expected to come upon Elijah as I opened it, but I was pleasantly surprised. No one was there to greet or accost me.

I got back into my truck and finally made my way back to the Benedict House.

Thirty-three

Whoever it is, we're in the dining room. Come eat," Viola called.

I hadn't gathered my backpack yet, but I slipped out of my boots and joined Viola, Claudia, Benny, and Lucy in the dining room, working very hard to normalize my expression. I wasn't ready to tell anyone but Gril or my mother what I now knew—or suspected, at least.

"Oh, it's you," Viola said. "Well. Always good to see you, Beth, but I was hoping for Gril or someone who could give us an update."

"I hear you. Nothing yet?" I asked as I sat down across from Claudia, who sent me a cursory glance before moving her focus back to the food on her plate. I seethed, but hoped I hid it well. For now.

"Not one stinkin' word." Benny handed me a plate.

I took the plate and filled it. I wouldn't be able to eat one thing, which was a first since my escape to Alaska. My appetite had suddenly disappeared.

"I did run into a dogsled and a musher," I said, keeping Claudia in the corner of my vision.

"Who?" Viola asked.

"A guy named Grant," I said.

Claudia deflated.

"A good guy. Did you ask him about Elijah?" Viola asked.

Claudia watched me again.

"He hadn't seen Elijah." I came close to telling them about his idea of checking by the airport, but I didn't want to risk sharing something I shouldn't quite yet.

If Elijah was near the airport and if he carried a cell phone, he might have a signal. If I mentioned his potential where-abouts to Claudia, she might try to call and tip him off. Even if I couldn't understand exactly what he was hiding from, I decided it was just more information I should save for Gril.

"Claudia, where would Elijah go?" Benny asked.

"Why are you asking her?" Lucy said, though by the tone of her voice, it was a rhetorical question.

I looked at Lucy, still not seeing one bobby pin in her hair.

"Because your sister-in-law was having an affair with our tow-truck driver," Benny said.

I thought Viola might admonish her sister, but she didn't even send Benny a sideways glance. Instead, her attention was also on Lucy.

"Oh, that's no surprise," Lucy said with a mouth-filled chuckle. "She'd sleep with anything that swung a di—"

"Lucy, not at the table," Viola said.

Another rule I hadn't known.

"Well, she would," Lucy said. She looked at Claudia. "You would."

"Shut up," Claudia said. "You knew what Ned was like. You grew up with him."

It didn't hit me right away, but as I absent-mindedly chewed a bite of tasteless food, a detail from the conversation I'd had with Lucy came back to me, one that suddenly seemed pertinent.

"Claudia, weren't Ned and Lucy separated when they were kids? I mean, sent to different foster homes?"

"Foster homes?" Claudia said.

"Oh, enough of this. I'm going back to my room. I may starve, but at least I don't have to take this sort of abuse." Lucy stood and threw her paper napkin down on her plate.

"Sit down," Viola told her. She looked at Claudia. "Answer Beth's question."

"There was no foster home. They grew up together. Their parents were just as bad as Lucy. Thieves. Ned left home about five years ago. We got married and came out here about three years ago."

Lucy tsked, sat back in her chair, and crossed her arms in front of herself. She looked at Viola. "So?"

Viola looked at me.

"You told me you went to different foster homes as children, that you were separated," I said.

"Again, so? What business is it of yours? I lied, but why would I owe you the truth anyway?"

"You wouldn't," I answered honestly.

"But you would owe it to me," Viola said.

"You didn't ask me those questions." She waved her hand toward me. "She was worried about my past. I told her what she wanted to hear—got her sympathy and all. I didn't tell her the truth, but maybe I should have. She'd eat up the stories about what our parents did to us, what Ned did to me. It wasn't pretty, let me tell you. None of it was. But blondie here likes drama, scary sad stories. I know her type, don't I, Elizabeth?"

Claudia flinched.

Before I could stop anyone, Lucy continued, "Elizabeth Fairchild."

"Who is that?" Viola asked.

"A writer," Claudia said, her attention back on her food. "A famous writer who was attacked down in St. Louis."

I had only a couple bites of food in my stomach, but I thought I might throw up at the table.

Everyone was silent as each person fell into their own thoughts. I was sure I could read them all, and they all had something to do with suddenly realizing I was that famous writer.

Fortunately, like Mill had said, I had some good people on my team.

"Shut up, Claudia, Lucy. Shut up and just eat," Viola said.

I wanted to confront Claudia, ask her so many things, but I didn't trust myself to speak. Not quite yet. She must have told Lucy who I was, or Lucy figured it out on her own, which didn't strike me as the way it had gone down.

Benny sent me a wary smile as Lucy rolled her eyes at me. Viola put her hand on my shoulder and patted it twice. Claudia stared down at her food.

The front door opened again and Gril called out, "Vi?"

"Dining room."

Gril came through. "Ferry's running. Let's go, Lucy. Now."

"What?" Lucy said, tears suddenly filling her eyes.

"I'm getting you on that ferry and out of here. Claudia, do you want to stay or go?"

"I don't have anywhere to go in Juneau. I'll stay."

"Suit yourself."

I wanted to tell Gril to stop, just wait, that I was coming to some conclusions, but they were far too fuzzy to nail down. It wasn't my job to come to conclusions anyway. And what did it matter that people had figured out who I was? It was bound to happen.

"I don't want to go," Lucy said. "Please let me stay here."

"No," Gril said. "Now. Come on, let's go."

"Have you found anyone?" Viola asked Gril.

"Not yet, but we will. One problem at a time. Now, Lucy."

"Can I get my stuff?" she asked woefully.

"Hurry up," Gril said. "Go with her, Benny."

Benny stood and followed as Lucy pouted her way out of the dining room. Her incarceration in Benedict was pretty cushy, comparatively.

The phone in Viola's office jangled. She hurried out of the dining room to answer it.

"Gril, it's for you," she called a moment later.

I followed Gril to Viola's office. If he noticed me behind him, he didn't say anything.

"Yeah," he said as he took the handset. "Shit. All right, well, if we have a window to fly, call the Harvingtons. I'll get her to the airport. Tell them we'll pay for a hotel if they can't get back." He hung up and looked at Viola. "Ferry's not going back, after all. Weather is on its way. But flights are good for two to three hours. I'll get her on the plane."

Viola nodded.

We heard the front door slam again.

"In my office," Viola called.

No one called back.

"Who's there?" Viola stepped around me and out into the hallway. She looked both directions and then back at Gril. "Lucy's door is open. Benny?"

There was no answer, but as we approached Lucy's closed door, I could hear muffled sounds.

We barreled through the door, now hearing Benny knocking and yelling from behind the bathroom door, where a chair under the knob had secured it shut.

Viola got the chair moved and the door open.

"She caught me off guard," Benny said. "She shoved me in here. I have my gun, but I didn't want to shoot. Did you catch her?"

"Jesus," Gril said as he put his hand on his holstered gun and followed Viola out of Lucy's room.

"You okay?" I asked Benny.

"Fine. Did she get away?"

Benny was fine, not even a scratch on her from what I could see.

"I'll be back," I said as I hurried to see what was happening.

By the front door, I noticed that my boots were gone again.

"She has my boots," I said, but Viola and Gril had already disappeared out the front door.

I was sock-footed but went outside, too. Viola was searching down the boardwalk as Gril ran across the main road, toward where I assumed Ned and Claudia's house was located.

I had another idea for where to look, but I didn't want to interrupt their searches—I could be very wrong.

And I had to find some boots to get me there first.

Thirty-four

There was no doubt in my mind that Lucy would say she'd rather die than go back to Juneau, but she truly didn't want to die, and she couldn't win a fight with weather exposure.

She wouldn't be able to survive for long. No one could if they weren't prepared. My boots weren't enough to save her.

I found some other footwear in my room, donned my winter gear again, and headed back toward the front door—Benny and Claudia were there and told me not to go, but at least Benny approved of my preparation.

"Tell Viola and Gril I'm going to the woods behind the Benedict House."

"I will," Benny said. "Don't go far. Come back quickly if you can."

"Don't confront her," Claudia said. "She's not . . . nice."

"If I see her, I'll try to talk her into coming back," I said.

We all knew that this probably wouldn't work, but it was worth a try, I supposed. My real hope was that if I found her, I could stall her long enough for Gril or Viola to help. If they didn't find her, I hoped Benny would send them to follow me.

Claudia nodded uncertainly.

I couldn't help myself. "You do know who I am, don't you?"

She looked at me a long moment before she nodded. "Yes. I mean, not really, but I know your name and . . . I told Lucy too, the first night she was here. I was just making conversation with her. Ned never knew."

"But Elijah knows who I am?" I said.

"He's the one who told me about you. He knows what you went through," she said.

"He had you write the note?"

Her eyes filled with tears. "No. I got mad at him for something and I was trying to find a way to get back at him. He'd asked me to keep it a secret. But I wanted to do something that would make him just as mad, so I wrote the note, not really thinking about the fact that it was your secret, not his. He'd told me that guy's name, the one who took you. I made up the address and put it on your desk, then told him I'd done it, just to get a rise out of him. I thought he'd go talk to you, be embarrassed or something, but he wasn't. He just told me that what I'd done probably scared you and I was the one who should apologize. But I never did, of course. I was just using you to get at him, but he wanted to keep your secret. I'm so sorry."

"How did you get into the shed?"

Claudia glanced at Benny, who looked sterner than I could ever have imagined. "I just slipped a credit card down in between the door and the lock. It's pretty easy."

I'd written such a thing in one of my books, but I couldn't remember which one. That old method of breaking and entering hadn't even occurred to me, but she was right—with the type of lock that was on the shed, it would have been a pretty easy thing to do.

"It worked?"

"I got right in."

"No, I mean, did it bother Elijah?"

"He broke up with me for a while. I'm . . . sorry. It was mean, but I didn't think about you at the time. I just wanted to get at him. It was just a stupid note."

"Why?" Benny asked. "Why were you so mad?"

"He wouldn't let me divorce Ned and move in with him. He said he loved me, but he didn't want me to leave Ned."

"Why not?" Benny asked. "I mean, did he not want you to leave Ned, or did he just not want to marry you?"

Claudia flinched. "I don't really know."

Benny looked at me.

"Would he have thought it better to kill Ned?" I asked. "Or could he have been pushed to do it?"

"If he killed Ned, he didn't tell me he was going to do it," Claudia whined.

I wanted to punch her in the face and at the same time to let her know that her apology to me was the most grown-up thing I'd heard from her so far.

"Is Elijah dangerous?" I asked.

"He's never been that way to me," Claudia said. "But I guess I don't know."

"Where in Missouri is he from?"

"Don't know. He might have told me once, but he never wants to talk about his time before Benedict."

"You wrote a town's name on the address. Why did you choose that town?"

She fell into thought. "I can't think of any other reason than Elijah mentioned it. I don't know anything about Missouri."

"You went out for a smoke the night Ned was killed," I said. "Did you see anyone else outside? Were you meeting Elijah?"

She shook her head. "I wasn't meeting Elijah, I swear, but I did see Donner and Gril. They were coming back from the direction of our house. I don't know why or what they were doing. I didn't see Ned's body out there, but it was dark over by Ben."

"Did Donner and Gril see you?"

"I don't think so. No."

"Did you overhear them saying anything?"

"Nothing."

"You didn't see Lucy outside?" I interjected quickly. I didn't want her to think about answering.

"No, not at all," Claudia said, surprised, but not as if she were lying.

"I'm heading out back to see if I can find Lucy. Will she hurt me?"

Claudia shook her head. "I have no idea. They weren't treated well as children. They both . . . lots of baggage there. I just don't know."

"Did you ever witness her being violent?" I asked.

"No, but she wasn't with us for long."

"Are you sure you don't want me to go with you?" Benny said.

I wasn't willing to let Benny leave Claudia alone.

"I'll be fine, and I won't be long." A thought popped into my head, though, and I made my way around them and through the dining room and into the kitchen. I pulled the handle on the knife drawer—it was unlocked.

"What?" Benny said.

I studied the inside of the drawer. "I'm pretty sure one of the big knives is missing." I looked at Benny and Claudia.

I wished I'd remembered to try the drawer again earlier, but I hadn't. And I doubted Viola even knew what knives she had. I spent more time in her kitchen than she did.

"I don't have it!" Claudia said as Benny and I turned our gazes to her.

"Might want to search Lucy's room," I said.

"Will do," Benny said.

I left them in the kitchen and hurried outside. There wasn't a soul to be seen outside the front doors. I saw parked trucks and other vehicles, even a snowmobile, but all drivers were inside the businesses as I made my way around the side and through the slot that would take me behind the Benedict House.

I spotted my boot prints immediately. New prints, not the old ones. Lucy had unquestionably run into these woods. I wished I'd been quick enough to let Viola and Gril know.

"Lucy!" I yelled as I followed her tracks.

It was as light as it was going to get for the day, which meant mostly soupy darkness all around.

"Lucy!"

No response, but I thought I heard something. I listened hard. As I'd learned since moving to Benedict, real quiet wasn't as silent as I'd once thought. Snowflakes made noise. The wind was always saying something, the trees creaking. I heard all those things now, along with my sped-up heart-beat, pounding away in my chest.

But there was also something else. Barking.

It was either far off or the forest was muting it some. The noise could be coming from the sledding path on the other side of the trees.

It wasn't a distressed bark, but it certainly seemed to be calling out for attention. I set off through the forest, my focus only on making it through to the other side.

I was relieved when I did.

"Gus!" I yelled, simply because it was currently the only dog's name I could remember.

Another bark sounded from somewhere down the track.

"Gus!" I set off in a run.

Out of the gloom, the dog's figure emerged. My first thought was that I was glad he seemed to be okay.

I fell to my knees as we met. In his exuberance, he would probably have knocked me over otherwise.

"Hey, boy." I petted him, inspected him the best I could. He was just fine. But his excited greeting transformed into a whine as he turned, as if he wanted me to follow him.

I'd been around intelligent animals before. I'd experienced the love between animals and their humans, but this was the first time I felt like an animal and I were truly communicating—at least anything other than those greetings.

I stood and told him to lead the way.

We ran only a short distance, coming upon a figure in the snow. It was a man, facedown, a pool of blood forming around his middle. There was no sled. There were no other dogs anywhere.

I knelt by the body, and without thinking I might hurt him, heaved him over onto his back.

Doug Vitner, the census man. I suspected he was dead, maybe for a while now. I'd glommed onto the idea that he was also Hugh Givens, but now I might never know.

Then he moaned.

"Hey." I shook his arm. "Wake up."

He moaned again but didn't open his eyes.

"Wake. Up." I pinched the skin on his exposed wrist.

His eyes fluttered open. "Who's there?"

"Beth. Wake up. Can you?"

"I'm not sure. Who's Beth?" he asked, still groggy.

"Doesn't matter. I need to get you to some shelter. I have no one else here. Can you help me help you?"

"What? Sure." He turned his head to the side and seemed to fall asleep again.

I looked around. I looked at Gus, who was sitting patiently next to Vitner's head.

I glanced all around the woods. "Mill! Are you there?"

No answer.

"I have to go back and get help. You want to come with me or stay?" I said to the dog.

I guessed the only word he really heard was *stay*. He remained sitting.

Why was Gus here? Where were Elijah and the other dogs? Was my mother with them? I didn't like the man on the ground in front of me, but I couldn't leave him out here to die. Apparently Gus couldn't, either.

A figure appeared from behind a nearby tree. "I'll help you get him back if you just let me go again."

I jumped but only a little. "Lucy, what's going on?"

"I don't want to go back to Juneau."

"I hear you, but we've got to get him some help. Have . . . have you seen my mother?"

"No. Do you want me to help you get him at least closer to the Benedict House? Then just let me go again."

I nodded. "Sure. Yes, but . . . why would you care about him?"

She shrugged. "He cared enough to check on me in the shed. I really do think that Ned's behavior made him worried about someone being held against their will. He cared enough to check and then leave me alone, keep me a secret."

I didn't believe her. I suspected she just didn't know where to go from here, but she knew for certain which way the ferry was docked. She needed to walk through downtown to get there. She probably thought I'd assist with that escape.

"All right. Help me." I'd take her help, but I wouldn't let her get away again.

He wasn't dead, but he was as good as dead weight. Someone had wrapped his wound, so it wasn't bleeding profusely, and his belly had been on the cold snow which might have also helped slow the flow of blood. I wondered if he'd done it himself and why he didn't just wait at the doctor's house. His behavior was wrong, that much I knew. I wanted answers, though, so I really hoped he lived long enough to give them to me.

Gus followed as Lucy and I managed to each get one of Vitner's arms around our shoulders. We dragged him more than anything else. Getting him through the trees was the worst of it. I was exhausted by the time we made it to the clearing.

Lucy released herself from the mix. I stumbled as Vitner and I both went down.

"I'm outta here," Lucy said.

I was incredibly tired, and I didn't think I could give chase until I rested for a few minutes. But I couldn't let her go.

"Lucy, please," I said as I breathed heavily, "just stay. You'll die out there. I'll tell Gril you helped. He'll take that into consideration."

She believed me for an instant—either that or she needed a minute to recover, too. But ultimately she just wanted to run.

"Later." She set off to make her way around the downtown buildings.

I had to make a choice. I needed to get Vitner inside or get Lucy first. I didn't have time to debate which was more important, but while she was still back here, trudging through the snow, Lucy would be moving slowly. I could grab her. I lifted myself up off the ground and followed. Gus was right there with me.

Lucy looked back and saw us. She tried to speed up, but it wasn't easy. I pushed myself and closed the gap between us.

"Come on, Lucy," I said when Gus and I were almost there. I hoped she didn't have a weapon, but since she wasn't wearing a coat, there was no obvious place to hide one.

"I'm not going to jail."

"I will work on it," I said as I reached for her arm.

She pulled it away just in time.

"Help me, Gus," I said, but he didn't seem to understand. I cut a path to Lucy's left, thinking I could intercept her better. We were almost around the buildings, to the spot where Claudia had taken a smoke break. Lucy tried to turn the other way but slipped. Tex had said I needed better boots if I was going to spend too much time out here. If they'd been better, she might not have missed a beat or two.

With a last push, I made it almost to her. I reached for her and missed again—but a second later, she and I were a tumble of bodies, with a dog on top. Gus had come up from behind her and jumped, pushing her into me.

"Good boy," I said as I tried to get purchase.

"Get off me, dog!" Lucy screamed. "I will kill this animal."

Those words, more than anything else, sent a wave of anger through me. "You piece of shit!" I yelled as I rolled and got myself on top of her. I had a small rope in my pocket, because I had been working on being more prepared. I had her arms tied behind her back and then around a tree only a few seconds later.

Then I got in her face. "You don't get to hurt an animal. Ever."

"I can do whatever I want," she spat back.

"Yeah, we'll see about that."

Taking Gus with me, and after making sure Vitner was still alive, I ran back inside and gathered some help.

Thirty-five

Waiting for Vitner to wake up made time do funny things. We all thought he must have some answers, at least those Lucy didn't want to share—and it was clear she truly didn't know all that needed to be illuminated. But until he was hydrated and warmed up, we weren't going to understand what he had been through or, hopefully, find out where Elijah and my mother might have gone.

As I sat in the dining room, a mug of coffee in front of me, every fifteen minutes that passed felt like an hour. I wanted to be back out there, searching, but it was impossible to know where to begin.

Tex had gone back to Brayn, but everyone else was at the Benedict House. Even Dr. Powder had been gathered to care for the man who'd so surprised him and his wife. Gril, Donner, Viola, Benny, Claudia, and Lucy—who was handcuffed to the front counter—were all in the building. The plans were to fly Lucy back to Juneau, but not for another hour. There was no reason to let her out of Gril's sight, and he didn't want to hang out at the airport while the rest of us waited for Vitner to become coherent.

Gus wouldn't leave my side—or at least the spot next to

my feet. I wondered if I'd ever be able to give him back to Elijah. I was really glad he was there.

My mind was racing, a million miles an hour in every direction, but more than anything I wanted to find my mom.

Viola, Benny, and Claudia were in the dining room with me. Gril and Donner were in another room with Dr. Powder and Vitner, who might be going to Juneau, too. Dr. Powder wanted to be certain he could make the short trip—depending on his condition, it might be better for him to remain on a bed in the Benedict House.

Dr. Powder had arrived with four bags of blood and the equipment needed to transfuse it into Vitner. I was surprised by the blood, wondered about any sort of expiration date, but no one else seemed to be concerned, and it was pretty clear that Vitner needed blood, so that's what he got. He'd been stabbed in the side, by a knife that must have had a two-inch blade.

The injury that had killed Ned was also from a knife, but if Dr. Powder had determined the size of that blade and whether it was the same one used on Vitner, he wasn't saying yet.

I took Viola to the knife drawer and asked her if she thought one was missing, but as I'd suspected earlier, she couldn't be sure. To be fair, there were a lot of knives in the drawer and Viola never did much cooking. Benny had searched Lucy's room, and no knife had been found.

"Viola, may I use the phone in your office?" I asked.

"Of course. You don't need to ask me, Beth. Use it whenever you want."

I nodded and stood. "Thanks."

We had some conversations ahead of us, but the least of everyone's concerns was what my name really was or where I'd actually come from. My problems weren't anyone's priority at the moment, even my own.

However, I couldn't help but wonder about . . . well, so many things.

With Gus at my heel, I made my way to the office and dialed the library's number.

"Benedict Library," Orin said, as he always did when he answered.

"It's Beth," I said.

"Hey! I've been trying to reach you."

"I know. I stopped by earlier, but you weren't there yet."

"Had some other stuff to get done. Are you okay? You sound funny."

"There is a lot going on and I would love to spill everything, but may I just promise to tell you later and let you tell me why you were trying to reach me?"

He hesitated. I didn't blame him. I'd want to know what was going on, too. But he finally said, "Sure. I have a picture of Hugh Givens. It's old, but my contact in Rocky Point sent it up. It was all she could find."

It wasn't that I'd forgotten about the picture from Stellan, but it had fallen onto a back burner. Now I would have two pictures of Hugh Givens. Would I recognize him? "Does he look like anyone we know?"

"That's the thing, I don't know. I thought so for a second, but it's hard to be certain. It's from a long time ago, and he's wearing a cap and sunglasses. The woman in Mexico said Givens wasn't currently around, but this picture is from about five years ago. It's not distinct, but it's the best we've got for the moment. You want me to just email it to you or do you want to come by?"

"Could you email it, please?" Vitner could have been in Mexico five years ago. He could have been anywhere. I would try to find that pocket of service in my room.

"I left a message for Gril. I want him to see it, too."

"Gril's here. If I can access it, I'll show him."

"That works. Should I just come over to the Benedict House?" Orin asked.

"There are lots of people here, but come over if you want."

He paused. "I'll stay out of the way. Okay, I just emailed the picture."

"I'll have to hang up and go to my room, see if I have a strong enough signal. Thank you, Orin."

"You're welcome. Let me know what's happening when you can."

"I will."

"How's your mom doing?"

I sighed. "She's not here. We don't know where she is."

"Oh? I do. At least I knew where she was an hour ago. I saw her going into the *Petition* shed."

I'd been sitting on the edge of the desk. I stood up so quickly that Gus started. "Really?"

"Really. You want me to go over there and get her?"

"No, Orin. Listen to me. Don't go over there. She's . . . dangerous. I mean, she's great and wonderful, but also dangerous. Promise me you'll stay away from that shed."

"Beth, I know how to handle myself. I really do."

"I know, but I'm going to have to be the one to talk her down. Let me do this. Please."

Another pause before he said, "Sure. I understand."

I hung up the phone. What was I going to do? If she was still at the *Petition,* she would only want me there. But would she really hurt someone?

For all I knew, she was the one who'd stabbed Vitner, and everyone knew she was capable of just about anything. I needed to talk to her, and I had some emails I needed to open.

Gus and I walked past the room with Vitner and then past the dining room. Lucy glared at me as we walked by her as well. It would be difficult to leave the building without everyone knowing.

I closed my door when Gus and I were inside my room and moved to the window, where I opened the laptop and held it up, hoping for a signal. There was nothing.

Thus I was particularly startled when my cell phone buzzed with a text notification.

I grabbed it from my pocket and flipped it open. One new message. It said, "I'm at your place."

I didn't know the number, but I had no doubt that it was Mill. I punched in a message and hit send. Chances were fifty-fifty it would get to her. *On my way.*

I hoped for another notification but nothing came immediately. I closed the phone and put on my winter gear again. I put my laptop in my bag and swung it over my shoulder.

"You'll need to stay here," I told Gus.

He sat at the word *stay* again, and I told him he was the best dog ever. Then I told him to come with me to another room.

We walked back toward the other wing. Again Lucy glared at me, and again I ignored her.

I glanced in to see that Vitner was still asleep as Donner, Gril, and Dr. Powder held vigil around him.

"Excuse me," I said. The three men looked at me. "I'm heading over to the *Petition*. I need to . . . do something."

"Beth, just stay here. There's no need," Gril said.

"I'll be fine."

"I'd like to find Mill and Elijah first."

"I'll be okay, Gril."

I wouldn't tell him where my mother was. I couldn't do that to her, no matter what, even if it was the wrong decision. But maybe my eyes could let him know that I would take care and would do what I needed to do with the hope that it was ultimately the right thing.

I think he got it. He nodded. "Call me on this landline if you need me."

"I will."

Reluctantly, I left Gus with the women in the dining room, and after a third glare from Lucy, exited the Benedict House and hurried to my truck.

The weather was still holding out. I hoped it would continue. I wanted to get Lucy on that plane. I wanted to get Mill on it, too. I didn't know how I was going to manage such a thing, but she needed to leave Benedict and if a plane flew, I wanted it to be the way she went.

My nerves had ratcheted up to about a million watts by the time I parked the truck and hurried to the shed's door. It was still unlocked, which I now attributed to carelessness on Mill's part. I knocked as I pushed it open. "Mill, it's me."

She lifted her head from her arms, which were resting on my desk. She wasn't hurt, but she didn't look well. She sent me a weary smile. "Hey, dollie."

I ran to her. "You okay?" I inspected her as she sat up.

"I'm tired. I was really cold, but I'm better now. But I'm so tired, baby girl. So fucking tired."

I grabbed her some water from the cooler, wishing she'd thought to get some herself. She took the paper cup and gulped it down.

"Are you hurt?" I asked as I went to the coffee machine and started it.

"No," she said as she watched me, her brow deeply furrowed.

"What happened? Tell me from the moment you left the bar."

Mill nodded in either defeat or resignation, neither of which I think I'd ever seen from her before. "I'll tell you everything."

I rolled my chair around to face her. We were practically

knee to knee. I reached around to the bottom drawer of my desk and pulled out some snack crackers. She took them with a grateful nod.

"I'll just start by saying that I was miles ahead of the police, as usual," she said after she chewed and swallowed one of the crackers.

"Naturally," I said.

"I got Hugh Givens's name about ten years ago. It was just a note in one of your grandfather's notebooks, but it was so random, and I figured out a long time ago that Gramps had kept things from us. Anyway, I figured Hugh was part of the puzzle. He wasn't all that hard to find. Didn't even need a special ops guy."

"Vitner?"

"No."

For some reason her answer didn't surprise me too much, because there was another possibility, though I'd ruled him out in my mind when Orin said he had a picture from Mexico from five years ago. Nevertheless, I said, "Elijah?"

Mill laughed once. "Good job. Elijah Wyatt is Hugh Givens. Imagine that, dollie, you picked the one place on the planet to run to where someone else from your past was hiding."

"Damn." I shook my head. "Hugh was with Dad. He's been here for fifteen or so years."

Mill shook her head. "Orin's intel hasn't caught up yet. Hugh did leave Mexico about fifteen years ago, came up here. But you gotta understand, it wasn't until Orin told me about your dad's being with Hugh that I learned that part. Sure, I'd found Hugh Givens in Alaska, but Orin filled in that missing piece."

"How did you find him?"

"After I saw the name in Gramps's notebook a long time ago, I just made a call to one of his people in Milton, told them I had a check for Hugh, some money from an old job or something. They gave me his address up here, along with his new name, like it wasn't even a secret."

"That seems so simple."

"I contacted him a long time ago. He told me he had no idea where your dad went—he lied about that part back then. I just chalked it up as another dead end."

"This is . . . wow."

"And, despite the fact that he lied to me about being with Dad, he's not a bad guy. Hugh cut ties with Travis Walker years ago. Sure, he pegged you for who you were the second he saw you—which was a few months ago, by the way—but his plan was to leave you alone." Mill shook her head.

"What?" I prompted.

"At least that's what he told me."

"I have so many questions." I stood and grabbed my backpack, pulling out my laptop and starting it up. "Both Stellan and Orin sent pictures of Hugh Givens. Orin's is from Mexico." I paused. "Did you stab Vitner? He's probably going to be okay. Wait, no, tell me what happened from when you were talking to Lucy in the bar. No, hang on—back up even more and tell how you got to Benedict."

I was startled when she stood. I thought she might leave, but she just went to the coffee machine and filled our cups. I remained silent while I assumed she was gathering her thoughts.

She handed me a cup before she sat again. "I didn't see a copy of the *Petition* in Homer."

"It was a stretch," I said.

"Yep." She took a sip. "After I shot Walker in the leg and disappeared, I just continued digging on things regarding your father—but I couldn't be seen anywhere, so it was all via the computer, the phone."

"Where were you?"

"I have a place" was all she said. "No one will ever find me there."

"Okay." What else was I going to say?

"My digging through all my old notes reminded me of Hugh, now living as tow-truck driver and dog musher Elijah Wyatt. I wasn't even considering coming up here, but then I remembered you told me you were in Alaska, and that number I got off Detective Majors's desk had an Alaskan area code. I couldn't trace the number, though."

"It's a halfway house. They get some extra privacy measures, I guess."

"I guess is right. I wonder if even your librarian could figure it out if he didn't know it already. Anyway, I was looking at Benedict pictures on some locals' Facebook pages, including Elijah's, and there you were."

"Oh no. In a picture?"

"In the background of a picture. According to the caption, it was taken at the community center, and you were there in the background, pinning a piece of paper onto a bulletin board. You weren't wearing a cap. All I had to do was zoom in a little and I knew it was my baby girl. I could even see the scar. Then I zoomed in more and saw that copy of the *Petition*. I made up my mind and my stories, and got up to Alaska. Hitchhiked the whole way, at least until the ferry here. I hid in car trunks when crossing borders. It was quite a ride."

"I bet."

"I thought the authorities might be watching you some since I was on the run and all, so I figured I should stay in Homer for a bit until things cooled down. Then the weather kicked in and I knew I had to take the first chance I could and get here."

"Why didn't you just call and tell me about Hugh or Elijah, whatever, or send me an email?"

She frowned. "Darlin', you're jumpier than a goose on Christmas Eve. I didn't want to scare you. And . . . well, I thought I needed to be the one to handle it."

Of course she did.

But she was right. I would have been terrified, and then I would have felt trapped if I couldn't get away. "So did you?"

"What?"

"Handle it? Did you hurt Elijah?"

Mill bit her bottom lip. "No, ma'am, I did not. When I left the bar last night, I went straight to that dog barn to confront him, though, ask him if he wrote that note that was left on your desk, if he was telling people who you really were. He knew who I was, too. He knows us both. He knew Eddy. Hugh's a good man. Now. He says he didn't write the note, but that he shared who you were with Claudia."

I nodded, but I sensed she'd rehearsed that story. Still, I couldn't find any argument with it. "That fits. Claudia said she wrote the note. He's okay?"

"That was the last time I saw him."

"When was that?"

"When I went to the barn, he knew why I was there. I wanted answers. I wanted to know what he planned on doing with you. He didn't have all the information I want, Bethie. He doesn't know where Travis Walker is, and though he admitted to going to Mexico with your dad, he hasn't talked to him in years."

My throat made a funny sound. "So Dad *was* alive then?"

"And well, apparently, but Elijah doesn't know if he still is. Cut ties good."

"God."

"I know. Anyway, as I was there talking to Elijah, he got a call from Vitner. Vitner had gotten stuck out in the middle of nowhere, had been trying to find a cell signal for hours. Got one little bar and managed to get through to Elijah."

I thought about where Tex and I had come upon the van. "I didn't see any tow-truck tracks and I stopped by the barn later. All the dogs but Gus were there. The truck was there."

"The truck wouldn't start. Elijah wanted to help Vitner, but all he had was the sled and a snowmobile. We grabbed Gus and the three of us went out to get him on the snowmobile."

"What happened? How did Vitner get stabbed?"

Mill held up her hand. "Right. We found him out by an old shed, the van off the side of the road. He saw us on the snowmobile and wanted Elijah to give it to him, but Elijah just said he'd give him a ride back to town. It would be a tight fit, but we could make it work. Vitner said he'd sprained his ankle. I volunteered to just walk back with Gus, but Elijah wouldn't have that either. Then he said we weren't far from the doctor's house, where we would find a phone and get help for Vitner's ankle. We snowmobiled to the edge of the doctor's property. But as we were walking up to the door, Vitner pulled out a knife, told Elijah just to give him the snowmobile keys, that we could get help from the doctor.

"Goddamn Elijah wasn't having any of it." Mill sighed with exasperation. "If he'd just handed over the keys, it would have been fine, but he kept trying to talk Vitner out of it. Vitner lunged at Elijah, but Elijah was quick and got out of the way, and when he went to grab Vitner's arm, it all went to shit and the knife went into Vitner's side. It was pretty horrible."

"Oh no. Did you just run away?"

"As that man stood there bleeding, Elijah and I argued. We had to get him to the doctor, but here was a man with an injury that Elijah felt responsible for, and I'm in trouble anyway. I told Elijah he probably was now, too. We had no choice but to run. Elijah went one way, I went the other, and we told Vitner to get some help with the doctor."

"Oh, Mill."

"Chickenshit, huh?"

"A little, I suppose, but Vitner really is going to be okay."

"That's good, I guess."

"Did Elijah kill Ned?"

"Oh, that. No. Lucy killed Ned."

"What?"

"Yep, Vitner told us the details." Mill sat forward and leaned on her knees. "You gotta understand something, and I tried to as well—this place was getting to Vitner. He was losing it, the claustrophobia, the dark and cold, he thought he'd never get out of here. He didn't like Ned—even though he'd met him only that once. He was glad to see the person 'visiting' Ned and Claudia wasn't being held against her will, and he wasn't looking for you, wasn't looking for anyone in particular, but he had Ned figured out quickly. Ned was a loser and an asshole. Elijah confirmed that for me, by the way."

"Elijah was having an affair with Claudia."

"That's true, but it was just a fling. Nothing serious."

"I think it was pretty serious in her mind."

"Well, not his." Mill shrugged.

"Okay."

"Anyway, Vitner watched Lucy stab Ned."

"Watched?"

"Best I can understand is that she got out of the Benedict House and went back to Ned's house mostly to get the jewelry back. Ned was angry at Lucy, blaming her for Claudia's leaving. He headed back into town to find Gril, tell him she'd escaped and that she had the jewelry.

"Vitner said that from the van he observed the murder near the statue, then told Lucy she had every right to do what she did, that Ned deserved it."

"Oh, lord."

"Yep, and then he helped her. He cleaned up the boots, then they went out back together, and she walked a path to the woods. She came back backward in the same steps, just to give the police something to distract them. He took the knife from her, got her back inside the Benedict House, and then spread a little of Ned's blood on a random doorknob."

"They were trying to frame me?"

"They were just trying to point suspicion somewhere other than Lucy. It wasn't personal."

"Do you know how she got out of her room?" I asked.

"The bobby-pin-a-rooney trick."

"I figured that out!"

"Nice." Mill smiled. "And now aren't you glad I got rid of the blood?"

I frowned but didn't answer.

"Also, Vitner went to the back window of your room and tried to be all creepy and shit. Said something like *come outside*."

"I thought I heard that the next night, but it must have been that night. I didn't imagine it!" I felt a small thrill at the idea that maybe my mind wasn't too messed up after all. "I bet that's when I fell out of the bed."

"I figured. The cheese thing was probably just because you were hungry. You're not going to walk in your sleep, Beth. You're fine. You were just being jacked around."

I wasn't sure if she was practicing some psychology on me, suggestive reasoning or something, but I believed it, too.

"Lucy killed Ned because he was going to tell the police on her? Why didn't she just dump the jewelry, hide it, go back to her room, ignore his threats?"

"Best I can figure is there was some pent-up rage with those two. It exploded, and she saw her opportunity. Oh, the jewelry she stole is in the van's glove compartment. The van Vitner drove off the road. He said he'd watch it for her."

"That's probably why she didn't run immediately. She needed to get the jewelry back. Dysfunctional family."

"Takes one to know one, I suppose."

I nodded. "I suppose." I sat back and crossed my hands on my lap. "Now what?"

Mill gave me a steady gaze. "Now I'm going to get out of here."

"You can't, Mill. There's nowhere to go."

"I'll figure it out."

"You'll die out there."

"No, I won't."

"Let's look at these pictures." I turned toward my laptop.

"You look. I gotta go."

I studied her, and I understood something else. "You and Elijah are going together?"

She shrugged. "If that happens, will you please make sure those dogs get the right attention? He has files on all of them, and inside those files are people who will take care of them."

I thought about telling her I would keep Gus, but I didn't have any right to make that decision.

"Where will you go? Really?"

"I don't know, but I'll be fine, I promise, and I'll be in touch. I promise that, too."

Tears welled in my eyes. I wanted her out of there, but I also wanted her to stay forever. "I'm going to miss you, Mom."

She laughed. "No you won't. You'll do better. You are doing better. You've found a great place, with great people. You are going to be fine."

For the moment I believed her.

"Mill, I think a plane will be flying out of here today," I said after I sniffed.

"Oh, yeah?" She smiled. "Think a couple of stowaways might be able to hitch a ride?"

"I don't know."

She shrugged. "Worth a thought."

She stood then and kissed the scar on my head. "Love you more than maple syrup, dollie."

"Love you, too." I sniffed again.

"Get a haircut, honey."

I laughed.

And then, like a million other times in my life, she walked out the door, leaving me alone again.

Thirty-six

moved to the corner of the shed, where the phone signal was best. With two bars, I rang the Benedict House landline.

"This is Viola. What?" Viola answered.

"It's Beth. Can I talk to Gril for a minute?"

She hesitated a moment. "Let me see." She dropped the handset, bumpy noises coming over the line.

A second later, Gril picked up. "Beth?"

"Vitner awake yet?"

"He is."

"My mom was here at the *Petition* shed, Gril. She's gone, but she told me what happened."

"Well, Beth, I'd like to hear her version. Any chance she'd come talk to me?"

"No."

"How about you come back and tell me what she said."

"I will, but first I want you to know that according to Mill, Lucy is Ned's killer. Vitner witnessed the murder, but didn't like Ned and told Lucy he'd cover for her."

"I see." He paused. "Vitner's kind of awake, and that's not exactly the story he's telling us."

I thought a second. "He's a wimp, Gril. If you push him,

he'll spill it, but I think Lucy is pretty dangerous. I wanted you to know as soon as possible. Oh, and this might help get him to talk. The jewelry Lucy stole is in the van's glove compartment. He said he'd watch it for her."

"I appreciate that, and I'll take care of it. Come back to the Benedict House, Beth. We need to talk again."

"I'm on my way."

We disconnected the call and I sat in my chair. Another few minutes wouldn't hurt. I looked over toward the library, where Orin's truck was still parked. Which email should I open first? I chose Stellan's.

As the picture came to life, I panicked a little when I realized one of the three men in the photo was my father and one was Travis Walker. The third man must be Hugh Givens.

The three of them couldn't be much into their thirties, all smiling, all with their arms around one another's shoulders. My dad was on the left side. He was so young. They were *all* so young.

My stomach fell as my eyes again landed on the man in the middle—Travis Walker. No immediate sign of the evil he would come to represent. I couldn't look at him for long.

I recognized the person on the other end of the picture, too. Hugh Givens. Elijah Wyatt. It wasn't immediate recognition, not like with my dad or Travis, but after a little study, I was pretty sure it was him.

What were the chances that I would go where Hugh had gone before me? God, they had to be billions to one.

However, I reminded myself that we weren't the only two runaways who'd found Benedict. The more I learned about my fellow townspeople, the more this seemed to be the perfect place to hide. Unless, I supposed, you were hiding from someone who was hiding there, too.

I sighed and looked at the picture again. Now I noticed

there was another person there. She was off to the side, only part of her showing. A woman—she was young, too.

"Mill," I said, my voice cracking.

She wasn't a part of the group smiling at the camera. Her own smile was directed at the men. No, it actually seemed more focused than that.

If I was seeing this correctly, Mill was smiling at Hugh—not at my dad, certainly not at Travis, but at Hugh.

Did that mean anything? It was just a picture, but I'd known she hadn't come to Benedict just to see me, or just to tell me about Givens in person. There had been other motivations. I still didn't know exactly what they were, but I had inklings, and this picture only gave them more heft.

Had she lied about . . . everything?

I answered my own question. "Probably."

Elijah had been at the dock with Gus when Mill had come to town. Had that been random, or was he there to meet her? Did he really need to leave town, too—Mill had said she told him he was in trouble now, but why would he be in trouble if he hadn't stabbed Vitner or if it had just been an accident? Why would he need to leave Benedict? In truth, had they been in contact for a long time? Had they planned this departure? What was going on?

I wasn't sure I'd ever know, but I'd have to think about it later.

I shook my head as I opened the picture from Orin, now anxious to see how Elijah had pulled off being in Mexico five years ago.

A bar was set up under an open space topped off with a palm thatched roof. There were many people in the picture, most of them with a drink and appearing to be having a good time. The bartender was circled. He wore a baseball cap and big sunglasses and was much older than from when I knew him, but I would have recognized my father anywhere. No matter all that had happened, all that I'd learned, I couldn't help but smile at the picture.

I quickly guessed that Dad must have become Hugh when Hugh became Elijah.

"Dad." I smiled at the picture that should not have given me any sense of happiness. Nevertheless, it did.

My phone buzzed in my hand, startling me. I flipped it open. "Hey, Orin, I just got the email. Thank you."

"Sure, Beth," he said, a strain in his voice. "Recognize him?"

"It's my dad, Orin."

"I see."

"What?"

"I have something else."

"What?" I said again as I steeled myself for bad news.

"Your mom just stopped by on her way . . . well, I don't know where she's going."

"Me either."

"She left something for me. She wanted me to give it to you. I have no idea how she got it."

"Okay," I said doubtfully, wondering why she'd chosen this method of delivery.

"It's a phone number. A Mexico number."

"Oh, shit. Did she get Dad's phone number?"

"I think so, but I haven't called it. I'll send it to you."

She'd probably gotten it from Elijah, but that was something else I wasn't sure I'd ever know. "Thanks, Orin. Thank you."

A second later, I was in possession of my long-lost dad's phone number.

At least allegedly.

Thirty-seven

I wasn't sure if or when I would call that number. I was overwhelmed and needed to get my head around everything else before I could even consider it. After talking to Orin, I hurried back to the Benedict House, where Lucy was loudly proclaiming her innocence. Vitner wasn't telling the truth, either, however he'd been asking for me when he heard I'd been the one to "save" him. I asked Gril if I could talk to him alone for a minute. Gril agreed but sat right outside the room door so he could hear everything.

"I hear you saved me," Vitner said as I walked in and sat in a chair next to his bed. "Thank you."

"You're welcome. I'm sorry . . . for all you've had to go through."

Yes, I didn't like the guy, but part of that was because I'd thought he was someone looking for me specifically. He wasn't. I needed to get answers, but maybe give the man another chance.

"I appreciate that," he said.

"Mr. Vitner, may I ask you some questions?"

"About?"

I shrugged. "Why are you here?"

"What do you mean?"

"I heard you chose to come to Benedict. Why?"

"Oh. That." He sighed deeply. "I needed to get away. I just went through a terrible divorce, lost any chance of even partial custody of my kids." He paused. "I'm not a bad guy."

"Okay."

"No, really, I'm not. I went through hell down in Washington and handled it poorly. I thought some time in Alaska would clear my head, but I'm afraid it did the opposite. I saw the census was hiring so I jumped in, requested this place and they sent me. But, man, it's so . . . primitive. I felt trapped. I still do, frankly, but I hurt too much to notice now. I . . . god, I just screwed up in so many ways."

"Who stabbed you?" I held my breath.

"It was my own damn fault. The weird thing is I knew I was losing it, things were getting to me, but I just couldn't stop my behavior. That tow-truck man tried to get the knife from me, and I fought him. This is my fault." He glanced down to the wound in his side.

I was relieved to know Mill had told me the truth about that part at least.

"How . . . how were they? Elijah and Mill. Did they seem like they were . . . together?"

Vitner studied me and then shook his head. "I don't know. I was so caught up in myself. When the van died, I convinced myself I was going to die out there. I wasn't quite right when they found me. I wish I could tell you more, but I didn't really pay them that kind of attention."

I nodded and swallowed hard. "Listen, I know you helped Lucy."

"I don't know what you're talking about."

I lowered my voice. "I have proof." I didn't. "Just tell the police what you saw. It will be better than if I tell them what I know."

"I'll be arrested," he hissed quietly.

The house felt strange with so many people inside it. Behind me, I could hear the rumble of conversations coming from the dining room, Lucy's continued protests. I hoped Gril was catching everything.

"I know the jewelry is in the van's glove compartment. I saved the blood. I used to work for the police. I managed to save the blood you put on my doorknob. I also got some fingerprints around the doorframe. I'm sure yours will show up."

His eyes got big. "I didn't put that blood there. Lucy did."

"I have your prints, Vitner. Do you want to be arrested for murder or for aiding and abetting? I would think the latter would be the better choice. Look, you've had a hard time up here. Maybe Gril can work with that, but only if you're honest with him. It's the only way, I promise."

If Gril had known about the blood beforehand, he would have used it the way I did. I was sure I'd hear from him later about not being pleased I'd kept it to myself.

Vitner sighed. "Get the police chief."

I smiled as Gril came into the room and Vitner told his story.

It was similar to what Mill had said. After being kicked out of the bar, Vitner had driven to the airport to use the internet access for a couple of hours. The airport was closed, but he parked outside it to get a signal. He spent some time sending emails and surfing the net. The last thing he'd wanted to do was go back to his room in Gril's house—the walls were closing in. But he had nothing else, nowhere else to go.

As he was headed back to Gril's and was near downtown, he thought he saw two people come out of the woods—the man who'd been such an ass to him and the woman who'd been in the shed. They stopped by the statue of Ben and argued. They didn't even notice Vitner park at the end of the buildings, turn off his headlights, and watch them.

He saw Lucy stab Ned. He jumped out of the van—to Gril he claimed he didn't even really know what he was doing. Lucy saw him and started to come at him with the knife. He stopped her by saying he'd help her. He took the knife, even cleaned off her boots (my boots). She changed into some clean sweats from the pile Viola had left for her and he took her bloody clothes. He agreed to keep the jewelry until she was ready to take it. Gril hadn't been in the Benedict House at the time—no one had seen Vitner come in or leave as far as he knew. He said he'd felt in a bubble of protection.

Gril had been in and out, searching, checking on Claudia. Viola had been upstairs working on the windows. Vitner and Lucy got way too lucky.

And as he was leaving the Benedict House, Vitner noticed blood on one of his fingers. He decided to wipe it on some random doorknob. Then he hurried around to the back of the Benedict House and said something outside my window just to give the police something else to worry about. He made his way to the van, taking the knife and jewelry with him. No one noticed him at all. I interrupted, asking if he'd somehow unlocked my door, but he said he hadn't. That part would remain a mystery.

"That man was an asshole, deserved to die," Vitner finally said to Gril.

Gril didn't respond, but after hearing Vitner's confession, I thought the police chief would do whatever he could to make sure Vitner's mental state was considered. I didn't like the census man, but I liked him better now than I had before. Gril probably felt the same, but he was still the one to enforce the law.

After he talked to Vitner, he talked to me, too. I quickly

told him everything, promising to write up the long version this afternoon. He didn't behave as if he was going to go after Mill and Elijah, but he probably wouldn't want me to know about that anyway. He'd looked the other way for Mill, and she'd done what she usually did, took advantage of his kindness. That might bother him some. Time would tell.

After more drama and proclamations of innocence by Lucy, Gril got everyone calmed down. He had to deal with the two criminals he had custody of.

A little while later, he loaded both Lucy and Vitner up in his truck to take them to the airport. Dr. Powder joined them. He'd make sure Vitner was set up safely in the plane. The doctor said that it would be better for Vitner to be treated in a Juneau hospital.

There were no goodbyes, even from Viola, who usually sent off even her trouble-making clients with some sort of positive words. She didn't have any today.

Without asking for permission, I loaded up Gus and followed behind Gril's truck in my own. It was a short drive to the airport, but it gave me a few moments of reflection.

My mother had blown through town and changed everything. Okay, to be fair, she hadn't been the main impetus, but I knew she'd come to town with more information or knowledge than I could grasp at the moment. I'd think about it some more. I'd talk to Orin again. Viola and Benny would be first on my list, though. I didn't have a good "team" in Benedict. I had a great one, and it was time for me to not only thank them but let them know how much they'd helped me.

As I pulled into the small Benedict airport parking lot and thought about my arrival to town, I felt the weight of the changes inside me. I wasn't close to the same person Travis Walker had tried to turn me into. I also wasn't the Elizabeth Fairchild I was before. I wasn't even the old Beth Rivers. I was turning into someone better than them all. This was a good place, better than I could have ever imagined.

From my truck I watched Gril and Dr. Powder get Lucy and Vitner loaded into the small six-passenger plane. No one questioned why I was there, probably because so many people went to the airport for internet and phone access. It wasn't a strange thing to do even after everything that had just happened.

But as the plane lifted up and into the air, I stepped out of my truck. My heart squeezed and I waved.

Just in case.

The plane flew into the clouds. I watched its blinking lights disappear, hoping that if my mother and Elijah were on it, they'd be safe. I had so many questions, but I had some answers too. A wave of gratitude swept through me.

I reached into the cab and petted Gus, who'd happily come with me.

"Well, do you think I should do it?" I asked him.

He nodded, panting.

I steered the truck to a spot in the parking lot where I was sure I'd get a good signal. I pulled the burner phone from my pocket and dialed.

Acknowledgments

It has only become clearer to me that writing books takes much more than just the writer. I'm eternally grateful for everyone who sticks with me, in my corner, even through some of the bumpier moments. Thanks to my fabulous agent, Jessica Faust; my perceptive editor, Hannah O'Grady; and everyone at Minotaur who had a hand in this book. I can't believe how lucky I am to work with you all.

Thank you to my readers who have continued to support me and my books. You are amazing, and I love taking this journey with you.

Thank you to my wonderful family, Charlie and Tyler. By the time this book is published, I will also have a daughter-in-law. We are all so lucky to have you in our lives, Lauren. I'm excited for you and Tyler and the adventure ahead. Much love.

Read on for an excerpt from

WINTER'S END

the next in Paige Shelton's Alaska Wild series, available
soon in hardcover
from Minotaur Books!

One

The End.

I looked at the words.

Then I grumbled and rolled the paper up the typewriter and grabbed the Wite-Out from my desk. It wasn't the end. Something was wrong with this story.

I just didn't know what it was.

I painted over the two words, then sighed. It was bad luck to leave them there for the universe to see if I was certain that the story wasn't finished or wasn't right, or something.

"What do you suppose the problem is?" I asked Gus. He was curled up on the dog bed next to my desk.

He raised his eyebrows over his husky-blue eyes. Even if he hadn't been a purebred, I'd have thought he was the most beautiful dog ever. I adored him and sensed the feeling was mutual, particularly when ear scratches were involved.

"Well, maybe I'll read the whole thing to you, and you can help me figure it out."

He seemed lazily amenable. I laughed. "We have a walk soon. Kaye and Finn will be here in about thirty minutes. That okay?"

At the word *walk,* he perked up, though he didn't rise. He

whined in agreement and then rested his head on his front paws again.

"Okay, I need to think about something else for a while. That's the only way to figure out what's wrong with a story, think about something completely different."

When I'd been tasked with finding homes for several dogs after their owner disappeared during the throes of the dark winter, local resident Kaye Miller had taken Finn. He was part Saint Bernard and part mystery breeds that were a concoction of smart and strong. The dogs had been members of a sled crew and had lived together for a long time. To give Gus and Finn a chance to see each other, Kaye and I had taken them out for a walk together once a month. When we'd first ventured outside, it had been mostly dark with challenging weather. Now, as we'd come into June, we were seeing much longer days and lots of thaw, which meant some mud but also temperatures that weren't always below freezing. It was still raining a lot but not today. The walk toward town down the road outside the shed might not be too terrible.

I looked forward to it, to seeing both Kaye and Finn. I couldn't say that Kaye and I were friends, but I'd enjoyed our time together, and I hoped we'd be able to walk the dogs more now that the weather might permit easier travel.

Truthfully, I was excited about *making* a friend, a woman close to my age, who based on our few times together, seemed to share a similar sense of humor.

I acknowledged that maybe excitement about such a thing was odd, perhaps immature for someone who was thirty. Did age matter when making friends? I really didn't know. I hadn't made very many of them over my lifetime. The strange turns of events in my life had kept me mostly a loner, though not an unhappy one.

"All right," I said to Gus, "I have thirty minutes for housekeeping."

I put attention to straightening my desk, making a few notes, and looking out the window. I hid the manuscript, including the page with the Wite-Out, sticking everything into one of the desk drawers. Though more people than just the local police chief, Gril, now knew my real identity, Kaye wasn't one of them.

I opened the top middle drawer to replace the red pens I used, and my eyes landed on a piece of paper with a phone number, stalling my tasks. It was a number I'd dialed more times than I could count since it had been given to me around the same time the dogs had become my responsibility. For a couple months, a generic voice mail had picked up. I'd left messages. But around March, the voice mail greeting disappeared. Now it only rang and rang.

It was allegedly my father's number, but I doubted I'd ever know for sure if it was or had ever been.

I closed the drawer but then opened it again. I hadn't tried the number for a week or so. I'd told myself I was going to stop calling it. My father had left my mother and me when I was seven. He hadn't responded to any of the messages I'd left at the other end of this number. At some point, I needed to accept that he was never going to come back into my life and didn't want to—hadn't wanted to for a long time. I sighed and then closed the drawer yet again.

"Pathetic," I said to myself, then looked down at Gus. "I'm pathetic."

Gus lifted an uncertain eyebrow, as if not sure whether or not to agree.

My circumstances weren't typical. My life hadn't been, so maybe this experience was simply my *normal,* not pathetic. No, I decided quickly, this continued sense of longing for a father who didn't want to be in my life was most definitely pathetic. Maybe a little justified, sure, but I needed to get over it. I was trying—and it was only one of the reasons my life wasn't *normal*.

I'd come to Benedict, Alaska, directly from a hospital in Missouri. A week or so before that, I'd thrown myself out of a van after being kept inside it for three days by Travis Walker, a name I hadn't immediately remembered and a man who hadn't been caught yet. I'd felt compelled to run away and hide, thinking that no one could find me here. I'd been wrong about that, but I still felt mostly safe, and as far as I knew, Walker hadn't made his way here.

One of the secrets I lived was my pen name, Elizabeth Fairchild, and my actual career as a thriller writer. Here, most people knew me by my real name, Beth Rivers.

I grabbed some files from the corner of my desk and straightened them. They were filled with details on local events and things I used for my cover job, editor of the local paper, the *Petition*. This shed, the home office for the paper and a place I could hide to write my books, had served me well.

No matter how I worked to distract myself by straightening up, the phone number kept flashing through my mind. No, I wasn't going to call the number today.

I had wanted something else to think about, something to get my mind off the book, but now I would rather have been obsessing about it instead.

I'd channeled some anger into this new manuscript, using the story as a way to maybe work out some of my own. Maybe I wasn't doing it right. Maybe I wasn't being honest enough about it. It would come to me.

I had a therapist now to help me through my traumas and resentments. Leia had encouraged me to journal, but when I told her I thought I could finally use what I'd been through in one of my books, she said it might be a good idea. *Might.* She'd had some reservations and wanted to make sure that whatever I wrote didn't send me into a downward spiral. It hadn't, but I sensed a roadblock of some sort—both in my real life and in the book. It was as if I could see what was ahead, but it was awfully blurry.

No matter what, though, Leia was glad I was ready to write it down—or as she said, "write it out of me."

I stood and walked to the other desk in the shed. I gathered a remaining pile of flyers I'd been putting up around town the last few days and neatly restacked them. Though I'd published the date of tomorrow's big event in the *Petition*'s weekly editions for months now, the flyers had been extra reminders. Everyone was required to attend the event. If they didn't, they'd be searched for and inquired about until eyes were put on them.

Tomorrow was Benedict's annual Death Walk, wherein Gril, the local police chief, and Donner, the other member of the local law enforcement team as well as a park ranger, took a head count, hoping everyone survived the winter, and then searched the community for those who didn't report in.

The Death Walk was not only important but also exciting. I'd heard many Benedict residents speak about it in expectant tones.

Don't forget about the Walk.

Unless you're dead, be there.

I'd learned that this was another reason the Walk was so important. It gave the community something to look forward to and talk about, a social event.

Just as my eyes moved back toward the drawer with the phone number, I heard the rumble of a truck engine approaching.

"Oh good," I said, grateful for the distraction. "That must

be them," I said to Gus as I made my way to the shed's door, happy to get out of my head, at least for a little while.

I opened it wide just as Kaye and Finn exited an old blue truck. I assumed the man behind the wheel was Warren, Kaye's husband. I hadn't met him yet. I stepped off the small landing from the shed, planning to introduce myself, but was stopped by Finn and his happy greeting.

"Hey, boy," I said as I scratched behind his ears and he and Gus also said hello to each other.

"Hi, Beth," Kaye said as she joined us.

In that short few moments, Warren put the truck in reverse and backed onto the road. He smiled and waved in our direction before he turned and took off toward town.

"It's great to see you both," I said, smiling at Kaye.

"You too."

Kaye's light brown hair was always smooth and had been pulled back into a perfect ponytail every time I'd seen her. Her skin was pale, and her bright brown eyes seemed unbothered by whatever challenges tugged on the corners of so many people's eyes out here. I'd only lived in Alaska for about a year, and some parts of me felt stronger, more youthful even, but I'd experienced the stress of the winter, and I wondered how much it showed on me.

"Warren will pick us up later," she added.

"That works. Come on in for a second. Let the boys say hello to each other. I'll change into boots." I turned back toward the shed.

It became crowded quickly. Bobby Reardon had originally set up this old hunting shed with a tin roof to house the workings of a weekly paper, the *Petition*. Bobby had been dead a few years now, but it seemed everyone thought of him fondly. He'd always had a chair and a full bottle of whiskey at the ready for any visitors. I'd tried to continue his hospitality, but I didn't think as many people stopped by to chat with me as they had Bobby.

He'd decorated the place with old black-and-white movie posters and a few typewriters atop two desks. I'd added my own Royal, which I'd found a long time ago in a Missouri secondhand store. All of my novels' first drafts had been typed on it. Subsequent drafts had been done on my laptop, but I doubted I'd ever change up the tradition of typing on the Royal, no matter how difficult it might eventually be to stock up on Wite-Out in Benedict.

Two big dogs and two adult humans made the space tight, but the dogs didn't seem to mind.

"How have you been?" I asked as I sat in my chair and reached for the boots under my desk. I'd slipped into tennis shoes earlier that morning.

"Oh, I'm good."

I looked up at her funny tone.

She sent me a tight smile. "No, really, I am."

Other than the fact that she was close to my age, I knew only that she lived with her husband and in-laws out west about "a good five miles." She'd told me a little about her husband, Warren, and how well they seemed to get along but not much about her in-laws. One time she'd mentioned that two of Warren's brothers also lived there, and I'd said something about that making for a lot of people in the house. She'd changed the subject quickly. I hadn't asked anything more about it.

I'd meant to ask my landlord, Viola, about Kaye, but with so much else going on I never had. That small, strained tone in Kaye's voice made me wish I knew more about her situation.

"Yeah?" I asked.

Her tight smile relaxed into something more real. "Yes,

definitely. Sorry, I do have something on my mind, but it's not bad. I'll tell you about it on the walk."

"Sounds good."

Once the boots, coats, hats, and leashes were in place, we left the shed and started down the road toward town. I was grateful it wasn't raining yet—and even more pleased that there wasn't a cloud in the sky. There would be soon enough.

"Warren reminded me to be on the lookout," Kaye said. "He's seen more bear cubs and mamas roaming around this year than in a while."

"Just yesterday I saw a mama black bear and two cubs walk right by the shed's window. It was quite the sight, and I was glad I was inside at the time. Gus sniffed curiously but didn't seem to be bothered by them. I could smell them through the window, and they were ripe."

Kaye laughed. "Finn isn't bothered by them, either. Elijah trained his dogs very well."

"He did." My heart sank a little at hearing his name. Everyone missed him and wondered where he'd gone. I was probably more curious than everyone else because I suspected that my mother had gone with him, and I wondered about her too, though she'd always been pretty good at taking care of herself.

Gus and Finn had both been part of Elijah's dogsled team. He'd taken care of his dogs, even to the point of keeping files on all of them with instructions where the dogs should go if something ever happened to him.

That's how I'd met Kaye. I'd called her one day to tell her she was listed as Finn's first possible connection and asked if she wanted to get together to talk about it.

She had. We'd met downtown at the one small restaurant, both ordering pancakes and coffee as we discussed if she was willing and ready to take care of the dog.

She'd been enthused. She'd owned dogs as a child but not

since moving to Benedict from Montana and marrying Warren. I'd asked her if she wanted Warren to meet Finn first, but she'd said he would be fine. I'd had a moment or two of concern that maybe I hadn't been as thorough as I needed to be in checking out Finn's new home, but Kaye had been so excited about taking the dog that ultimately I'd accepted things as they were.

All the dogs had been placed in good homes, but nothing was perfect around here. There were no dog parks, and a veterinarian came through town only twice a month if the weather permitted. Wild animals were always a potential threat.

But I knew that the dogs were with people who would love them and do their best by them. I figured that was about all anyone could ask since I didn't think I could take care of all of them myself.

"How have you been?" Kaye asked as we set out. "I haven't seen you since our last walk. As small as this place is and with the weather improving, I thought I'd see more people over the last few weeks."

"I'm still in my first year. I wasn't sure what to expect. I have been out more but not a lot. Since I live downtown, I'm either there or here at the shed." I nodded back toward the building. "I felt moments of isolation during the winter, but it wasn't as bad as I thought it might be. Since I live in the same building as Viola, we had each other's company and our own rooms if we didn't want company. Downtown only shut down a few days, so most of the time we could walk a short distance and see someone else. How did you and your family do?"

Kaye smiled, but I wondered if it was forced, too. Maybe I was imagining things. "We did okay. It's a house full of people, and every winter I actually wish to get away"—she laughed once—"for a little isolation."

320 • PAIGE SHELTON

"Do you all get along? I mean, I'm not trying to be nosy, I just . . ."

"No worries. Sure, we get along. I mean, we all like and respect each other and for the most part we are cordial, but all that closeness can get old. You know?"

"I do. How do you get away when you want some alone time? Is the house big enough?"

"I take walks, I guess. The house is a funny place. It started as a cabin built by my father-in-law's father. It's been added on to for years. We all have our own spaces. I call them pods sometimes, but they're just added rooms and such. From the outside, to me it looks like something from a Willy Wonka movie but less colorful."

"How many people?"

"Six," she said with a notable eyebrow raise. "My husband, me, his parents, and two of his brothers."

"That's a lot of testosterone," I said, hoping to keep it light.

"I'd say. Even Camille, Warren's mother, seems that way." She laughed again, more genuinely this time.

It was such a gleeful noise that I laughed, too.

"Oh, it feels good to be out," she exclaimed. "Away from . . ."

"It does feel good." I paused. "Away from? Is that what you were talking about in the shed? What was bothering you?"

She nodded and then looked off into the distance to her right. It was a westerly glance, so I suspected she was thinking of her home. Or maybe not. Downtown was that direction, too. I recognized something in her profile. Though not as much as just a few minutes earlier when Warren had dropped her and Finn off, she looked bothered, something pinched her lips, squinted her eyes. There's immeasurable beauty to this land, but there can also be a void, something dug out by the dark and the cold. I'd felt it, though that space had been replenishing with the nicer weather. I wondered if she experienced the same thing, but I wanted to let her answer on her own time. I waited and watched as her expression relaxed some. She turned back to me and smiled weakly. "And I already feel much better."

I couldn't help but note that in addition to being outside, she was also away from her husband. Was that part of what had transformed her so quickly? She truly did appear to be a different person than the one who'd been dropped off only a few minutes earlier. Freer, maybe.

"I could do this all day, just walk," she said.

Maybe she just liked the outdoors.

"I hear you," I agreed.

We continued down the road in companionable silence for a short distance.

"Beth," Kaye said a few beats later. "Do you ever feel like you want to run away?"

I glanced at her. She didn't backpedal or try to shrug off her words.

"I've had that feeling before, yes. Why? Is that something you've been feeling?"

She sighed. "Oh, it's probably just the winter thaw, but, yes, I have been feeling that lately. Maybe I'll hop on the ferry and spend some time in Juneau. I don't know; I just need a getaway." She smiled almost apologetically. "I think I go through this every year. I can't be sure because I never remember this sense of melancholy—that's what Warren calls it, and he tells me it's an annual thing, whether I remember it or not. I really don't remember it. Isn't that strange?"

"That you don't remember it or that you go through it?"

"That I don't remember it."

I shrug. "I don't know, I think that's normal. I hear women forget the pain of childbirth, because if they didn't, they would never have another child."

The dogs had found something intriguing to sniff on the side of the road. We'd come to a stop. Kaye looked at me for a long moment, as if she was taking time to dissect my words. I thought tears might have sprung to her eyes, but she blinked them away before I could be sure.

Finally, she spoke, "That is an incredibly good point, Beth."

I nodded, and wanted to say, *It is?* but I didn't.

"And it makes me think I should work very hard never to let myself forget my melancholy again," she added.

"Well, forgetting can be a form of protection."

"Or a path directly to denial."

I knew all about that, but there was something much bigger going on here than Kaye's winter blues, though I knew that blues on their own could be debilitating. I didn't want to steer her wrong. In fact, I didn't know her well enough to want to steer her in any direction at all, but I had one idea.

"Have you talked to Dr. Powder about how you feel?" I suggested. "He's a wonderful listener."

She frowned and shook her head. "No, I'm afraid not." She looked around the woods. There wasn't another soul in sight, not even a bear. Nevertheless, she lowered her voice, "The Millers don't believe in doctors."

"Oh."

In a few months, if things went as I hoped and Kaye and I became actual friends, not just amicable fellow dog walkers, I would tell her that her family was being dumb. Okay, well, maybe I wouldn't use that word specifically, but I'd do what I could to convince her that doctors were sometimes necessary.

We weren't there yet, but I couldn't stop myself from speaking the next question that came to me.

"Why?" I asked.

"They don't trust them. They think they can handle

everything by themselves. To be fair, they've done pretty well so far. Camille isn't a terrible nurse."

"Is she trained?"

Kaye shrugged. "She reads books."

I nodded. "Well, if there ever comes a time when you or someone in your family needs serious medical help, I hope you call or go see Dr. Powder. He's very good, and he can be trusted."

I did trust him, but I couldn't rightly attest to his medical abilities. He was unquestionably the best doctor around, for miles and miles. Being the only one will give you that superlative.

This time I was sure that tears filled her eyes as she looked at me again.

"What is it, Kaye?" I asked.

Almost violently, she wiped away the tears and sniffed once. She forced a smile. "It's just so good to talk to someone . . . else. You know? Not a Miller or . . ."

"You can talk to me anytime. I'm either downtown or at the shed. Look for my truck and you'll find me nearby. Anytime, Kaye."

She nodded.

The rumble of an engine caught our attention. We hadn't been walking for very long, I thought, but that was Warren's truck coming this way.

"Oh, shoot," Kaye said.

"I can take you home if you want to keep walking. It's no bother at all."

She lifted her eyebrows briefly as if that sounded like a great idea but then she shook her head and wiped her fingers over her cheeks again, seemingly just for good measure. "No, I'd better go with him."

The truck came to a stop next to us. Warren put it in park and then hopped out and came around.

"You're Beth," he said as he extended his hand.

"I am. Nice to meet you, Warren." We shook.

"I should have gotten my lazy butt out of the truck and introduced myself earlier. Apologies if I was rude."

"Not at all."

Warren was handsome in a shaggy sort of way. He was trim, but his shoulders were wide, and his arms were clearly muscular under his plaid jacket. His dark hair was slightly too long and unbrushed. His teeth were crooked but made for an appealing smile. His beard was short, more two-day stubble than anything.

He looked at Kaye. "I'm sorry to cut your time short, darlin'. Pops called for me at the bar and needs me to get home."

"I could bring Kaye home later," I offered. I meant it sincerely, but I also wanted to see how he would react.

He didn't miss a beat. "Oh, that's all right. My mom needs Kaye's help with the bread. Today is bread day. There's plenty to do around the house. Thank you, though."

Kaye smiled apologetically and nodded. "It *is* bread day."

"Okay, well, see you both tomorrow, right?"

"The Death Walk? We wouldn't miss it for the world, unless we were dead, of course." Warren laughed.

Kaye and I smiled. Some version of that joke had been heard around town all month.

He seemed like an okay guy, but I couldn't shake the impression that my time with Kaye had given me. Was it something about Warren or his family that was bothering Kaye, or was it just the seasonal blues she spoke about? I would make an effort to find her tomorrow and see if she seemed better. I suddenly looked forward to meeting the rest of Warren's family, just to see what they were like.

They hopped into the truck. I noticed how Finn sat between Kaye and Warren, and then I noticed how Warren didn't even look at the dog. He didn't seem bothered by him, but he didn't acknowledge him either, not with a "Hey, boy" or a quick scratch behind the ears. Finn didn't seem bothered by Warren, either. He didn't seem anything by Warren.

These were observations I would never have made before I'd been put in charge of finding homes for Elijah's dogs.

Gus and I watched them drive away. We were only about a quarter mile from the shed. We could see it, could see the blue sky above.

I was pretty sure Gus felt as much disappointment that Finn was gone as I did that Kaye was. I hoped we'd get the chance to walk the dogs, or just hang out, again soon.

"It's okay, boy," I said.

He looked at me as if he'd believe me for now, but I should probably do better at making sure he got to visit with Finn. I laughed at his expression. "I'll work on it. I promise."

I lifted my face toward the sky. The sun wasn't shining from above, but it was light outside, and the brightness was comforting underneath my eyelids. My face was cool but not cold. I'd been thawing out over the past few weeks. I opened my eyes and peered down the road, thinking that maybe Kaye was doing the same.

I heard a sound that might have been a twig snapping in the woods behind us. I turned quickly and looked out into the trees. I also sniffed but didn't smell anything, including the ripe scent I'd noticed with the wild animals.

I didn't see anything, either.

But I felt something. "Hello?"

The hair stood up on the back of my neck. I was sure someone was out there. So was Gus. I had hold of his leash as he focused his concentration toward where the noise must have come from, wanting to explore but knowing he couldn't unless I let him. The woods were thick, almost impossible to travel through quickly. They made for easy hiding places.

Someone was out there, I was sure, but that didn't mean

it was someone being sneaky. It just meant that they didn't want to show themselves. Around here, that could be for reasons that had nothing to do with me specifically.

"Hello?" I said one more time, again to no avail. I muttered to myself, "I know you're out there."

Gus looked up at me.

"No. Come on, let's get back to the shed."

I kept watch behind us as we made our way, but no one emerged from the woods. Once inside, I locked the door, checked it twice, then slipped a chair under the knob.